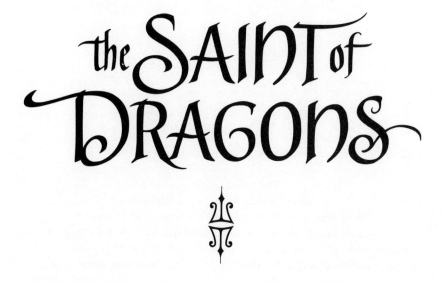

the SAINT of DRAGONS

JASON HIGHTMAN

An Imprint of HarperCollins*Publishers*

Eos is an imprint of HarperCollins Publishers.

The Saint of Dragons
Library of Congress Cataloging-in-Publication Data
Hightman, Jason.
The Saint of Dragons / by Jason Hightman.— 1st ed.
    p. cm.
    Summary: After a lonely childhood at the Lighthouse School for Boys,
thirteen-year-old Simon learns that he is descended from a medieval
dragonslayer, and that his father needs his help to face the last of these
evil monsters.
    ISBN 0-06-054011-7 — ISBN 0-06-054012-5 (lib. bdg.)
    [1. Dragons—Fiction. 2. Fathers and sons—Fiction. 3. Knights and
knighthood—Fiction. 4. George, Saint, d. 303—Fiction.] I. Title.
PZ7.H543995Sai 2004   2003025132
[Fic]—dc22

Typography by Larissa Lawrynenko

3   4   5   6   7   8   9   10

❖

First Edition

For my mother and father

With thanks to:

Ruth Katcher, Ori Marmur, Bryan Burk,

Peter Guber, and of course,

my family

CONTENTS

INTRODUCTION

You've been taught to believe they are dead. Figments of an ancient imagination. But one lonely schoolboy at the Lighthouse School for Boys, who has never known his family, and who has never known adventure, is about to have a rude awakening.

Dragons are real.

And they have . . . *evolved*.

They exist in the world today and are every bit as evil as they ever were. It is only their appearance that has changed. Their eight-foot bodies now resemble men much more than before. With their reptilian faces hidden in a cloak and hood, you wouldn't look twice at one crossing the street hunched over, perhaps pretending to be a homeless man pushing a grocery cart. But make no mistake: these Dragonmen are highly dangerous.

They still have scales for skin, slithery tongues, lizard tails, sharpened faces—and they are secretly responsible for most of the worst fires you hear about, using their wicked magic for no reason, burning buildings just for sport.

They live hidden away, in luxurious apartments in New York, London, or Paris, underground in Beijing, or beneath the sands of Egypt, in boats anchored in Venice or Tokyo, or in homes built inside water caves in Africa or South America. They back organized crime, military dictatorships, and cruel multinational companies, or they act as lone killers, secluded and hermitlike in mountains or deserts. Their exact number is not known. No two of them are alike. But they are powerful. And it will take all the strength the human world can muster to end their reign.

It is a time of opportunity for them. All the magicians are dead, and people no longer believe in magic. Spirits are low. To make matters worse, the Dragons have the ability to cloud people's minds so that they don't see them in their true form.

You might see a little old lady or an expensively dressed businessman, but the person standing next to you could be, in reality, a monstrous beast. At certain times, people can see through this magic. For a moment you might glimpse the flash of Serpent eyes behind the steam of a coffee cup in a local café—but it's like a mirage. The next moment, it's gone. Their trickery is rampant.

They sometimes move among us in ordinary ways. It is impossible for the average person to know for certain where they are. But there are signs, both large and small.

The modern Dragon is that person at school or in the workplace who hides his true self, who secretly speaks badly of others, who can't be trusted, who brings misery to those around them, who delights in the failure of friends. The modern Dragon is not content to be rich, but wants others to be poor. Beneath this person's outward appearance, there is very likely Serpent skin. And a vast desire to do harm.

Few people realize these dark forces surround us.

But the numbers of those who know the truth are about to grow.

Chapter One

SIMON ST. GEORGE

I T WAS AUTUMN. OCTOBER. It was the edge of a wicked season, and Christmas was a far-off thought. The amber-crimson colors of fall, and its pumpkin-spice smells, surrounded Simon St. George like a vast, bewitching fire. There had never been an October that felt so perfectly suited to Halloween.

There was a chill in the air that was worse than normal for this time of year, and a fog hung around the Bay, and the houses in the Bay, with a cruel persistence. The trees seemed to hunch over in sadness and wish for their leaves back to keep them warm. All the pumpkins in Ebony Hollow's fields seemed rotten, and to ache from their own rottenness. The factory smoke from over the hill swept down into town, and the gray daylight seemed to give way after only a few hours to a deep, intense nightfall. No one wanted to be out much. And no one could sleep.

Simon St. George had only the faintest sense of all this. The idea that something wasn't quite right just skittered over his mind between thoughts of tomorrow's Halloween masquerade and a girl in town whose name he did not know.

For him, Halloween was more than just fun and games. The masquerade was something everyone had to go to at his school, a tradition, and everyone had to be in costume. Simon wasn't sure why he needed a costume; he seemed to disappear in a crowd easily enough without one.

No matter what he did, no one seemed to notice him or take him very seriously. He was an average kid, a bit smallish, which made him easy to ignore. He had an upturned pug-nose, and blond, wiry, slept-in hair that made him look even younger. But he often kept his head down, so you never got a really good look at him; to the other boys, if they thought of him at all, he was something of a mystery.

Simon went to an elite academy that was called the Lighthouse School for Boys, because it was just for boys and it was made from a giant old lighthouse. It was a boarding school, where children slept and ate and lived, at least for most of the year. It was perfect if your parents wanted you to be strong and independent, or if they didn't have time for you. Simon St. George had parents who didn't have time for him. They paid for his school, but he didn't know who they were, hadn't seen them since he was two years old, and he didn't like to talk about it, if it was all the same to you.

At this moment, it was hard to see the Lighthouse School. There was just its shining light, laboring to cut through the mist. On most days the Lighthouse School could be seen from almost anywhere in town, because it was on a high promontory cliff and it was huge. In this same way, the school had dominated Simon's life. It was the only home he had ever known.

He stood at the corner of the misty street and stared at the little novelty shop on the opposite corner. He could just make out the shop window filled with strange, hand-painted masks, and the daughter of the shop owner at the counter. Simon had hardly ever said a word to her, but she kept his secret, that he liked to collect toys and marbles, because her shop was where he bought them. He was thirteen. She was maybe two years older.

Simon watched the girl adjust the masks hanging in the window. He gathered up his nerve and stepped off to cross the street.

As he did, the foghorn bellowed at the edge of the bay with a low moan. And something else happened.

Simon turned to look for traffic, and saw at the next corner, crossing the street going the other way, a very tall figure, hunched over as if from a deformity or sickness. He wore a long trench coat with the collar pulled up tight around his neck and an old hat pulled down close, so none of his face could be seen. It was just a quick moment, but as Simon looked, the wind picked up and blew the man's coat open. Although the man quickly tightened it around him, Simon could swear he saw a clawlike foot and a thick tail slapping the ground, a tail like the largest snake on earth.

It was hard for Simon to get a good look through the fog. The man was no more than a shadowy profile. In the next second, the figure had moved on, around a corner, and couldn't be seen, and the idea that some sort of creature was roaming the streets of Ebony Hollow was too ridiculous to investigate.

So Simon caught his breath and went inside the novelty shop, feeling around in his pocket for money and feeling around in his head for something to say to the girl behind the counter. He stood at the doorway and managed to catch her gaze for about a second, and that was it.

His eyes scanned a glass case that held a series of tiny knight figures made of metal, a kind Simon collected. He didn't know why he liked them, but he did. No one else his age ever wanted these.

He bought a little black knight and a Halloween mask that matched it, and he was just starting to talk to the girl about the masquerade when he was interrupted.

With a bang the shop door opened, and a group of boys from his school herded in, noisily, arrogantly pushing Simon aside as they argued over costumes. The girl almost instantly forgot about him, and after trying to be heard over their voices, Simon left the boys and the shop behind. Today just wasn't his day.

It was a relief to get out. His face was burning red from embarrassment at having the knight toy in his hand with the other kids around him. He didn't dare glance at the girl, for fear she was looking at him like he was an overgrown little boy.

The fog had gotten worse since he'd gone into the shop. Cars crawled along like wounded soldiers on a battlefield. The street-lamps were nearly useless, their pale light illuminating nothing except more fog.

Going home to the Lighthouse alone did not seem like such a wonderful idea in this mess, Simon was thinking. The morning had taken a turn for the stranger. Simon saw a German shepherd bounding up over trash cans and working its way to the roof of a store. All over town dogs had retreated up to the rooftops, howling. He could see their forms dimly in the fog. Something had scared them beyond belief.

Then something shuddered in the air, the sound of flapping wings. A torrent of white shapes flashed by, white *bats*, descending to land at the town clock.

Simon eased back into the space between two buildings. Watching them. The bats seemed to stare down at him.

Before anything else could happen, the other boys clanged out of the novelty shop.

"It's gotten cold out here," one of them said. Simon fell in behind them, hiking his jacket collar up against the weirdly icy breeze. He thought he heard the bats shuffling in the distance. He didn't have the nerve to look back.

He was about to ask the others if they'd seen the bats, but it was a rare thing for him to be part of a group, and the boys shot him unfriendly glances before he could even speak. Feeling unwelcome, he trailed back, letting them go on without him.

They were stuck-up kids, the richest of the rich, and they tended to torture Simon with constant questions about the St. George family. Simon never had any answers.

At the Lighthouse School, kids knew every branch of their entire family tree, going back to their great-grandfathers and great-great-grandfathers, and before that. These were boys from families with histories to be proud of, and futures all mapped out for them. If your dad was a doctor, you'd be a doctor; if he was a banker, that was your lot. There was a sureness to this that made the boys feel strong and at ease. There were not many of them who questioned what was laid out for them.

Simon had no past and no certain future. There was a blankness all around him. At his age, you're supposed to have *some* idea of what you want to do in life. Supposedly.

He finally glanced back at the strange white bats, but the town clock was nearly buried in the pearly air.

He followed the boys down a familiar sloping street, a street that sank down a hill to an old streetcar stop. The boys stomped through the gloomy day, slapping the poles, kicking down trash cans, and doing anything they could to keep from thinking about how creepy the weather had become.

Simon stood apart from them, waiting in the cold for the streetcar. Even though the boys knew it was coming, when they heard it deep in the fog, approaching with a clang and a rattle, everyone jumped. It was that kind of day.

Simon started to join them at the trolley stop, but something stopped him.

The boys. They were staring, the looks on their faces changing from curiosity to a kind of horror. For an instant, Simon thought it might be a stupid trick, but then he saw they were looking at his feet. Looking down, Simon saw *beetles* flooding the street in the pale light, flowing down the hill, swarming around them!

Behind him the streetcar tore out of the fog with a clang.

The first boy stepped back in surprise. All over the metal car, *more* beetles were swarming. Hundreds and hundreds of tiny white beetles. There were so many they were tumbling off the roof and scattering about their shoes. The boys were so stunned all they could do was stare.

"Get inside!" someone shouted. They rushed aboard, pushing through the rain of beetles, and the door closed behind them.

They were safe. The car was warm, very warm. It was like

stepping into a greenhouse on a June day. The lights inside flickered strangely. The boys noticed that lights in the nearby buildings were flickering on and off as well.

Simon was the last to board the streetcar. As he got on, he could swear he heard the roar of some tremendous animal far off in the gloom.

It was the strangest thing.

It sounded familiar.

Chapter Two

THE ORIGINAL DRAGONHUNTER

DAYS BEFORE THIS, IN an old suburban town near Chicago, Illinois, far from the Lighthouse School for Boys, five men rode their horses down a street frosted with autumn leaves. The sight would have been a strange one had anyone bothered to look out their window. No one did. It was a quiet part of town. Quiet folks lived there, mostly old people, and they minded their own business. It was as if a spell kept them half asleep most of the time.

But if anyone had bothered to look out their window, they would have seen that it wasn't just the arrival of horses that was strange. The riders were dressed in dull, iron-colored armor with ornate writing carved into the metal, a runic writing so old and so secret no one would have recognized it.

The man in the middle was tall and strong, though not as stocky as the others. He had the beginnings of a beard that would have been gray if he'd let it go further. His hair was black and gray, and long and greasy, and he kept it swept back, out of his way. His face was handsomely chiseled, if you could see it under the dirt and the occasional scars. He had not washed for days. He had been on the road a long time.

"This is it," he said to the other men. "The time is now." His voice was deep and painted with an English accent.

He looked to a taller Englishman, who nodded. The tall one gave the others a grave smile and said, "Aldric is right. Let's not give the wretch time to think."

The men put on their helmets. They were now covered head to toe in armor.

Each helmet was an angular box with tiny slits for the eyes, in the Crusader style. They were marked with a small symbol looking like a cross mixed with the fleur-de-lis; every warrior's symbol was a different color.

The horses were in an awful state of agitation. They fidgeted backward and side to side, preparing themselves for the fight ahead.

Ahead of them lay a stone wall and a wrought-iron gate, and a stone house taller than the others nearby. The place looked haunted. It had two round turrets with long windows, though the curtains were always pulled shut. Rarely did sunlight enter this home.

The trees in the yard were dead and rotting. Beetles swarmed around their exposed roots. The twisted branches were home to the skeletal remains of many birds that had died in them as soon as they landed. The house itself smelled rancid, and whoever did the gardening, such as it was, constantly replanted perennials to cover the stink, but these flowers always died.

The riders moved forward, and the lead man pulled at his

horse so that it reared up with its huge front legs and smashed open the front gate. There was no point in being silent. A surprise attack was virtually impossible. The thing at the heart of the house would have known they were coming no matter what. Its teeth would have started to ache the moment the men came within a hundred yards. It could sense them closing in.

The horses clomped across the dead yellow grass. It was getting hot now. The men were sweating in their armor. They each carried a long metal lance, which they now raised into position.

The lead horseman pushed open the front door with his lance and urged his horse forward. The others followed close behind.

The house had a long entryway and then a set of stairs. Little could be seen in the dim light. The smell was almost overpowering. The thing had not moved from this place in years.

"It's not coming out," said one of the horsemen. He was Irish. "We'll have to ferret him out."

"He's coming," said the leader.

"Indeed I am," said a chilling voice. It seemed to come from their right, and then their left, and even behind them, offering no clues to the beast's whereabouts.

"Come out, worm," said the leader. "This waiting is pointless."

"On the contrary," said the voice, and again it was as if the walls themselves were talking. "I can smell the fear on you. It is growing minute by minute. You never really lose that fear, do you? Just a hazard of the job, I suppose. . . ."

The lead man, Aldric, rode his horse deeper into the house. Now the light from the doorway no longer helped him to see.

"Do I seem fearful to you?" he said to the darkness.

"Oh, do be brave," whispered the thing, mockingly. "Do come in closer. And by all means, do rush forward *valiantly*."

The lead horseman hit a trigger on his lance, and an iron cylinder shot into the room. It was a kind of white flare, and it lit up with more intensity than any ordinary light could ever manage. But there was nothing to be seen. The voice was coming from nowhere.

"I'm not here, brave warrior," said the voice. "I am sending you my voice from far away, and your search has been in vain. I have already fled to the caves of a South American country, and you have come all this way for nothing. You will have to begin again."

Inside their helmets, the horsemen looked crestfallen. If this was true, untold hours had been wasted tracking and hunting this disgusting beast. Starting over would not be easy. Their hearts sank.

The lead man held his nervous horse. "You are a perfect liar," he said.

"Yes, I am," said the voice, and from out of nowhere, a rush of heat knocked into the horse, which squealed terribly—and the man was nearly knocked from his mount. A claw had torn into his arm, right through his armor. The thing would not material-ize, but the men could feel its heat, and could see smoky, wavy lines like that of a mirage where the creature's invisibility magic was wearing thin.

"Oh, but our games are fun," said the creature.

The man was thinking they were anything but fun. Through his helmet, he could see waves of smoky heat ahead of him, marking the creature's trail. His boots jabbed at his horse, and as they rushed down the hall, his lance slashed into the space just ahead of the smoky heat marks. Whatever was there made a splunking noise, as if the lance had struck against some kind of flesh, and the wall behind it collapsed. The sound that came out of that space was horrible, like a set of furious, squealing hogs, joined together with the cry of an eagle and the roar of a lion.

To the man it was beautiful, the sound of a wretched and terrible thing dying.

The man on the horse could not believe his luck. It had never been this easy before. His enemy must be an old one. Older than he thought, and frail.

"Be careful, Aldric," said the tall man behind him. "Let me handle this."

The Knight growled back, "No, Ormand, the thing is mine."

But Ormand went past him, rushing on foot into the wall's broken space.

Aldric followed behind him, trotting his horse forward into the hole in the wall. He was now in the kitchen.

He could hear the wheezing breath of the wounded creature. Still, its magic was strong enough to keep it largely invisible. That might not wear off until hours after its death. You might not be sure where the dead ones were. Sometimes the smell was the only thing you had to go by.

The kitchen was filled with the stink of rotting meat. The creature liked to let the meat go bad for weeks before it ate any of it. The man could smell pungent spices and sickly odors best left undescribed.

Above the kitchen counter, ironwork held pots and pans and dozens of sharp, sharp knives and cleavers and meat forks. They rattled and scraped as if trying to get loose. Then they *did* get loose. Six knives flew at the tall man, and another four hit the man on the horse. The blades clanged off the armor, falling to the floor.

This was the last of the thing's magic.

The engravings on the knightly armor glowed dimly, as if fighting to regain its magical strength. Each battle wore down the strength of the steel.

It was time now for the tall man to lay his hands upon the beast and call out the spell that would destroy it. This was the tricky part. He would have to get in close to the thing. First the man on the horse slammed his lance down into the invisible reptilian skin once more.

The thing gave out a painful howl.

If you had known all the evil things that this creature had brought about in this world, you would have been happy to know its life was at an end.

The creature's shape began to show under layers of billowing gray smoke.

"Its strength is passing away," said the horseman.

The tall man nodded, and moved closer to the smoky shape.

"It should be mine," said the horseman. "I should be the one to end this."

But the tall man frowned back at him. "A child could do this one, Aldric."

The other horsemen, alert in the doorway, relaxed.

Until the wheezing voice of the unnatural beast came scraping through the house. "I'm not . . . ," said the voice, "finished. . . ."

A light began to glow in the smoky shape in the center of the kitchen. This was the heart of the creature.

Aldric pulled at his reins to halt his frightened horse.

Ormand moved in fearlessly over the light. "It's over," he said. "Your deceit is at an end." And he put his hand on the glowing space, whispering with a touch of awe, "The heart of a Dragon. The heart of evil . . ."

"Careful," said the horseman in the glowlight. "I've never seen that before."

"His lifeforce, I'd wager," said the tall warrior, "draining out of him."

With that, the tall Knight began to recite words that would have sounded bizarre to anyone except those gathered in the house. They were words that brought death to these creatures. Words of great magic. The light beneath his naked hand burned, but the tall warrior did not flinch.

The horseman who watched above him did not know anything was wrong. But his horse was thrown into terror. With a squealing neigh, the horse pranced backward but could not get through the hole he'd come in.

"Whoa!" shouted Aldric, but any control over his horse was gone. In panic, it launched forward and jumped over the downed beast.

As man and horse leapt over the glowlight, it suddenly burned more intensely.

The light grew hotter and fiercer, and the nearly invisible Dragon rose up with its last strength and began a fierce rush toward his attacker. The creature was old, wounded, and could not see well, but it was full of wild rage and energy, and it blew

Ormand backward, carrying him toward the other horsemen in a giant growing wave of flame. The tall man flew backward helplessly.

Meanwhile, Aldric threw his wild horse on its side as the heat rushed over and past him, sprawling outward. It was a fire like no other. The only way to describe the explosion is to say that it screamed.

The rumble of that explosion was heard for miles. Mirrors cracked. Pictures fell from the walls. Dogs yelped and hid themselves away under furniture. In all the homes around the blast, for sixteen miles, milk curdled into a disgusting cream.

At the center of the blast, much of the house was left in rubble.

The lead horseman was the only one left.

The fire had risen high, and spared him.

He woke up and nudged his horse. It was knocked out. Leaving it behind for the moment, the man got up and walked toward the destroyed front of the house.

What he saw outside shocked him.

The fire from the dying creature had lasted only a second, but it had demolished the huge stones that made up the front of the house, it had burned away the yellowed flowers in the garden, it had knocked down the iron fence. It had even burned foliage down the street.

In the scorched trees above him, his fellow horsemen were spread out, draped in the ugly branches. Their armor had been burned to black and still smoldered, sending smoke into the air. Their lances were twisted corkscrewlike, or splayed in two, and hung loosely in the bony trees. The horses were gone; they had no armor, so they had vanished instantly in the blast. The man took some comfort in knowing they had felt no pain.

It was the only comfort the man had left to him. The other Knights were dead. His friends, the closest people to him in the world, were gone forever. They had been through so much together. It would not be easy without them.

The man stepped through a trail of red ash to find the skull of the terrible beast. As its spirit died, he heard its insufferable voice.

"Ssshame the boy won't carry on your work," taunted the voice. Aldric was stunned, and leaned closer. "Oh, we know about the boy. . . . Sweet little child . . . not long for this world . . ."

And then it was dead.

At first, Aldric's mind rejected what he'd heard. How could anyone know about his boy?

But he felt fear rising inside him, a growing sense that the Serpent's words were true.

Angrily, he lifted the skull. It broke apart in his hand, turning to crimson ash.

There was a sound behind him. The snort of an animal. He turned in alarm—only to find his horse in the smashed doorway.

The next moment, Aldric was riding away from the scene with all possible speed. Police would be coming soon, and emergency people. He couldn't wait around answering questions.

How did the thing know he had a child?

The thought tore at him. Fighting emotion, he galloped through the quiet town in a rush, down an alley filled with old cars, avoiding the wailing sirens on the streets. Autumn leaves floated past him.

His mind was racing even faster than the horse.

The creature had outwitted them. Playing at being weaker than it was, it had fooled them into taking their time, and it had let loose all of its powers as it died. The spell had indeed killed it; but the beast had a dangerous death rattle. They should have let it *weaken* first, before getting closer. Always full of tricks, the things were. *I must learn from this,* the man thought. *I must strike harder, move faster. I must bury my feelings. I must fight with all that's in me. And have nothing left over.*

It *knew*, he thought. The creature knew. Its spies had found his child. The thing had said, We know about the boy. *We.*

He tried not to think anymore.

But in his heart, he knew three things to be true.

He was the last Knight on earth.

His son was in danger.

And he had one more Dragon to face.

Chapter Three

THE SCHOOL IN THE LIGHTHOUSE

FOR SIMON, THE INCIDENT of the beetles swarming the streets had been a dreamlike event, and none of the other boys seemed to feel right talking about it, either. Life slipped back to normal. No one ever listened to Simon much, anyway; his voice never seemed loud enough to get attention.

He was known for only one thing. It had long been a rumor that Simon was poor and that he was allowed to stay at school for free, out of charity to orphans. The rumor hurt him deeply, but everyone had come to believe it.

He had always been treated like a pauper. With no parents to pick him up on weekends or holidays, Simon had come under the care of the lighthouse keeper and his wife. The lighthouse keeper naturally ended up giving Simon all kinds of chores, so the boy came to be known as something of a junior janitor. To the rich snobs at the Lighthouse School, Simon seemed like a servant, a second-class citizen.

He didn't even sleep in the regular rooms with everyone else.

Simon lived in the lighthouse. He stayed in the little two-story building next to the beacon lamp with the old lighthouse keeper and his wife. That's the way it had always been.

It was another reason Simon didn't grow close to the other boys: He lived apart from them.

His room in the lighthouse was plain and simple, often quite cold and drafty. The only thing notable about it was a fireplace, which he was never supposed to use without permission.

The other kids were down the hill in dormitories that had once been used by Revolutionary War soldiers. So even the *buildings* had a past, which Simon was left out of.

Simon did get some use out of the fireplace when he could get away with it. He loved the way the flames shivered and swayed, making little sculptures, how they created flickering shadow plays on the wall.

Recently, he had gotten caught several times and punished with cooking duty. He had started taking more chances in the things he did lately, that was certain. The principal had given him a stern talking-to. Old Denman the lighthouse keeper, who was Scottish, had tried to explain to Simon that fire was a terrible thing, the most awful, sickening thing imaginable to a wood-and-brick place like the school.

"You know how we feel about you, boy," Denman had said, his wife looking on. "We've watched you since you were a little child. We've never tried to step in and replace your true parents. We've never looked at caring for you as anything but a job, to be done well and without complaint. And we've done it. But you listen to me: Fire is nothing to play with. Don't you ever harm this old lighthouse . . . it's your sanctuary."

These were more words than the lighthouse keeper had ever said to Simon at one time in his entire life. They didn't talk much. They worked together tending the lighthouse and had the shared sense of accomplishment that came with it, but the old man was not a father figure. His wife was not motherly. Both of them had seemed old and tired since as far back as Simon could remember.

They were tired of Simon's questions about his family.

Maybe the rumors were true: Maybe he was a poor kid, an orphan, allowed to stay at school for free. Wouldn't someone have told him if his parents were dead? Or was the school sparing him from the truth? For Simon, it was a depressing possibility. All he knew of his family came from the few things Denman had told him, that they were good people, that they cared about him, that they wanted the best for him. They felt he was better off here than living with them, for reasons Simon didn't understand.

No one else at school knew much, either. The day after the beetles, on Halloween, Simon had sneaked into the school office to get a look at his file while everyone was out decorating for the masquerade. The file had nothing interesting in it, but the principal and his secretary passed through, and Simon heard them talking while he hid out of sight.

"He claimed he was Simon St. George's father," said the secretary, and at this Simon perked up to listen, "but you should have seen him. He was a wreck. His hair hadn't been washed for Lord knows how long, he had dirt and grime all over his face, he was wearing the shabbiest secondhand clothes you ever saw, and he had these wild eyes like a madman!"

"What did you tell him?" the principal asked.

"Well, I sent him away, of course," she said. "I think he was a homeless man who had rifled through some of our garbage and found Simon's name. Probably wanted to snake out some of the boy's money. Of course, the money's all set up in a trust fund, and no one can get to it. His parents set that up years ago so they wouldn't ever have to mess with him."

"Scam artist," muttered the principal. "He chose the wrong boy on that one. If Simon St. George's father *ever* shows up, I'll have a cardiac arrest."

Then they left, and, hiding in the darkness, Simon tried not to feel bad. What they had said was true, after all. But it spooked him to know that someone was asking for him.

There was little doubt that the man was an imposter. In all his years at the Lighthouse School for Boys, Simon had never heard from his parents. Not once. They clearly did not want to hear from him. He didn't even have an address to send them a Christmas card.

There was simply no reason for his father to appear out of nowhere after all this time.

At least that's what he thought.

Later that afternoon he was cleaning the lighthouse windows, hanging from a rope tied to his waist. Below him was a cliff that dropped off to the sharp rocks of the shore. It was one of the dirty jobs he did from time to time for the lighthouse keeper.

Boys had walked by earlier, and he heard them making fun of him. Even his friends, such as they were, avoided him when he was working. He was completely alone.

Simon was scrubbing the grimy film off of the windows and

thinking how badly they needed it. They had not been cleaned for months. He was listening to the wind whistle around the giant circle of the lighthouse when suddenly a hand reached out and grabbed his leg. He screamed and looked down in horror.

Standing on the narrow cliffside was a bright-eyed man who was in sorry need of a bath and a shave. The wind was blowing hard enough to carry him off the cliff, but still he stood there.

"I need to talk to you," he whispered loudly.

Simon couldn't believe it.

"They don't believe I'm your father," he whispered again.

"*I* don't believe you're my father," said Simon, and he kicked loose from the man's hand. The man had to catch his balance to keep from falling off the cliff.

"Just don't scream," said the man. "I only want a chance to tell you who you are."

"You're out of your mind," said Simon, clinging to the rope.

"Don't you see a family resemblance?" the man called.

Simon turned back, his heart drumming. The man looked crazy.

"I can answer so many questions for you," the man said, and Simon could see he was desperate to talk. He seemed tired and in a hurry at the same time. "You could be in danger. Listen to me. I care what happens to you."

"Then you are definitely not my father," Simon called back, and he clambered up the rope and escaped to the lighthouse deck. When he looked back down, the man was gone.

Simon didn't tell anyone about him. He didn't want the man thrown in jail; the poor guy probably just needed a few bucks. And he surely didn't want anyone thinking that *was* his father.

But what if he was telling the truth? He wondered if it was possible. Why had he looked so run-down—didn't he have plenty of money? And why couldn't he prove his identity to the principal?

The questions nagged at Simon all day.

The answers came during the Halloween masquerade. The lighthouse had been surrounded with jack-o'-lanterns and orange lights had been put up all over school. The library had been transformed with ribbons and banners and decorations, and there was music, but nobody danced. Girls from the nearby private school congregated around one punch bowl, and the boys stayed at the other. All of them were nervous, even though they were disguised in their costumes.

Once Simon looked out the window and thought he saw the man staring back at him . . . but when he looked closer, it was just the reflection of his own black knight mask.

Simon noticed that the girl from the novelty shop had come to the gathering, but before he could approach her, other boys moved in, and he heard them making fun of him. At first he thought they couldn't see him under his mask. Then he realized they were joking about his costume. Someone said he was the shortest knight in history. The girl didn't laugh, but Simon slipped outside to escape them all anyway.

He was going to head to the lighthouse or the stables, where he often went to be alone, when he heard voices. He peeked around the building and could see a man dressed all in pale white, along with other men, servants perhaps, talking to the principal. Simon leaned forward, hearing only pieces of the conversation.

". . . Simon St. George here?" he heard the man in white say.

"Is he in some kind of trouble?" asked the principal, but the man answered that his father was inquiring about him.

His father? Simon tried to hear more. Then he glanced down and saw several rats. They had been scurrying beside the building and were now stopped, staring at him. Very large white rats with red eyes.

Simon froze where he was, afraid to get bit, afraid to scream and give himself away.

"I'm very sorry to bother you at this late hour," he heard the man in white say. "My plane arrived late, and I just desperately wanted to speak with the boy."

Simon winced as a rat began to crawl onto his foot. He was going to scream after all, but something the man said stopped him: "Has the boy been doing well?"

He strained to hear the reply, that Mr. St. George had nothing to worry about, the boy was doing fine, acceptable work, but he was curious as to why the family had never come to see him in person.

At this the man in white sounded sorry, as if it hurt to explain. "If he ever asks about that, you just tell him his father would like to see him very much, but work has taken him far from home, and you know, as time has gone on, it's become harder for his father to simply show up out of nowhere. It's difficult, as I'm sure you realize. His father thinks it might be better to stay away than to stir up a lot of angry feelings, especially if the boy is doing all right without him."

Simon leaned out to look at the man's face, but he couldn't see clearly, not in the dim light. All he could see was a coat, a hat, nothing more.

"I can tell you," said the principal, "the boy is doing well; you can be sure of it."

"Well, that's good," the man said. "Because I have concerns for him."

"Concerns?" the principal asked.

"There is always a certain kind of rabble who are drawn to a boy from a family of means," said the man. "Rotten, disreputable people. I just want to make sure you turn away anyone . . . unsavory . . . if someone should come around, looking in on the boy. You know, I suppose I should probably talk to him myself. Is Simon around?"

"Yes, of course. He'll be thrilled. He's here somewhere," the principal said. "Might take me a moment to find him."

"Well, now, wait a moment. I don't want to interrupt all this if he's having a good time," said the man in white. "I can't imagine a worse way to meet him, come to think of it. I didn't know you were having a party here. I'll tell you what. I'll be back tomorrow, and maybe I can get away with the boy for a while."

He smiled at the principal, shook hands, and headed for an old white Rolls-Royce.

For a moment, Simon just stared. He had never heard a word from his father, and now *two* people wanted the job in the same day? The well-dressed man certainly fit the part in Simon's mind, but he had no time to weigh the matter—the rats at his feet were squealing murderously.

Simon stepped away from them, backing up into the field, where dozens of masqueraders were now leaving for the library to hear ghost stories. The younger students were all carrying jack-o'-lanterns, and a little boy handed one to Simon.

Simon stared blankly at the pumpkin, as above him, the sky clouded over in a sudden desire to make a storm.

Panicked that he had missed his chance to see his father in person, Simon scrambled through the throngs of boys with their pumpkins, hurrying to catch the man in white.

Simon ran across the field, but the ground was slick with mud, and he nearly fell.

As he hurried to catch the man, he did not notice the lizards—several of them—that had slithered out of the underbrush to get to him, just missing. He did not see the bats that had gathered above him, swarming in a tangle of moonlit motion. The boy was focused completely on catching his father.

Simon ran down the lane from the building, but he could not see the landscape well, even with help from the lighthouse and the stern glow of the moon. There was no sign of his father. No sign of anything; the car had vanished. The awful emptiness of the night slammed into him with the power of the ocean wind.

Whoever he was, the man was gone.

Simon stood there, watching the boys continuing to pass over the field, and with a confused sort of feeling, he joined them. He couldn't think. He just started moving with them.

They began to walk across the dark field, with only their jack-o'-lanterns, a few flashlights, and the lighthouse itself lighting their way. The lighthouse beam would sweep across the field, and then it would spin around and light the ocean, so the field would go dark.

Flash. Flash. Light. Dark. For most of the boys, it was a weird and perfect end to a Halloween night.

Light. Dark. Light. Dark. The boys could hear the ocean rushing back and forth against the rocks. Simon thought he could hear something else, too. Thunder. Not the usual kind of thunder from a rainstorm, but something somehow less real. Then he realized it was not thunder he was hearing at all. It was a horse's hooves.

Walking at the end of the long group of boys, he stopped to listen. "Do you hear that?" he said to the boy in front of him. The boy turned, and then all the boys turned.

"What is it?" said the next boy.

"It's a horse," said Simon, "somewhere out there."

Everyone turned around, searching the foggy night. They could hear the thunder of the horse's hooves getting closer and closer.

The lighthouse spread its beam across the cloudy field. Suddenly a shape launched out of the fog. A man on a great horse. In a second he had swooped up Simon into his arms and thrown him atop the horse.

The boys screamed and ran. Lanterns were dropped. Before anyone knew it, the horseman had rumbled off into the fog. The librarian called out to Simon, but no answer came. As the light-house beam swept past the boys again, the light showed them nothing but the whiteness of the fog. The beam did not fall on the horseman, nor on Simon St. George.

Both of them had vanished.

Chapter Four

※

ST. GEORGE, THE ELDER

SIMON COULD NOT YELL. He was in a panic, with no air in his lungs. The horseman's face was nearly all covered in a long black scarf, and his great black trench coat was fanning out from the wind, like giant black wings.

Simon clung to his back, afraid of falling. In that quick moment, Simon felt a strange flash of fear that the horseman was the hideous creature he had seen crossing the street—a creature with a long snaky tail. But now the horseman's scarf fell down from his face, and Simon could see it was the shabby man who claimed to be his father.

For some reason, this made Simon feel better.

Suddenly, he heard sounds up ahead. Shouting. In the grayness near the cliff, he could see three men rushing at the horse. The horseman drew a long sword, heading for the first man, who may have held a gun. It was hard to tell.

But then, *behind* the three men, came another, out of the fog, who slashed at the attackers with a long wooden staff. The staff slammed into the first two men, throwing them to the ground. Then the man with the staff attacked the gunman, knocking loose his weapon.

It was the old lighthouse keeper, there, in the thick of the battle, brandishing his long walking cane! The old man was holding back the three attackers! Simon gaped in surprise as the horse galloped past the fight.

"Go!" the old man shouted.

The horse galloped into the safety of the fog shroud.

Gone into the night.

When Simon finally found himself able to breathe and speak more than a whisper, he was a long, long way from the Lighthouse School for Boys. The horseman said not a word, urging his horse on through the fog. He must have gone a very long way, because Simon did not hear any sirens, and he knew the principal would have called the police immediately.

"Where are you taking me?" Simon managed to say.

"Don't worry now," said the horseman comfortingly. "You'll be safe."

That was all he said, and the horse galloped onward, down the coast, through muddy forests, empty fields, and past lifeless piers, with the dark ocean calling after them.

Simon had no chance to yell for help. They did not go near any houses. Even if he was able to call out, Simon wasn't sure he wanted to. Once the shock wore off a bit, he started to think this was the most exciting thing that could have happened. If this was his father after all, what exactly did he have to tell Simon?

They reached a long, empty dock. There were no buildings

around, just a big sailboat that looked like it had been made a long time ago. The horse trotted over the wooden pier and stopped at the boat with a snort of exhaustion.

"Rest now," said the man, and Simon thought he was speaking to the horse. "There's a place to sleep onboard," he went on.

"You're talking to me?" said Simon in amazement. "I can't just . . . I'm not going to . . ."

"You know who I am," said the man. "And I'd like to stand here all night and tell you the story of my life, but it's not safe here. We've got to move on."

He led the horse on board. Standing on the dock, Simon looked around. He could make a run for it, but he doubted he would get very far. He didn't even know which way to go; the fog had obscured everything around them.

"Are you coming?" said the man, annoyed, and he put out his hand for Simon to take it.

"I didn't know I had a choice," said Simon.

"You have a choice if you want to get *eaten* out there" was the reply.

Not sure what he meant by this, but knowing that indeed he meant it, Simon turned to look behind him. He heard a rattling in the bushes, and fearing that it was the dangerous men from the lighthouse, he reached out and took the man's hand. He was pulled aboard the ship, and they set sail.

The thing was, Simon thought he might be able to trust this man somehow. Without knowing why, the boy was willing to go with the unknown. . . .

It was too foggy to see the cliffs as the boat drifted away, but Simon could see the giant light-beam from the Lighthouse

School, slicing through the darkness. It got smaller and smaller as the night went on. Ebony Hollow was being pushed away, and with it, Simon's old life.

Part of him was sorry to see it go. He had few friends, but the Lighthouse School was his whole world. He had no idea where he was headed.

He had a moment to think about his schoolmates, the lighthouse keeper, and to wonder just for an instant about the name of the girl at the novelty shop, but as that thought flitted away, he felt ready for whatever came his way.

The man behind Simon coughed. "Well," he said, "if you're not too tired, we may as well get some work done."

He went inside the cabin.

Simon turned back, not sure he wanted to follow. But the time for regrets had passed. Simon went in.

In the tight quarters of the galley, Simon found the man hard at work, making something to eat. "First things first. I hope you like eggs," grunted the man. "That's all I'm cooking."

"I'm not very hungry," said Simon.

"You ought to eat whenever you can," the man replied. "You never know when you won't be able to."

Simon was confused. *Is he ever going to explain himself?* He went to sit at a tiny table, not knowing what else to do. The ship lurched a bit, and Simon fell, embarrassingly.

"Don't tell me the tide knocked you over," said the man. "The water's calm as can be tonight."

"I'm fine," said Simon, and he started to realize the man might be insulting him.

"You're small," the man added, sizing up Simon's frame, and

he seemed touched by that. "I didn't think you'd be small."

Simon decided to be direct.

"Are you going to tell me what's going on?" Then he added a threat. "My father is waiting for me back there. He isn't going to like this. He's a very . . . he's a very wealthy businessman. Very powerful."

"Businessman? Is that what you were hoping?" said the man disdainfully. "Would've expected more imagination from you. You're not going to spook me. You can stop with the petty threats. Next time use a little foul language, put a bit of punch in it, so you don't sound like such a prep-school toughie."

He broke eggs into a bowl. "Old Denman, your lighthouse keeper, he might've gotten hurt out there tonight, protecting you. He's done a good job looking after you all these years—wish I could have thanked him proper. He knew the enemy might come looking sometime, with its spies out all over the world. He's a good man, a good warrior. I hope he's all right."

The lighthouse keeper, working for this man? Nothing made any sense. Simon decided just to listen.

"I don't want to scare you off, but this isn't like playing war in the woods. You need to be sharp. Pay attention. Listen and learn every step of the way. There is a hallowed place for each one of us after death, but I don't plan to get to mine for a very long time, so you better not hasten my passage. Certain people have a mission in life, and there's no changing it, halting it, or reasoning with it. It's just the way it is."

Maybe the man was insane. He acted like it. This fancy way of talking about his work, whatever that was, and the way he grunted his words. He did not look very clean, either. His clothes were ragged and dirt-ridden. He seemed distrustful of everything. He was like a homeless man, Simon thought. His eyes did not seem crazy, though. They seemed kinder than his voice. Did he think he needed to be harsh with Simon?

"Eat."

Simon followed his orders. Scrambled eggs. Plain, unsalted, but they tasted good. Turned out Simon was hungry. How late was it now?

"You're going to need all your strength," the man said again, gobbling his own meal with a wolfish hunger, "and all your skills. Do you have any skills?"

Of course he had skills, Simon thought. What skills would this man find useful?

"I can do . . . woodworking," Simon tried.

"Don't need it."

"I can read French."

"French?"

"I speak fluently. My teachers say I'm very good."

"Probably not helpful. What else?"

"I don't know. I can pretty much operate the lighthouse. I had to cook sometimes in school, so I know a little about that. And I'm good with horses."

"Good, I guess that's something," the man said. "That school had the best fencing instructors in the country—you never took fencing?" The man's eyes shot over to Simon.

"Fencing was going to be next year. This year I took art."

"Art." The man sighed. "Didn't you take anything practical? What about archery?"

"Since when is archery practical?"

The man almost smiled. "Depends on your line of work." He looked at Simon for a long moment, taking him in. "Denman must've kept you away from all this sort of thing. We never thought you'd come into this."

"Do I get to know your name?" said the boy.

"My name is Aldric St. George," he answered. "And I am your father."

He seemed proud of the fact. But it also seemed to be a warning.

"You've said that before." The boy eyed him. "I don't suppose you have any proof."

"Proof?" The man looked angry. "We've got the same eyebrows, the same nose . . . You hear it in your voice, you see it in the way you move—the proof is in your blood, boy! You are a St. George!"

Simon tried not to react to the man's thundering.

"And if I had any proof with me," Aldric continued, calming, "it could prove deadly to you. Why do you think I haven't been able to talk to you all these years?"

"I figured you didn't want to."

Aldric St. George looked very upset for a moment. "Of course I wanted to talk to you," he told Simon, "but it wasn't safe. I've been wondering about you since the day we said good-bye."

"*You* said good-bye. I was too little to talk," Simon said plainly.

Aldric didn't like to be corrected. "There was no other way," he said, and then his anger came back a bit. "The Lighthouse School had the best reputation anywhere. I trusted Denman. Didn't that school take care of you?" At this he seemed to lean forward, worried about the answer.

"I guess," the boy admitted.

"Well, all right, then," said Aldric, relieved.

"But I would have liked it if someone had told me who my mother and father were," Simon grumbled, not wanting his father off the hook so easy. "I would have liked it if I knew where they had gone. And why."

"The 'why' is easy," said Aldric. "You'll understand all that soon enough. It's the reason I'm here now. I need you to join me on my quest to fight the evil that dwells among us. It has been with us for centuries. It was with us when you were born. We had to send you away to protect you from it."

"From *what*?"

"From the Serpents. From the Draconians. Whatever name you choose to use."

"Choose a name I can understand," begged Simon.

"Dragons."

There was a moment now when no one said a word. It was such a bizarre thing to say, Simon almost laughed. But his father said it with all the truth he had in him, he said it with such fear and disgust and such wildness in his eyes that it was clear he truly meant what he said.

"You were protecting me from Dragons?"

"Don't look at me like that," said Aldric. "I am telling you the truth. A truth few people in this world have ever heard."

"I'm listening," said Simon.

"The Dragon is a creature of unspeakable evil. It is a monster. A wretched liar, an insatiable thief, and a despicable killer. I say 'is' because this creature isn't an animal made up out of the imagination, or from the distant past. It is real, it is alive, and it is at work in the world today. Living out there somewhere in the shadows."

He pushed away his plate. "Fact is, up until recent times, there were great numbers of them. I've spent my life hunting them down, one by one."

"You hunt down Dragons," said Simon doubtfully. "The giant scaly reptiles. With big wings and huge teeth."

"No," said Aldric. "They haven't looked like that for centuries."

"What?"

"Well, Dragons haven't stayed the same since the dawn of time," he explained. "They've moved on like everything else. They've changed, evolved. They look like men now, mostly. They stand two or three feet taller than an average fellow, unless they're hunched over. They walk like men do, on two feet. They have two heavy, muscular arms. Their bodies are smaller than they used to be, so they can hide under a big coat, but their skin is reptile skin, and their blood is green, and warm to the touch. Their heads are man-sized, and their faces reptilian. Their eyes are glassy green or yellow or pitch-black ugly.

"We don't even call them Dragons, that's how different they are now. They're more like Dragonmen. We call them Draconians, or Reptellans. Some people call them Serpentines, or Pyrothraxes."

"Pyro . . . ?" Simon tried to say it.

"Pyrothraxes. Pyro, meaning fire," Aldric rattled on, as if all of this was everyday knowledge. "They use fire as their chief weapon, but not because they need to. These days, Dragons have hundreds, sometimes thousands, of ordinary people working for them. Dragons can be found in business, in politics; most are in charge of organized crime at the top levels. They can be found in every country on earth. Their men do their bidding now with knives and guns and bombs just like all criminals, but the Dragon has a special place in his heart for fire. They simply love fire, and can never get enough of it. You can never be sure what they'll do with it. You'll learn about that.

"Most of them are rich, too. That makes it hard to find them, to catch them. But they like to walk the streets—most people have walked right past one without knowing it—and sooner or later I pick up on where they've been. Their magic leaves behind unwanted side effects. Wherever there are strange things going on, you can bet a Dragon has been in the vicinity."

"And you destroy them?" asked Simon.

"Every single one of them I find," said Aldric, with a gleam in his eye. "In fact, I think I've gotten just about the last of them."

"Sounds like you've done pretty well out there on your own," said Simon, trying to humor him. "What do you need me for?"

"You," said Aldric, "are about to join the family business. *Dragonhunting.*"

Chapter Five

A Brief History of Dragons

"SOME THINGS YOU'LL LEARN on the job," said Aldric, and he took out an old curly pipe, relaxing for the first time since Simon had met him. "And some of it you need to know right away."

Simon reclined against the wall. The ship swayed gently, and pipe smoke filled the room with a pungent smell.

Aldric began. "Nobody knows when the first Dragon was sighted, but it must have been a very long time ago. They began their lives right after man began to walk the earth. They were born when the first man had his first evil thought. They grew like a tiny worm in his head, and when the man died and was buried, they went into the ground and spread. From this tiny beginning, many more of them grew from tough, leathery eggs hidden deep in the earth. White, like a spider's eggs, they were, but giant. When the young Dragons hatched, they crawled their way to the surface. They have caused constant trouble for humankind ever since.

"What does a Dragon want? It wants nothing more than to cause people pain, fear, and sadness. The Dragon feeds on these things. It is attracted to human misery—it thrives on it, in much the same way that plants need sunlight and water.

"Whenever a person feels down, the Dragon wants to be nearby. It crawls underground and feels with its tongue for vibrations of sadness. It sucks up the sadness right through its skin, and this makes the creature stronger. In turn, a Dragon, through his magic, can make people *more* unhappy. Whenever a person feels self-doubt, whenever a person thinks he or she cannot succeed, that life is not worth a penny, it's a good bet a Dragon is behind it. Nothing causes more evil in the world than self-hatred. When a person hates himself, he will do terrible things. He wants everyone to feel as bad as he does. A Dragon loves to make people hate themselves.

"Dragons have always wanted to dominate mankind. They need us, but they look at humans as if we were rats or cockroaches. They see us as pests. Vermin. There are so many of us that the Serpents have never been able to wipe all of us out. But they try. They try to thin our numbers. They try to get us to wipe ourselves out by tricking us into hating each other. There were only two thousand Dragons at the height of their power, and they could never get rid of the millions and billions of people in the world.

"You see, Pyrothraxes see themselves as better than humans, superior in intelligence. Stronger. They cannot stand humans because to them, humans are weak.

"Add to that the fact that humans hate fire. Pyrothraxes love fire. Their favorite place is inside the heart of a good blazing fire.

They play with fire, they eat fire, they sleep in fire. Most of the time when you hear about a building going up in smoke, it was a Pyrothrax having some fun.

"The worst part is, they can't help themselves. They are *addicted* to fire. They have to have it, and more and more of it every time. If the Pyrothrax had no fire, he would go mad. He couldn't stand it. And, since humans are the enemy of fire, Dragons are the enemy of humans.

"For a long time, there were warriors who would fight Dragons alongside certain magicians who had learned about Serpent trickery. Each warrior had a magician to help him. In ancient Egypt, magicians banished the most terrible beast, the Serpent Queen, into a never-ending slumber, and sent it away into a shadow realm, never to be seen again. Dragons have never forgiven the humans for doing this.

"Over the millennia, Dragons were hunted down until there weren't many left, and very few females to continue the species. So the Serpents went away from man, into hiding. Slowly they changed themselves. They made themselves smaller and out-wardly more like us, so they could live in cities and towns and not be noticed. They learned a kind of magic that would make people see what the serpents wanted them to see.

"Today, because of this magic, a man could look a Dragon right in the eye and not see it for what it really is. The Dragon can make itself look like another ordinary human being, unless it's an old Dragon, or a weak one. Then its magic might wear thin. But you and I are special, Simon. We can see right through that magic.

"In the past few years, the Serpents have grown very strong.

They have turned the tables on us. They have hunted down all of the magicians, every last one. There are no magicians left. And there are only two Knights left. Me . . . and you, Simon."

"Me? I'm not a Knight." Simon recoiled.

"You will be," said his father. "It's your duty. You see, in the Middle Ages, the Knights did battle with Dragons and destroyed most of them. A very great Knight named Saint George killed a very nasty Dragon in the Arab desert, and from that day forward his sons and their sons, and the entire family for centuries and centuries, went after the Dragons to protect the world. We are his descendants, Simon. And the job must go on.

"It was the tradition of the Order of Dragonhunters to bring their sons into the battle when they reached the age of fifteen. When a boy reached fifteen, he was ready to become a Knight. But I have need of you now."

What about what I need? Simon thought to himself. *What if I don't want to do this?*

"I've no one to turn to," Aldric added. "My fellow Knights have all passed on. Even my brother Ormand has been killed."

"Your brother?"

"The bravest of us all. He was older than me. Smarter. Trustworthy. Good-natured—everyone loved him. I made strategy, and he held the Knights together. They were from families that long ago pledged to defend the Dragonhunters. I don't know if they would have followed me alone, had they lived. But they are all gone now. And I have work left to do."

"You want me to fight Dragons with you?" asked Simon, bewildered.

"I don't have any choice. You have to come with me, there's

nowhere safe for you to go. Don't worry, boy, I'll be with you all the time now. The challenge is real, but we're up to it. And there's good news. There's only one Dragonman left to find."

Well, that *was* good news. Simon couldn't believe this. It was the craziest thing he'd ever heard. And since when could he count on his father for anything? If this *was* his father.

Simon did his best not to upset the man, father or not. "I think," he said, coughing from the awful pipe smoke, "you'd better take me back now."

Aldric looked displeased. "That place is not safe for you. You couldn't stay there if you wanted to. The Pyrothrax is looking for you. It has spies all over the world. It knows that I am the last Knight, and if they get rid of me, and you, there will be no one left to stop it. We can identify the creature—do you think it would allow that? It owes a great debt in blood to the St. George family. It would love to find you and get its revenge on all of us. That old lighthouse keeper is getting older—you think he could protect you? Don't you see? The wretched thing knows where you are. All these years I've kept you secret, but now they know you exist."

Simon's mind flashed back to the strange man in the trench coat crossing the street, the man who seemed to have a tail. But that was just a shadow, surely. Was the man in white one of the Dragon's agents? *This simply can't be happening*, he thought.

Aldric interrupted his musings. "I'm sorry all of this is rushed, but I'm on to something. I think I know where the Dragon is. I was closing in on him weeks ago, but my brother called me away to help with a Serpent he'd found in the heartland. That was when I found out you were in danger. We've got to get back on the hunt. You are the only one in the world I have left. Your mother passed away years ago, and there is no more family except for you, the last of the bloodline."

Simon was shocked. He had imagined he wouldn't like his mother, whoever she was, but he always figured she was alive, out there in the world, sipping fancy wine on a big yacht and never giving him a thought. It shattered something in him to know that he would never meet her.

"We have very little time," continued Aldric. "If the Pyrothrax knows we're on his trail, he'll move on, and we'll miss our chance."

Simon was now convinced the man was off his rocker. But then Aldric added something: "I don't expect you to swallow this story without any proof. I'm going to show you what I'm talking about."

Simon's head hurt from so much information. It must have shown on his face. "In the morning," Aldric said. "In the morning I will show you proof that the Creature is real, and things will be much clearer."

Smoke burned in Simon's eyes, and he almost wanted to faint.

"Now get some sleep," he heard his father say, but he was already slipping into dreamland, worn out. He wanted to hear the rest of the story, but his brain had shut off. It had had enough.

The real shock was that morning would prove to be even more amazing.

Come morning, he would indeed be joining the family business. . . .

Chapter Six

※

THE FAMILY BUSINESS

SIMON FELT A LARGE tongue licking his face. He was being eaten.

In shock, he opened his eyes and rolled on the floor! He scrambled to his feet, ready for battle. But the creature he was looking at was not a Dragon. It was a horse.

Aldric must have moved Simon into the hold of the little ship while the boy was sleeping. He had put him down to sleep in the hay. *Not very comfortable*, thought Simon. *Not very nice.*

Nevertheless, he had slept without waking once, even with the tilting and swaying of the ship. He must have been totally drained.

He backed away from the horse and looked around. The hold had a tidy and sizable space for the animal, and along the wall there were some chickens in pens.

"Good, you're awake," said a voice from above. Simon looked up at the hatch that led to the galley. His father threw down a bunch of apples. "You can feed the horse."

Simon looked up at him, but all he could see was his shape, lit by the bright sunlight flooding into the hold. Simon picked up the apples. He'd been awake two seconds, and already he was doing chores.

"Give her some oats. You'll find them in the wood bins on the port wall," Aldric added, disappearing somewhere up above deck.

Simon threw some oats into the horse's stall and held an apple out for it to eat. The horse chomped the apple eagerly. Simon was hungry himself. He took one of the other apples, sinking his teeth in for a big bite.

"DON'T EAT VALSEPHANY'S APPLES," came a warning from upstairs. "SHE'S EARNED EACH AND EVERY ONE OF THEM."

Guiltily, Simon swallowed. But he was still hungry, and it made him a little angry.

"Does anybody care I'm hungry enough to eat Valsephany?!" he said loudly.

His father came back down with a look of fierce annoyance on his face. "Eat Valsephany?" he repeated. "Eat Valsephany?"

"It's an expression," said Simon mildly. "You know. In America, we say, 'hungry enough to eat a horse.'"

Aldric plucked the apple away from Simon and went to his horse. It gave a thankful neighing, and fed from his hand.

"Valsephany is the greatest animal a man could ever have," Aldric said. "Very few steeds on this earth could withstand what she has withstood. Not many would be able to look a Dragon in the eye and hold its course. Most horses would bolt away. Or their legs would buckle, and they'd fall to the ground in fear. It has taken ages to prepare Valsephany for battle. She's priceless."

The horse seemed to understand, raising its head with a

whinny of pride. Simon made a mental note. Never joke about the horse.

"I didn't know she meant so much to you," said Simon.

"We've grown up together," said Aldric, putting his face against Valsephany's. "We were trained for battle together by your grandfather, Veritus St. George. Fascinating creatures. Did you know that thousands of years ago, horses were wee small little fellows, the size of terriers? Now look at them. You see? *Everything* evolves."

He may not have a sense of humor, Simon thought, but Aldric's knowledge was impressive. From all his talking the night before, he got the feeling Aldric knew a *little* bit about a great many subjects, but probably not a whole lot in depth about anything. He wondered if his father had ever had the benefit of the education he had gotten at the Lighthouse School.

"A horse is a perfect companion. When you get your steed, you'll understand," said Aldric. A horse? For Simon? His heart leapt at the mention of it. But before Simon could be sure that's what he meant, his father brought up something more pressing.

"If you're hungry," said Aldric, "there's a plate of food over there on that old box. I was eating it while I watched you sleep."

Simon looked at him with curiosity.

"I came down once in the night. I had to be sure you wouldn't try to jump overboard," his father said to the unasked question. "I need you for battle."

Simon frowned. *Oh, it was distrust, not concern*, he thought. He reached for the plate, which was piled with meat, fried potatoes, and onion.

Suddenly, a large red fox darted from the shadows and stuck

its snout onto the plate.

Aldric looked over disdainfully. "Fenwick. I guess I should have introduced you. Did I mention a horse was the greatest of all the animals?"

Simon stared at the fox, which seemed to be glowering unhappily.

"An old English fox is probably the worst," muttered Aldric, shooing the animal back.

"He's hungry," Simon said, and held out some food, which the fox took quickly.

"Oh, poor thing," Aldric mocked him. "He'll eat when he's earned it. This stable is a mess, Fenwick. I have to tell you, Simon, he spends most of his time fishing alongside the boat, and he stinks at it. As a matter of fact, he just plain stinks."

Fenwick gave what seemed to be a scowl. Then, to Simon's surprise, the fox scurried its furry red body into the stable and began cleaning up, pulling tools back into their spots, using its nose to push boxes into place. Fenwick, apparently, had been expertly trained.

"I'm sure this wasn't exactly your idea of a wonderful Halloween," said Aldric. He looked at the black knight mask in the hay. Somehow it had made it through the ride, in Simon's satchel. "Interesting choice. It wouldn't offer you much protection, though. Our armor is strong as titanium—it's overlaid with an alchemical resin created by my magician friend Maradine, who died long ago. There's still enough of it left for your armor, if I can adjust it for your size, but I doubt you'll need any of it on this trip."

"Why is that?" asked Simon, munching on a hard piece of

black meat. He was thinking a suit of armor would be a very remarkable thing to own.

"This Dragon we're after, he's an urban Dragon. We'll have to disguise ourselves. The armor is what gives you away. The strong magic in it makes the Dragon's teeth ache. He knows when you're coming. So we end up with a choice. Protect ourselves and lose the element of surprise, or go in with a tremendous shock, but with no armor to protect us."

"This is unreal," mumbled Simon. Shining armor, urban Dragons. He realized he was actually starting to believe this insanity.

"I assure you," said his father solemnly. "The White Dragon is very real."

"White Dragon," Simon repeated. "Is that what you call it?"

"Yes. He's the last of the bunch. That's his brother you're eating," said Aldric, casually.

Simon had been chewing on the tough, greenish-black meat for some time. Now he felt sick.

"I'm eating it?"

"Yes, with some pepper."

"I'm eating Dragon meat?" repeated Simon.

"Well, why not?" Aldric asked him. "Dragonmen eat humans every chance they get. They do it for pure pleasure, just to spite us. We are a delicacy to them. They cover us with a hot milky syrup."

The Dragon meat tasted like very old beef. Between the motion of the ship and the bad meat, Simon thought he might throw up.

"I'm not feeling well," groaned Simon.

"I thought you wanted proof," Aldric replied.

"This isn't exactly proof," said Simon. "This could be old deer meat, or dead alligator. It just doesn't taste good. What are you trying to do to me?"

"Just keeping you from hunger. It took time to clean that off my sword and cook it up right," said Aldric. "This one was called the Vermin Dragon, because he had a fancy for eating garlic-covered rats, and he ended up tasting rather good, if you ask me."

Simon looked at him with utter disbelief. "Well, you sure have thought a lot about this."

The older St. George looked irritated. "In a few hours," he said, "we need to be ready for combat. I had hoped my word would be enough for you."

Simon didn't know what to say.

"But I did promise I'd show you the truth."

He motioned Simon to follow. "I didn't want to frighten you, but if you insist, so be it." He walked to the back of the hold and opened a series of locks on a heavy metal door. "In you go," he told his son.

Simon wasn't sure he wanted proof any more.

The room ahead was dark as a shark's belly, and it gave off a musty smell of being closed up for a long, long time.

Fenwick, the little fox, had found business at the back of the ship, cowering fearfully.

Simon stalled, looking at Aldric: "Shouldn't you be running the ship?"

"It runs itself."

"Runs itself?" said Simon. "You have that kind of machinery on board? You don't even have electricity."

"The ship runs on magic," grumbled his father, "using devices made by my late friend Maradine, and they know the way. Now, quit stalling."

"I'm not stalling. I just had some questions."

"It isn't pretty in there, but you need to see it," said Aldric.

Simon swallowed hard.

"You *asked* to see it," said Aldric.

"I know."

"Then go!"

Simon entered the dark room. The ship swayed to one side, and it spooked him even more. Aldric entered behind him and clicked on some dim brass lights. The first thing Simon saw was a giant set of teeth. He almost jumped back from the shock. They were set in a skull the size of a small car. It was like the skull of a *Tyrannosaurus rex*, but it had long, goatlike horns jutting upward from the head. The eyeholes alone were big enough for Simon to walk through. The boy stayed at the door, clearly disturbed.

"Oh, come on, don't be afraid," said Aldric in disgust. "You can see it's dead. Dead as Friday's mutton. For heaven's sake, you're going to have to show some guts. We're going after the real thing in a few hours."

"But it's so big," said Simon. "I didn't know it was so big."

"That's an old Dragon," said Aldric. "It's six hundred years old. Haven't you been listening? Dragons today are man-sized. They don't look anything like this."

The bones around the mouth and nose of the skeleton were black. The fire it spewed out must have burned the bone over time.

"What do the Dragonmen look like?" asked Simon.

"Like this," said Aldric, and he thrust another skull into Simon's face.

Simon almost screamed, but he held it in, just to keep his father from the satisfaction. The skull in Aldric's hand was indeed smaller. It was quite a bit larger than a human skull, though, and shaped like a little replica of the giant fossil nearby.

"This is the skull of the Dragon of Seville," said Aldric. "The first Dragon I took on, when I was about your age. He was an ugly Pyrothrax. Had six rows of teeth. See? Like a shark." Simon ran his fingers over the old teeth. Still sharp. "Father and I went in together. It was the first time I'd been out of England. Easiest Serpent I ever killed." His voice took on a melancholy tone. "The next one would put an end to Dad." He took the skull back and set it on a shelf with at least a dozen more such skulls.

Simon's eyes were drawn to several steel cases with glass doors on them. Inside the cases were lighted torches. Some of the torches burned green, some blue, others yellow.

"Serpentfire can burn for a very long time if the magic is strong," said Aldric. "It's hard to handle, that kind of fire, it seems to have a mind of its own, but it can be a good tool if you have nothing else. You never, ever want to use it unless you need it. I keep it around in case of dire circumstances. I hate to admit anything Serpentine can be useful." Absentmindedly he picked up a Dragon's claw from a pile of them on the table, and used it to scratch his neck.

The room had a smell like old leather. On several cabinets, and hung on the walls, were layers of Dragonhide. Simon reached out and touched the closest. It felt leathery and tough, and scaly like a snake in parts.

"Serpent skin resists fire," said Aldric, "unless the fire is from another Dragon. Another good reason to keep serpentfire around. It used to be that the best way to kill a Dragon was to introduce it to another Dragon."

"Really? They don't like each other?"

"Oh, they despise each other. They despise everything, really. They're just gluttons for hatred," Aldric revealed. "It all goes back to the Queen of Serpents. Once she vanished, they turned against each other, all blaming the other for what had happened."

"That was thousands of years ago," recalled Simon.

"Yes, but they've never gotten over it" was the answer. "They've got a long memory—they're like the Irish that way."

"They?"

"It. I keep forgetting, there's only one of the terrors left," smiled Aldric. "We're soon to be out of a job, aren't we? Maybe we'll go into the fishing business. Or, who knows, maybe this last one has a treasure we can make off with. But we're getting ahead of ourselves."

He took the Dragonhide from Simon. "It's nasty material, this is, but you can drive a silver sword or a silver arrow through it if you move fast. You need the right weapons."

With that, he clicked on another light, and on the far side of the room Simon could now see an entire wall filled with suits of armor and Dragonfighting equipment. There were swords of every kind, crossbows, shields, bows and arrows—everything made of silver.

It was an amazing sight. The boy's jaw dropped.

He felt something brush against his leg, and looked down to

see Fenwick carefully moving in next to him.

"Get out of here, you fish-mongrel," Aldric yelled at the fox, to no effect. "He seems to like you."

But Simon's eyes were on the weaponry.

"The favorite weapon of the Dragonhunter," explained Aldric, "is the silver crossbow." He went over to the wall and handed one to Simon. It was heavy, like holding a bowling ball.

"This one is yours."

Simon stared at it in disbelief. "This is how you slay Dragons?" he asked.

"No, this is how you *harm* Dragons. Silver can hurt a Dragon, but their skin regenerates over time. There is only one way for us to eliminate a Dragon—to destroy him completely. And that is with a deathspell."

"A what?"

"Long ago magicians discovered that every Dragon has a spell that will bring it to an end," Aldric related, "and every spell is written into the book of Saint George. I know all the words to the spells; I've committed them to memory, and so shall you, for the last of the creatures. Each Dragon has a weakness. A soft piece of flesh in the middle of its chest, right over its heart. Its weakest part. You lay your hand on its heart, press against this skin, and call out the deathspell. And the Dragon will . . . expire."

"What happens then?"

"They all go down differently," said Aldric. "You'll see it for yourself."

Simon could hardly believe it. He was really going to hunt a Dragon. He looked at his silver crossbow and noticed for the first time that it was covered in spell-writing. Runes. An enchanted protection of some kind.

Then he noticed a small piece of glass fitted over the middle of the weapon, and inside that glass was a small, burning light, a silver oval that was beating like a heart. The crossbow had a heart!

"It's alive," said Simon.

"Of course it's alive," said Aldric, "everything enchanted is alive. It will try to help you as best it can."

The boy scratched his head, unnerved.

Fenwick sniffed at the crossbow. He seemed worried.

"Will you show me how to use it?" Simon asked.

There was a glint of pride in Aldric's eye when he nodded.

"Our first and last hunt."

Chapter Seven

A Manhattan Dragon

THE WHITE DRAGON WAS, indeed, purely white. Its leathery skin was white with tiny cream speckles, and it had small white plates on its back that stuck up in the air like the plates of a miniature stegosaurus. Its long fingers were tipped with white claws. Its teeth were white. Its amber-white eyes had a protective translucent white eyelid. Even when it closed its eyes, it *saw* whiteness.

It lived in a luxury building in New York City that overlooked Central Park. Everything in its very large apartment was white: the floors, the walls, the ceiling, the drapes. The furniture, including the chairs, the tables, the sofa, the bookcases (and the books in them), as well as the telephone, the television, all of the furnishings everywhere, all were shades of white. The kitchen and all of its tools were white. The bedroom and the bed and the nightstands were all white. So was the bathroom.

Nothing was ever written down in the home of the White Dragon. The White Dragon liked blank white paper.

Nothing was ever dirty. The White Dragon made sure anything dirty was thrown out unless it could be made clean and white.

Nothing was ever eaten that was not white. The White Dragon ate white cream soup or white clam chowder, stone-white crackers, white bread, white vanilla ice cream, white mashed potatoes. White meat. His favorite: white goats, swallowed whole. If the Dragon was eating a human being, he used his magic to grind it up until the person was a white powder that could be sprinkled easily over nice, white food.

It took great pride in its appearance. It spent most of its time in a massive white bathtub filled with white bubbles. The one reason it enjoyed going out into the world was to return home and wash it all away with white soap.

The White Creature had grown rich from criminal activity, mostly from the art world. Its human partners spent all day stealing money from people through art forgeries, and forcing other people to steal money from still more people. The White Dragon gave the orders, then all it had to do was sit back and receive reports of how much money it had made that day.

The rest of its day was spent contemplating whiteness.

All about the place were small white boxes with small white cloths inside that the creature could use to clean up tiny bits of dirt or dust that might somehow have fallen onto his pristine skin.

It spent hours polishing its teeth. It even scrubbed its eyes with soap, no matter what the pain. It had read somewhere that harmful dust can collect in the corner of the eyes and go unnoticed. It did not go unnoticed in the home of the White Dragon.

The creature stood eight feet tall, and could hide easily under heavy clothing and a long trench coat. It walked on two feet. Its head was fairly small, and though its neck was a bit longer than a human's, it could retract.

The Dragon had a white tail, long, full, and strong. It kept its tail curled up against its back so it could be hidden under a coat. Its white wings could also be kept hidden, but it rarely flew. That required too much energy, and dirt particles would fly into his eyes.

When at home, naturally, the creature hid nothing. It stretched out its long tail and its baggy old body and lay around in its pricey little kingdom, listening to the radio tuned to no particular station. White noise, of course. The ultimate lounge lizard.

The only matter that troubled the Dragon was that it liked to sleep in flames. He would spew fire into the massive fireplace, and sleep inside of it, with fire all around him. This was delightful to him. In the morning, however, there would be all that mess to clean up. Fire makes things black.

To keep things clean, a small army of workers was employed at all times. They did not know for whom they worked. They only knew that the fireplace must be kept perfectly clean at all costs, every single day. Only white ash was allowed to remain.

Even the creature's fire was white. It was magic fire. The old Serpent liked to make the fire grow like a white vine, like ivy, in long strings that would crawl on the wall and branch out in thin, glowing strands. He thought fire was lovely. He could make it come out of his mouth or his eyes or his hands or his fingers, but after that, it might do whatever it wanted. Dragonfire is an unpredictable thing. After a few seconds in the air, it can actually come to *life*. From time to time, the Dragon would unleash a fire just to have someone to talk to. The living fire would laugh with him, and speak of rotten things. It sometimes took the shape of a blobby man with no real face, and it would walk around the room, scorching everything. The Dragon hated the messes it made.

The creature had other ways of making messes. It had developed an interest in art. Its new joy was painting pictures.

They were pictures of the color white.

If his paint should ever drip off the canvas, it only added to the white in the room.

The painting he was currently working on was a pride and joy. Like the others, it used various shades of white to create a subtle white abstract effect. Blobs of colors from white to off white, to egg white, to cream, to vanilla, to ivory, to almost-a-color, to tannish white to grayish white, all fell together on a big canvas. A white canvas. It was wonderful. The creature was certain he was on the verge of something brilliant. Art *is* white. Anything else distracts from the art.

The creature cheated at his art, as he cheated at everything in life. No one else in the world would be much interested in a painting of shades of white. So as he worked, the White Dragon touched the art with magic. Anyone who looked at a White Dragon painting saw exactly what he wanted, dimly reflected under the white paint, and everyone saw something different. The artwork was just enchanted enough to capture your heart, without a drop of extra enchantment left behind.

Each one was worth a small fortune.

The Dragon smiled at its work. Captivating, even to him. The only thing more marvelous was the work of that delicate woman across town, at the modern art gallery.

You see, the Dragon had one other interest. A lovely lady, an art collector. To him, she was as beautiful as the art that surrounded her.

The White Dragon had made himself somewhat well-known with his own paintings, and the woman had placed many of his art pieces in the gallery where she worked. She was a painter herself, so the two had much to talk about.

The pity was that no one else saw the quality of her paintings. The woman had displayed them in her office discreetly, and the Dragon passing through the gallery one day had taken note of them. Her paintings were scratchings of green colors laid out over odd symbols, runes that were brushed in with shades of gold. Most people thought her works were quite strange. Not the Dragon. He loved them. He made a habit of calling her to tell her how much he loved them.

The two had only spoken on the telephone. He had seen her only from afar.

He decided it was time to introduce himself formally.

But he was low on energy. He had used his magic quite a lot recently and needed to rest. The White Dragon had been to a town called Ebony Hollow, looking for a boy named Simon St. George. An amazing discovery: The Dragonhunter had a son. The White Dragon's dying brother had sent him word through one of his spies. An unusual act of cooperation, but they were brothers, after all. It's a shame the spies weren't up to the task of *destroying* the Knight, but that was a pleasure the Dragon wanted for himself anyway. Always hunting each other, they were. The game went round and round.

The St. George family was a curse to Dragons. St. Georges were faster, smarter, and stronger than other humans. They could see through Serpentine magic.

The true power of the child was not known. But it did not matter, thought the Dragon; the boy will no doubt amount to nothing. His Dragon spies remained on the job. They'd find him.

Or, better yet, he thought, *maybe he will come right to me.*

Across the City of New York, this was precisely what was going to happen.

Simon St. George was preparing for battle.

Chapter Eight

⁂

THE WOMAN WHO FELL IN LOVE
WITH A DRAGON

THE BOY AND HIS father had docked the Ship with No Name in New York Harbor and made their way quickly—Simon would say *too* quickly—through the streets by taxicab to a perch in a giant tree in Central Park. Aldric scaled it quickly, but Simon struggled with the climb. No one could see them because they were so high up, and the tree was deep inside the park, thickly covered in autumn colors.

Aldric St. George had set the area up nicely for their needs long before his trip to the Lighthouse School. Stuck away here and there among the branches were little gunnysacks of food and water, small flashlights, a clock, some books, and below, at the trunk, two comfortable easy chairs that Aldric had salvaged in a trash bin off Park Avenue, and which would serve now as a place to sleep, something Simon found depressing. Lodged in the tree were two old brass telescopes, positioned to see in every direction around the Park.

"What are we looking for?" Simon wondered.

"The signs. He's been here, you can tell. Lurking."

"How do you know?"

Aldric's eyes passed over the people below. "You can see it in people's faces. Everything weighs heavy on them. Their hearts beat slower. The fire that drives them through life is burning low. Look at them, Simon. Nothing reaches past their sadness—not the landscape, not the movement of the city, not the souls around them. . . . They've lost something and they don't know what it is. Some haven't noticed what's missing inside, but they know enough to suspect that the city has stolen something from them. You can feel their anger. These people don't want to be alive any-more. The gloom is falling down around them like rain."

Simon looked. He saw ordinary people, doing ordinary things.

Aldric pointed down. "The cabdriver at the corner, yelling at the woman crossing. The old woman in the gray coat. The priest. Don't you feel it?"

Quiet filled the tree as Simon tried to sense what his father described. The city was just a city. Finally he had to admit, "All I see are a bunch of ticked-off New Yorkers. I thought that was supposed to be pretty normal here."

His father frowned. "These are the signs of a Dragon presence. Be alert to them. Now, then: Over there, on the eighteenth floor of that building, is the home of a woman named Alaythia Moore," said Aldric with a touch of sadness Simon didn't quite understand. "She lives there alone, and rarely has visitors. She works for a modern art gallery. She is an art curator, and an artist in her own right, I understand, though I've never seen any of her work. She's too shy and private to show off her own paintings."

Simon started to swing his telescope toward her building, but Aldric stopped him. "No, no, no! You can't stare in people's windows! Don't you have any manners? Watch the street. We don't bother the lady!"

"Then why exactly are we hanging outside her house?"

Moving to his own telescope, Aldric answered him. "Because she is in great danger. She doesn't know it, but the Manhattan Dragon has taken an interest in her."

"The White Dragon?"

"The very one. He is sending his paintings in the mail, for her to display in her gallery. And she has found them to be to her liking."

"Hmm," said Simon. "Are Dragons very good at painting?"

"Don't be absurd," snapped Aldric. "He uses enchantment to lure the woman in. She can't help herself. The paintings are magic. He's fallen in love with her."

He's not the only one, thought Simon.

"Is she pretty?" he asked.

"Dragons don't like ugly women," answered Aldric, "unless it's dinnertime."

Simon laughed. His father didn't.

"When a Dragon falls in love with a mortal woman, it is a terrible thing," he told Simon. "Worse if he decides to marry. When a Dragon takes a human bride, he bathes her in fire, consuming her ever so slowly, until she is burned away. It's an elaborate ceremony, a show of ultimate honor. The beasts have a strange way of showing respect."

Simon grew somber.

"I don't know where in this city the White Dragon lives," said Aldric, scarcely taking his eye off the telescope, "but he's here. His agents have been sending her artwork, but I haven't been able to find out where it originates. I've been in that gallery, I've heard the woman talking to him on the phone. He won't make a move on her there, with so many people around, and risk destroying his own artwork besides. But sooner or later, the thing is going to come to get her, and we've got to be here to stop him."

They had no idea the White Dragon was just a few buildings away, across the Park.

All they had to do was turn their telescopes around.

Simon sneaked a look through his telescope and found Alaythia Moore's apartment on the eighteenth floor. It had to be hers. Her home was simple and cozy, but filled with paintings, her own and others. They were leaning against the walls, hanging on the walls, propped up in easels and sitting in chairs, even lying on the floor. It looked like art ruled the house. But there was no sign of the woman.

The day passed slowly. The pale sun snailed across the sky and was nearly on its way to bed, and still there was no woman in the house.

Simon was getting bored. He opened up one of his father's old, old books that he'd taken from the ship. The Book of Saint George was filled with information on Dragons. It was mostly out-of-date, though. The book had been written by the original Saint George and the Knights who came after him. There were parts of it in Old English, and some in Latin and a runic language Simon didn't understand. But it was clear the Dragon of the modern world was very different from the giant monstrosities that had roamed about in olden times. Simon looked at the pictures of the immense flying beasts. Too bad they hardly ever used their wings nowadays, he thought; it would have been amazing to see one fly. It drew too much attention, it seemed, and was too exhausting. The White Dragon was not likely to leap into flight, and it was the last one left.

There was no illustration of the Serpent Queen in the book. He wondered if anyone knew what it looked like.

He paged through the book, munching on a crunchy little food he'd discovered on the ship. Turns out that Dragons' nails are absolutely delicious when they're broken up into a bowl and salted and peppered. At first they stung his tongue, but after a bit, he started to like them. Only problem was, they left him with a terrible case of Dragon-breath.

"You're not at your post," Aldric rumbled, and Simon scrambled back to the telescope.

"Well, there's not much happening."

"There *will* be," his father said urgently, "and we've got to be ready. You have a mission to fulfill. This isn't a father-son picnic."

No, Simon thought, *it's definitely not that. We don't want to spend all this time getting to know each other. That would be a real waste of energy.*

Aldric added quietly, "It will surely be a waste of effort if we both end up dead because we aren't ready for the Enemy."

What do you need me for? wondered Simon, but he couldn't say it out loud. "You seem to have everything under control," he said at last.

His father leaned closer to Simon and looked apologetic. "I know this isn't the best way to start things off. I wanted it to be different, but we're here now. If anything goes wrong, I want you with me. And right now, I need you to use your eyes. I can't see *everything* that goes on. I need you to look for anything unusual."

"Like what?"

"Beetles."

"Beetles? You mean, like bugs?"

"Yes, like bugs, insects. They tend to swarm all around whenever a Pyrothrax is present. Haven't you been listening?"

Simon remembered the beetles that had swarmed over the streetcar back in Ebony Hollow. He had a sinking feeling he'd been close to this Dragon before.

"I don't see any beetles right now," said Simon, staring through the eyepiece.

"Not just beetles. Anything strange or out of the ordinary," said Aldric. "A Pyrothrax can't contain all his magic—it flows out of him in heavy, invisible waves, like heat waves. Because of this, there are side effects wherever the Dragon goes. Odd things happen to nature. Dogs and animals get frightened or behave in strange ways. The weather can go crazy."

"How?" asked Simon.

"You'll know it when you see it."

"Well, that's no help," Simon complained.

Aldric looked at him in frustration. "I'm not a teacher, I'm a warrior. You seem more comfortable with your nose in a book than a sword in your hand."

Simon was offended. "Well," he said quietly, "I *would* have a sword in my hand, but you haven't *given* me one. You seem to be afraid to let me use them."

"Nonsense," Aldric groused, and he threw Simon one of the

scabbards hanging on the tree trunk. He seemed to regret doing so, as Simon carefully drew the sword. "Be careful not to cut yourself. And watch you don't cut me, either. And don't drop it on someone's head down there."

Am I supposed to be a Dragonhunter or not? thought Simon, trying not to look too excited. "Dropping it on someone's head," he muttered doubtfully. But then, it almost slipped out of his hand.

After a moment, he realized the base of the hilt had a tiny silver heart inside that was beating. *Of course*, he thought, *it's alive, it's enchanted.* And then it occurred to him, proudly: *It's mine.*

"The crossbow is more suited to you," said Aldric, pointing at Simon's silver weapon. "You use it at long range. It helps you stay clear of the Pyrothrax."

"I can't practice with the crossbow," said Simon. "I can't shoot arrows around Central Park. People would have me arrested."

"At least you can get used to carrying it," replied Aldric, "so it's not so heavy in your hands."

"I like the sword better," Simon said, and he slashed the sword over Aldric's head, fighting the evening air.

"You don't need the sword," said Aldric. "Most likely, I will do the fighting. I need you to watch for the Dragon's approach."

"That's boring," said Simon.

"It's part of the job!" snapped Aldric.

His voice rocked Simon, who immediately put the sword away. He slunk over to his telescope. He knew he'd said too much. He knew his father meant only one thing: *Take this seriously.*

Neither spoke for quite a while, and then Simon got up his nerve.

"There's only one Dragon left, right?" asked Simon, and Aldric nodded. "Then, what do you say after this one, you let me go back to Ebony Hollow? If I help you now, you let me get back to school."

School, he was thinking, was not so bad after all. He could deal with being lonely and not fitting in.

"Fine," said Aldric, sick of talking. "The one Dragon, and then you go back."

Simon didn't answer. He had just noticed that it was starting to rain, even though there wasn't a cloud in the sky.

"It's the Serpent," hissed Aldric, rushing to the telescope. "It's around here somewhere. It's on the move."

Of course the thing was close; it was after the woman, and she was just now coming home from work.

"There she is!" Aldric cried.

Simon turned his telescope toward the street to see her. She was very pretty, dressed nicely in a gray dress and a gray coat, with her hair pinned up, and she walked in a slow, thoughtful way.

Indeed, her mind must have been miles away, because she walked past her own apartment building and would have kept going, but the doorman shouted to her. Simon liked her at once. He almost didn't notice that the green grass of Central Park was now completely covered in worms.

"It's the Dragon," he realized. "We've got to warn her."

His father looked pale. "You mean talk to her?"

"Yes." Simon was bewildered. "You have to tell her what's going on, don't you?"

Aldric looked at the woman. He seemed terribly reluctant. Simon's thoughts immediately returned to the girl at the novelty shop. It seemed the St. Georges were not very good at dealing with females. Brave in battle, timid in love.

"It would just scare her," said Aldric. "I've tried before. I only got a little out. She seemed to think I was crazy."

That was logical enough. Simon figured Aldric's ratty outfit alone would make the woman think twice. He swiveled the telescope to look at her again.

He could now see wisps of hair that seemed to be spraying out rebelliously. Her coat had some odd little shoulder and elbow patches. It was homemade, or a repaired hand-me-down or something. Besides that, she did not seem to notice there was a dollop of paint on her cheek, perhaps from some after-hours painting she'd done. She was half elegant career woman, half out-of-control mess. But she carried a kind of casual strength, like someone who could take on anything.

"Our best strategy is simply to wait," said Aldric, "and go on the assault when we see the beast."

As the St. Georges continued their vigil, the woman disappeared inside, entering her apartment just in time to receive a most interesting phone call.

From the White Dragon himself.

It was a pleasant voice. A friendly voice. It sounded like someone you'd want to invite for dinner.

"I was thinking maybe I would invite you over for dinner," said the woman.

"If you did," said the playful Dragon, "I would be there in an instant. With my latest work, by the way."

"You have a new painting?" said Alaythia, bursting with curiosity.

"I've just finished it," said the Dragon. "I think, if I do say so myself, it is my finest yet. That's no small accomplishment. There are so few artists who move the art form to a new level. I, on the other hand, have a way of doing just that every time I create a new work. It's because I'm in touch with the animal inside me. All the great artists have to tame the wildness in them. This latest painting is even more beautiful than the others. It may actually change the world. And no one has seen it yet."

"No one has seen it?"

"You would be the first," said the White Dragon, who went by the name Venemon.

"I would be honored if you would bring it to me," said Alaythia. "I'd be absolutely honored. I'll even cook you dinner."

"Wonderful," said the Dragon. "Perfect. Eight o'clock. And maybe sometime I'll return the favor—and have you over here for dinner."

Alaythia laughed pleasantly at the idea, and the line went dead.

Outside, Simon and Aldric were going mad pondering what the wretched thing would do if it got its claws into her.

"She doesn't know what she's getting into," said Aldric.

"Where *is* it?" asked Simon. Already his heart was racing.

Within minutes, a long, white, old-fashioned Rolls-Royce rolled down the street and stopped at the home of Alaythia Moore. Simon was startled. He recognized the car as the one he'd seen in Ebony Hollow. Out stepped several strong men in fancy gray and dull-white suits. They were frightful men, with scarred faces; they had the mean glare of criminals. One of them opened the back door, and a tall man dressed all in pale white stepped out.

His face was covered with a white scarf, his head with a white fedora. He wore a costly business suit and tie, and shoes made of albino alligator skin, imported from Italy. A long grayish-white coat draped over the rest of his body. People who saw him saw a gentleman. So did the men who worked for him. Aldric St. George looked and saw something else: a modern Dragon.

Beetles poured out of the gutter, wishing they could follow him.

But he had already vanished from view.

The White Dragon was here.

Chapter Nine

THE BATTLE WITH THE WHITE DRAGON

LDRIC WAS ALREADY RUSHING down the tree with sur-prising swiftness, but Simon was slipping on the slick branches. "Quickly," said Aldric. "It'll tear her to pieces."

The Knight ran across the swampy grass toward her building. Rain was jabbing the Park, and by now it was nighttime, so Simon had trouble seeing where his father was going. The boy ran as fast as he could, but he was weighted down with the cross-bow in his arms and the sword now hanging from his belt.

Wait, he wanted to yell, but he knew Aldric wouldn't.

He strained to get across the field, slipping on thousands of slimy worms.

Finally, Simon slowed down, slipping past the doorman and the gathering of the White Dragon's guards, just behind Aldric. They ran into the elevator, the doors whipping shut behind them.

"Eighteenth floor," Aldric muttered, pushing the number. "When the lift stops, I go first. It'll be to our right about fifty paces, the door facing east."

The elevator seemed to take forever. Simon watched Aldric close his eyes, seeming to calm himself. Clearly he had some feeling for this woman. Simon wondered if it would cloud his judgment.

Inside the woman's home, Venemon, the White Dragon, had just sat down for a cup of hot chocolate. White chocolate.

To her, the Dragon looked like an older, extremely handsome, white-haired gentleman. He had made his magic just right for her. His clothes and scarf simply made the illusion easier.

"Don't you want to take off your coat?" asked Alaythia, pouring his cocoa and trying not to seem too eager to please.

"I don't think so. There's still a bit of a chill in the air."

"Really?" asked Alaythia, wiping her brow with a badly tailored sleeve. "I was thinking it was surprisingly warm."

"It's comforting to me. I come from a cold place," said the Dragonman.

"And where is that?" The woman smiled. "If it's not prying too much . . . "

"I consider my true home to be in the icy cold of northern England," he said. "That's where my ancestors come from. It's very beautiful, and I miss it. All that pristine white sand on the beach, the foam at the top of the ocean, so perfectly white. But, as you know, art is my passion. The best place in the world for art is in New York. And perhaps in this very room. You have some terrific works right here."

Alaythia blushed. "Most of them are just my own doodlings."

"They show great talent," said Venemon, his amber eyes flicking around the room.

She sat down in the chair beside him. She had never been given a word of encouragement for her own art, and his kind remarks had left her a bit dizzy. Dizzier than usual.

Little did she know the Dragon was actually thinking the room was painfully messy. It made his skin crawl to think how dirty it was making him. This woman was very beautiful, and he simply adored her, but her apartment was awful. She spent too much time on art, and not enough on dusting and pursuing whiteness, as far as he was concerned. There was a smell to the place. It almost smelled of . . . magic, he thought.

He was so caught up in watching the woman and her slightly jumbled hair, he did not realize he was smelling Dragonhunters approaching.

But would they ever get there? Simon and Aldric were aghast to see the elevator stopping for a little old lady.

"We don't have time for this," threatened Aldric. "Wait for the next one."

The little old lady pushed inside with her cane.

"Back off, little man," she squeaked. "I've got a date."

Aldric pulled Simon out of the elevator. "We'll take the stairs," he said. They had six flights to go.

Meanwhile, Alaythia's guest rubbed his hands together with contained excitement.

"I believe you promised me a bite," he said, smiling broadly.

"Yes, yes, of course," said Alaythia. "I've just put in a roast beef."

"Rare, I hope," said the Dragonman.

"Oh, yes," she answered, her eyes sparkling in the candlelight. "As rare as that artwork you've brought me tonight." She was trying to prompt him to open the package he'd carried in.

"You want to see it now?"

"A brand-new Venemon? I want to see it more than anything in the world."

"Maybe we should wait till after dinner."

"No, no, no, I think we should open it now, right now."

"Right now, this minute?"

"Right now, this minute, of course. You're toying with me."

Finally, he nudged her. "All right. Go on, open it."

She rushed to the package with trembling hands. "The gallery will be so lucky to have it."

The old reptile felt a thrill in his bones. The woman was soon to be his.

Slowly she peeled back the plain wrapper, to gaze upon a large white canvas painted with white blobs and dabs, flecks and flicks, spatters and spetters. It was a monument to blankness. To nothingness. To emptiness.

"It's ravishing," she whispered, for what she saw in the painting was something quite lovely and perfect. It was a great nothing, like all of his works, but this one was made just for her. And the magic was working.

The White Dragon licked his reptile lips with a long forked tongue.

Life could be as perfect as the color white.

Climbing the stairs, Simon and Aldric had finally reached the eighteenth floor. Simon was out of breath, even without armor.

Aldric didn't have any that would fit him. "I'll protect you. Just stay out of the way," he warned Simon, drawing his sword.

He rushed down the long marble-floored hallway, and his coat flew up behind him, exposing his dull-gray metal chestplate. He was not in full armor this time. He had decided to go light and wear only half the protection. He was still wearing the baggy gray painter's pants and long boots he wore on the ship. Hardly anyone's idea of a knight in shining armor. He had even left off his helmet.

But he moved so fast and smoothly, Simon was amazed.

He felt sorry for the Dragon.

Aldric muttered something, that the small apartment called for close combat tactics.

Simon pulled his own sword from its scabbard and slung the crossbow over his arm.

"Put that thing away," snarled Aldric. "If I need you, I'll tell you. Just find a corner where it can't reach you. And catch up, for God's sake."

Simon ran to catch up to his father, who had stopped at the door of the apartment, listening.

Inside, Alaythia was staring at the painting and slowly losing her will to stay awake. Her eyes fluttered. She stood without moving a muscle. She was aware of nothing but the white painting.

She was not aware that the Great White Dragon had risen to its full eight-foot height and was slowly moving in behind her. The creature was so excited its fangs dripped sizzling white drool onto the carpet. He could almost taste her already.

What a beautiful prize she will be, he thought. *What a beautiful flame she will make.*

"What do you see in it?" he asked her in a low whispery voice, right over her shoulder.

Alaythia was so entranced by the artwork, she did not notice her neck being burned by the white strands of drool that had fallen from the Dragon's jaws onto her skin. "I see . . . a knight in shining armor," she said dreamily, and she seemed a bit confused by that.

"A Knight?" growled the Dragon, and he leaned his long neck back to strike at her.

Just then Aldric and Simon bashed through the door, swords drawn.

"Leave her, Vermin!" said Aldric in a voice Simon barely recognized.

But what Simon saw was not a Dragon at all, just a man in white clothes. Was Aldric completely mad?

It was the man in white. From school. The man who said he was Simon's father!

Then Simon watched in amazement as his vision blurred, and he briefly saw the man in white in his real form, a lizardly man with all-white skin.

"Murderer," hissed the Dragon, looking at them with utter disgust.

Aldric rushed in with his sword, calling out a war cry that would have scared the devil himself—and the White Dragon stepped back two paces on its curved, *Tyrannosaurus*-like legs.

Simon wanted to help his father. But the boy had never felt so small. His legs wouldn't budge. He could hardly breathe. The beast was absolutely terrifying.

The Dragon leaned back its neck and its long, sharp face, and it looked at the rushing Knight with disdainful calm. Then its narrow jaws shot open, and a tide of white fire flooded from its throat.

Aldric hit the ground and rolled right into the Dragon, dodging the rush of fire. The white flames stretched over the floor, wiping out the paintings lying about and lapping at Simon's feet. The heat was incredible.

Aldric pushed against the Dragonman, knocking him back, away from Alaythia, who was still locked in her sleepy enchantment. She didn't even move as the Knight drove the Dragon against the wall.

"She's mine," the White Dragon whispered in Aldric's face.

The Knight drew back his sword and slammed it into the creature's belly. The White Dragon roared and dripped flaming spittle on Aldric's hand. Aldric dropped the sword.

The Dragon roared, and shoved the Knight back, clutching its midsection.

Simon threw his sword to his dad. "Finish it!" he shouted, and Aldric slashed into the Dragon again. Howling, the creature stumbled back, out of the window, which shattered with a shimmering crash. The creature landed on the balcony, shaking the rain of glass off of its head.

Aldric rushed again. But he was forced to retreat from the creature's snapping jaws.

Suddenly the Dragonman's bodyguards appeared at the door. They ran past Alaythia, who was now down on her knees, still staring at the painting on the floor. One of the men shoved Simon down. The boy landed just inches from the burning paintings. White fire licked at his eyebrows.

The men ran at Aldric, but he kicked them away with stunning skill. Simon was in awe. His father really *was* a Knight.

One of the men fell into the fire and went running out of the room, howling. The others had seen enough. They fled from Aldric's gleaming sword. They vanished down the hall and soon melted back onto the street.

Angrily, the Dragon lunged, but the Knight banged the creature's head with the hilt of his sword and got free. Aldric's sword began slashing with so much speed Simon could hardly see it moving. It took everything the Dragon had to avoid the blows.

Simon finally had his wits enough about him to get his crossbow ready for action. Trembling, he fired a silver bolt across the room, but it slammed into the wall, missing the beast.

The Dragonman's bright amber eyes flashed over to Simon, seeing him as a danger for the first time. Simon felt himself retreat a step, withering under those eyes.

But as his father drove the Dragonman back onto the balcony, the creature swung at him. Each of its claws was covered in white fire.

Aldric pushed in closer, stabbing at the Serpent, but the heat from the fire was almost too intense to bear.

People on the street stared up in bewilderment at the Knight and the Dragon, fighting eighteen stories up, at the lit-up corner building.

Finally, Aldric dived right at the heart of the Dragon—and slammed his open hand over its soft skin. The Knight had barely begun the words of the deathspell—

"Tyrannis mortemsa writhicus—"

—when suddenly the Dragon fell back, and with a hum of

power, the monster's chest glowed white. The White Dragon couldn't believe it. Its eyes went wild. The Knight had done him in.

Aldric backed the stunned creature away, forcing a retreat from the night air, into the apartment. The creature fell into the room on its back. Aldric fell on its chest, his face bathed in the shocking white light.

He stared at his handiwork.

The last Dragon on earth was dying.

The White Creature wheezed out his last breath, his weakened eyes staring at the human who had destroyed him—

Aldric, his face bathed in the shocking white light, looked up at Simon.

"Run!" he shouted. "We've got to run!"

The flame-tattered apartment was filling with smoke. Alaythia was already unconscious. Simon grabbed her under her arms and pulled her toward Aldric. They couldn't reach the door in the fire, so Aldric lifted her, and they all rushed for the balcony instead.

Running past, Simon had an instant to see the rolling white eyes of the Dragonman as the white fire at its chest grew brighter and brighter—

"Simon," Aldric yelled, "grab hold."

He knew the Dragon's heart could explode at any second.

The Knight had torn loose a large cable from a flagpole meant to hold a giant American flag over the street. Aldric pulled the cable over to the balcony and gripped tight. He held the unconscious woman and Simon held on to him.

As Simon glanced back at the Dragon, all of a sudden it shot out a wall of white fire from its jaws and its body seemed to give way to a tremendous white explosion.

Half of the apartment blew up. The Dragon, the wall, the furniture—all of it vanished. The fire blew over everything on that side of the room.

Simon could only stare.

In the next instant, he felt himself shot forward, and his eyes took in a soaring view of the city at night, as he realized Aldric was swinging them across the wide street, high up in the air, a spider on a string. On his left he saw Central Park blurring by. The apartment behind them burst open with fire.

Simon looked down—the traffic was just a glimmer of tiny lights.

Behind him, he could sense the fire reaching for them.

But Aldric had given them enough speed, and the cable slammed all three of them into an apartment across the street as the humongous American flag billowed out in the night air.

They landed on a balcony with unexpected smoothness.

Simon stared at his father with awe. "You did it," he whispered.

"I told you to stay out of the way," he said. He glanced Simon over, for injuries.

Then he turned and put out his hand—and astonishingly, from out of the flaming building his sword *flew* over the street and directly into his grip! *FWIPP!* He caught it and scabbarded it quickly. "It knows how to find me," he said. Then he handed back Simon's own sword. Its tiny heart was beating fast.

Alaythia's eyes gently opened.

"What happened?" she muttered.

"You've had a fire," Aldric said. "We've got to get you out of here."

"Come on!" said Simon. "The fire's growing!"

They ran, all of them, out of the balcony, into a stranger's empty apartment, and out again, down the stairs.

It was not until they were all the way outside on the street that Alaythia realized her guest Mr. Venemon, the man in white, had disappeared. She didn't remember a thing.

"Don't worry about him," said Aldric. "He didn't worry about you. He was out of there in a flash."

Alaythia looked terrible. Her paintings were going up in smoke.

"They'll be burned. I could lose every one of them," she realized.

"I'm really sorry," said Simon.

"It's not mine that matter," she said with a cracking voice. "We'll lose several priceless Venemons."

Aldric scoffed. "You could have lost a lot more than that," he said over the sound of the sirens. A crowd was gathered now, people who had fled the burning and those who'd come to see it. He knew he had to leave immediately. Cops meant questions.

"Whoever you are, I want to thank you for getting me out of there alive. I just wonder what caused the fire to begin with," Alaythia said.

But she was speaking to the cold night air.

Simon and his father had slipped away.

Chapter Ten

SOMETHING TO CHILL YOUR BONES

FOR SIMON, THE NIGHT had been a stomach-churning trauma. The creature could not be denied. It had been as real and absolutely terrifying as his father had promised. It took hours before he could stop shaking. When he and Aldric finally left Alaythia and got down the street, Simon was mortified to find himself throwing up out of pure fear.

Simon wanted to die. His legs buckled; his arms were useless. His fears had overcome him.

But Aldric did not humiliate him. He did the kindest thing Simon could imagine. He kept his stride, and did not mention it directly. He simply said the body has a way of turning against you in a panic, in car accidents, or in warfare, and that Simon had done passably well under the circumstances. He said what they both needed was a good bath, a fresh set of clothes, and a night's rest.

He delivered on each of them, back at the ship, except for the restful part. Aldric handed Simon oversized, homemade clothes, saying he had once worn them as a child himself. Then the Knight fell into a sentimental mood. And as the night wore on, drinking an old wine he'd saved for the occasion, Aldric grew happier and more pleased with himself. He told Simon stories, though few were about himself. They were mostly about his brother, Ormand, and how Aldric wished he'd seen the final outcome of their work.

"We finished the last of them," he said to the sky with weary joy. "They're gone, Ormand. Mankind can sleep." He turned to Simon. "The White Dragon is dead. And you were with me, right there till the end."

It wasn't really praise, but Simon felt privileged. He'd seen what no one else on earth could have witnessed—the darkest of its evils destroyed. It was only when Aldric thought of the future that his mood turned bleak. "It's all going to be different now. Don't have much use in me, I'm afraid," he said. "My talents aren't exactly in demand. I just never really thought it would happen. No more Dragons to slay. No horizons to conquer. I may end up missing the wretched things."

Simon felt bad for him, but wasn't sure how to say it.

"I'm not exactly sure what I'll do with myself," Aldric said into his cup. "I suppose I could teach fencing at your fancy school."

Simon wasn't sure if he was joking. Aldric's combat style would not be welcomed there, and his edgy way didn't seem right for a teacher. Thankfully, he seemed to realize it.

"Maybe I'll find work as a bodyguard," he mumbled. "That's good pay, you know. A decent living. So don't be looking sorry for me—I'll be fine."

They stayed awake until the early hours, learning about one

another, and listening to the lapping of the water against the boat whenever there was silence. They didn't get up until late morning.

"The woman," said Aldric, waking slowly.

"What?" asked Simon groggily.

"We might check on the woman," said Aldric. "People don't always fare so well after an encounter."

"Oh," said Simon, hopeful. "What was her name? Amathia, Arathia . . . "

Grumpily, Aldric brushed Fenwick the fox away from the kitchen, and Simon heard him say rather worriedly, "Alaythia."

Alaythia had been busy while they slept. She had spent a restless night in a hotel and returned to her apartment early in the morning, against police orders. She found the place a sorrowful mess. Half of it was gone, and only a few of her paintings survived.

No one would miss them. They were a loss only to her.

Her paintings were just streaks of green and amber, overlaid with strange, runelike writing that she had painted feverishly since she was a little girl. She didn't know what they meant, but she couldn't stop painting them. Nothing else had ever seemed important enough to paint.

Today, looking at her half-burned paintings, it seemed as if the little runes made sense, as if she could almost remember what they meant, like a song she'd forgotten the words to. Her art was trying to speak to her.

Suddenly, a big gust of wind plundered the apartment, soaring in through the giant hole in the wall and throwing everything about. Most of what she had gathered up blew away again. As Alaythia watched the ashes of her life fly about in the wind, wondering how she was going to make herself feel better, she looked up to see two figures in the doorway.

Simon and Aldric were relieved to see that the strange white fire was gone, and with it, any trace of the White Dragon. The firefighters had not put the blaze out. None of their water or special chemicals had done them any good. The fire just suddenly disappeared. As if it had gotten bored with burning and retired for the night.

Alaythia told the whole story to her visitors, who said they had come back to help her.

"It was good of you to come," she said, looking over her ash-filled home.

Simon could see Aldric looking intently at her face, as if he found it hard to look away.

"We just want to help," Aldric said, picking up the pieces of an old picture frame.

"You know, you look familiar," Alaythia said to the Knight. "I feel like I saw you. . . . I mean, before the fire—I just can't remember where."

Simon was looking at the odd runic symbols in Alaythia's paintings, strewn about on the floor. He began to wonder what else might be hiding in the ashes.

Strangely enough, the only things left perfectly untouched by the fire were the paintings by the man in white. Somehow they'd survived without a scratch. As Alaythia marveled over this with Aldric, Simon saw something glint in the ashes by the giant broken window. Careful not to get too close to the window, where wind was still whistling into the room, he dug into the ashes and pulled out a couple of quarter-sized coins marked with unusual writing.

He turned to Aldric. "What're these?"

Each coin had a hole in it. Perhaps they were meant to be medallions, but their leather straps had been burned away.

Aldric came over and took hold of them. Slowly his face became rigid and pale.

"Do you recognize them?" the boy asked.

Aldric did not answer. He ran his fingers over the markings and turned the coins over. On the other side was an image of a flying Dragon.

"Is it something important? What does it mean?"

Still his father did not reply.

"Do you remember that deal we made yesterday, about you going back when we stopped the White Dragon?" Aldric asked at last.

"Yes."

"Well, I'm about to break that deal."

The look in his eyes gave Simon a chill.

"This is a Dragon's medallion," he said. "Dragons used to give these to others as tokens of friendship, in ancient times, when they made alliances."

"What does it mean?"

"I'm not sure," said Aldric, and he moved closer, away from Alaythia, who was combing through the rubble on the other side of the room. "Each of these was marked with a runic message of goodwill on one side, and on the other there was a special emblem signifying the Dragon the medallion had come from."

"It's kind of pretty," said Simon.

"This one," Aldric said, "has the mark of the White Dragon. But this one," and he lifted the other, "I've never seen before. It doesn't come from any known Dragon in the book."

Now things got very quiet.

Simon could feel the cold fear in the room.

"The Book of Saint George lists all the Dragons in creation," said Aldric. "All of them, every last one. When a new Dragon is born, its name appears in the book with its deathspell. It is an ancient, infallible magic. All the Serpent bloodlines are in the book. I have hunted them all. They should all be gone."

Simon tried not to shiver.

"There is another Dragon out there."

The words hung in the air. The sound of street traffic floated inside, and gray ash stirred on the floor.

"What is a symbol of friendship from one Dragon doing with another?" whispered Aldric in frustration, staring at the medallion.

Simon's voice shook. "They were working together?"

"To do what? It just doesn't happen. These creatures hate each other. They don't collaborate, not anymore. I don't know what this is doing here, but we need to find out."

Simon could see that his father was scared. And that chilled Simon even more. A danger that is known is one thing. An unknown danger is another.

"There is no one we can go to for help," said Aldric. "There is just you and me."

Simon's mind froze, and he couldn't think of what to say. For a second, he wondered what Alaythia might be thinking of this strange conversation, but then he heard her moving distantly in the apartment and was relieved.

"Good God, we won't even have a deathspell for him . . . ," Aldric said. "I'm going to need you. I'm going to need another tracker."

Simon liked the sound of it. But he did not smile. He gripped his sword hanging at the belt under his coat, and he knew he would use it soon. He was a long way from Ebony Hollow.

In the space of a minute, the world had become a darker, colder place.

Out there somewhere, a great evil was roaming free.

Chapter Eleven

※

A HIDDEN EVIL

THE SHOCK OF WHAT they had just discovered had barely settled in when Alaythia approached them. "Is something wrong?" she asked Aldric. "You look pale."

"I feel terrible we couldn't save more of your things," he answered.

"Oh, but you saved my life. Whatever caused this fire wasn't your fault. Things can always be replaced."

"Fair enough," said Aldric, barely listening, and he began moving toward the door. Simon could see he was distracted, his mind on the medallions in his pocket.

"Except my artwork," said Alaythia, looking around. "Can't replace that, of course, though I don't know who'll ever miss it."

"Well, we won't keep you from it," said Aldric, pulling Simon toward the door. "It's best you get right back to work."

"On what?" she asked.

"On rebuilding, something new," mumbled Aldric. "Maybe all of this will be an inspiration."

"I thought you said you were going to help me pick things up," called Alaythia.

"We did," murmured Aldric, going out the door. "We picked up all sorts of things."

And they were gone.

What they had picked up were artifacts that could change everything they knew about the world of Dragons. As soon as they were on the sidewalk, Aldric took the unknown medallion out of his pocket and examined it again.

"You could've been a little nicer to her," said Simon.

"We don't have time for niceness," said his father, squinting at the medallion. "I was in a hurry to get out of there. I don't even know what I said."

Well, that's obvious, Simon wanted to say, but didn't. *Have you ever spoken to a woman before? Because it didn't look like it.*

Aldric wouldn't have listened anyway. His fingers were tracing the shape of the Dragon on the medallion. "Very good craftsmanship," he murmured.

The image of the Dragon caused terrible memories of the real thing to come flooding back to Simon. A whisper came out of him. "I can't do this."

Slowly, Aldric brought his gaze to bear on the boy.

"Can't?"

There was an edge in Aldric's voice, and Simon didn't meet his eyes. "I just . . . I don't know what I can do . . . ," he said.

"Look," Aldric said quietly. "There is no running away. This thing is out here. And it will be coming for you. No one will understand, no one will believe us. I am the only one who can protect you, but if I should go down fighting, you will be the only one who knows their secrets. The only one left to stand against them. You have to learn their tricks, and how to fight so that it counts. We have this power. We must use it. There's no choice in the matter. It is as God wills it."

He put the medallion in the boy's hand.

"We have to find him—before he finds us." Aldric's voice left no doubt. Simon had taken on his profession.

"It's kind of, you know, sort of artistic," Simon said sadly, peering at it more closely. There were many strange marks on the medallion. "It sort of looks like her artwork."

Aldric was deep in thought. "What?"

"The writing on the thing. It looks like her paintings, the ones up—"

"There you are," said a woman's voice.

Simon turned. Alaythia was following them, coming down the street with a confused look on her face. "I'm wondering if I look stupid to you." She caught up to them and sighed. "I mean, it's obvious you two are concealing something—you're acting completely strange."

Aldric looked annoyed. "We just felt we were in your way."

"I feel somewhat certain that you took something from me," said Alaythia, not sure how to confront them.

Simon gripped the medallion behind his back.

"What's that?" wondered Alaythia, and she coolly cocked her head to one side, trying to see Simon's hand.

Simon stammered, "It's just a thing . . . a souvenir thing."

But she snatched it away efficiently. "Hey, it looks like it's been burned," she observed. "Did this come from my house?"

Simon swiped the prize back, but Alaythia's eyes had locked

on to its curious writing. "What is that? That writing?"

Aldric took the piece from Simon. "It's nothing of your concern."

"Oh, I think it is," she said, staring back at him. "I know that writing, I've seen it before."

"That's impossible," said Aldric, but even as he said so, she held up some small scraps of paintings she'd recovered from the fire. Right there on her canvas tatters was the exact same writing.

"I've been painting those symbols since I was a child," she said, "painting them everywhere, all the time, drawing them on paper, on old newspapers, on cereal boxes, etching them into the wood of my desk, seeing them in my dreams—if you think you can just wander off out of my life after tossing something like that in my face"—at this she motioned to the medallion—"you're out of your mind."

Aldric still did not say anything, brooding with his arms crossed, thinking.

Simon was amazed. Somehow she carried off all this ranting with a quiet and confident grace. Even when she was pushy, she was delicate.

"You painted these?" Aldric asked her.

"All my life."

"Do you know what they mean?"

"No," she sighed. She stopped, staring intently at the medallion now.

"This is a gilt-edged coin," she said, pointing to the gold around its edges.

Aldric looked at her.

She looked back, curious. "This coin is meant to look old, isn't it? A replica? I've heard of artists who do work like this, fine art coins. This kind of engraving is very distinctive." She took it from Aldric, turning it over in her hand. "Cross-thatches on the edge. Lots of little scratches, looks like a secretive maker's mark."

Now it was Aldric who was coming closer. "Would you know where it came from?"

"Well, I don't know *exactly*, but the style is Italian. It was popular there a few years ago, in certain weird little circles. There's a school of artists that I know of who do this kind of metalwork. Except for the edges, this is pewter. It's a dead giveaway. You know where you get work like this?" She smiled knowingly, making him wait. "Venice."

Simon watched his father's eyes rise to meet hers. "That confirms my suspicion," said Aldric. Simon saw his father was lying. He clearly didn't trust the woman yet. "Can you say anything else about it?"

"I can say it's the most fascinating thing I've ever seen. Whoever made this is using *my* abstract symbols. And I never show anyone my work. Where did you get it?"

"I'm a collector, too," said Aldric vaguely, taking it back. "And my fortune is tied up in this particular piece."

She looked back, trying to figure him out. "You want to know where this came from. And so do I. Well, I would imagine the rest of the mystery lies in Venice."

"That's where we're headed," Aldric replied. Simon's heart jumped. They were leaving America?

"If you want to know where that coin medallion came from, you need someone who knows the art world. Give me some time to pack," said Alaythia.

"We're leaving now," said Aldric. "And I don't think we need a third."

"I can't leave the rest of my paintings and those Venemons up there in that apartment!"

"I can," said Aldric.

As his father pulled him down the street, Simon looked back sadly at the woman, who seemed to have given up so easily. Then, all in a rush, she went after them, crossing in front of Aldric.

"I'm a part of this. I want to know where that coin came from, too," she said.

"We don't know what we'll find," said Aldric. "It could be dangerous."

"I owe you for saving my life, and I'm going to pay you back one way or another. I've never owed anybody anything. You're taking me with you."

"I'm not sure that's a good idea," said Aldric, but his face was softening now.

"Let me pack some clothes. I need something warm."

Simon thought she seemed prepared for any possible climate. She was wearing a light dress but a big, burdensome coat, with a scarf tucked into a pocket. Aldric glanced at her outfit.

"Warm enough," he said, and kept walking.

Alaythia took a deep breath. It was now or never. In a moment, the boy and his father would be around the corner, gone, vanished. Something inside her settled. She didn't even look back at her apartment. She just went forward. Like she always did.

Simon grinned when she joined them. Now he wouldn't be

alone with his father's crazed ramblings. "I'm not going to worry about my apartment," said Alaythia. "We have some kind of destiny together. Truth is, I've never been one for logic anyway. What is logic? It's an excuse for wallflowers."

Simon looked at her. Wonderful. He'd be traveling with *two* crazies.

Chapter Twelve

A Ship Made for One

NEEDLESS TO SAY, ALAYTHIA was not happy to discover that she had been hunted by the White Dragon of Manhattan, or that she had invited him over for roast beef. She was even more disturbed to learn that there was another Dragonman out there in the world and that they were on their way to see him. A Serpent in Venice.

Sitting around the table in the ship, with Fenwick puttering about the kitchen galley like a short-order cook, she realized she had to be prepared to accept anything.

"I ought to be terrified of you two," she told Aldric and Simon, "gallivanting around the oceans with your fox and your horse and some total insanity about hunting Dragons—but I'm not sure you *are* crazy. I've seen things in the past few days I don't fully understand, fires that appear and vanish, pieces of dreams that come true. I've had a feeling inside I can't quite explain. Like something big is going to happen, all over the world, and you two are involved in it somehow."

Simon nodded gravely. "I know exactly how you feel."

"Well, you're in this now, too," said Aldric in a low, hushed tone. It was as if they were talking and conspiring against something that could hear them everywhere on earth. "That language you've been writing is Dragonscript. They're ancient rune-words the Dragons used in dealings with each other."

Alaythia remained doubtful. "I thought it might be Celtic or something. Why do you think I'm writing it all the time?"

Aldric shook his head. "I'm not really sure. Some people are very sensitive to the forces around them. It's likely you've encountered Dragons before, perhaps in childhood. You might have been living next to one for years. Its power seeped into you in some way, probably from long-term exposure. I don't know, but it would be of some assistance if you could read the language. Not that I'm happy you're tagging along," he added crustily. "I don't need another mouth to feed."

Simon rolled his eyes at Aldric's customary rudeness. But Alaythia seemed to find his gruffness amusing. "Speaking of mouths to feed," she said, gliding to the kitchen, "I plan to earn my keep around here. It so happens I'm an excellent cook."

She was, in fact, a horrible, dreadful cook, but she insisted on making their meals all the way to Venice. There was no getting her out of the kitchen. Simon was dazzled by the number and manner of ways that a simple dish like eggs and bacon could be mangled beyond all human recognition. She did things to eggs that were simply terrifying. There was so much smoke in the ship's galley that Fenwick took to sitting on one of the masts, as far from the smell of her cooking as possible. But for whatever reason, Aldric allowed Alaythia to fill up the ship with her smells.

Simon welcomed the food, but not for the taste of it. Alaythia's edible disasters were proving to be highly entertaining. At least she had a sense of humor about her fiascoes, and her endless determination to do something right cheered them all up. The nightly gatherings were bringing them together, and though he grumbled, Aldric found one or two reasons to laugh now and then, Simon noticed.

He had little enough reason during the rest of the day. His mind was clearly on the mystery ahead. Aldric refused to believe the White Dragon was working with the Serpent of Venice, but whoever the Venice creature was, he had probably tangled with the White Dragon, which meant he was powerful. They would have to find him and cast him down. Aldric spent his time practicing in the stables with sword, shield, and bow.

The rest of the time he trained Simon, who found his new tools heavy and hard to use. Nothing he did impressed his father. Alaythia was the only one to give Simon any encouragement, but he often felt he was in her way. She had set up a makeshift easel to make and study her Dragonscript runes, and Simon was no help in figuring them out.

Still, Simon certainly wasn't wishing for his old life back. He did wonder what the other kids at the Lighthouse School would say if they knew where he was. It gave him a little thrill to think they'd never know where he'd gone. He had just vanished into the foggy night. Now he would be a legend there.

He found himself worrying a lot about what lay ahead, and the sea was no friend to him, turning vicious as the trip wore on. The ship teeter-tottered in heavy swells of water, and up ahead on the horizon, dark rain clouds were getting ready for battle. It was as if something didn't want them to get to Venice.

The Ship with No Name was a sailboat, but it was handled by old machines, rods and boxes and switches, which ran themselves. Simon saw how they toiled against the wind.

As rain began to fall, Aldric worried the old machines would not be able to survive the weather. "Hand me that oil can!" he shouted to Simon.

"Magic machines need oil?" asked Simon.

"Of course they need oil. They're not perfect."

Simon watched as Aldric squirted oil on the strange boxes and gears and levers that covered the ship. His efforts did not seem to make much difference. The metal parts continued to squeak and moan, adding their noise to the rainfall and thunder.

"Are they going to keep working?"

"They'd better," called Aldric over the rain.

"Let me help," Alaythia interjected. "I've been watching how it all works. I think I've learned a thing or two about this old boat."

Aldric groaned, not even bothering to be polite. If she handled a ship as well as she handled a kitchen, they would end up at the bottom of the ocean in no time.

She started to adjust the sails, but Aldric roughly stepped in front of her. "I don't need you messing with the ship. Maradine made these machines, and they're working just fine."

The machines creaked and squeaked. Alaythia and Simon looked at Aldric with very little confidence.

Lightning struck the sea all around them. Simon watched in amazement as the crackling splinters of light stabbed at the water and cut it open. Then he looked up and saw the lightning weaving over the ship's masts and metal. Saint Elmo's fire.

The lightning glow seemed to sweep all over the boat, right past Aldric and Simon, drifting over Alaythia, as if it were searching, looking things over.

It was entirely possible, Simon thought, that the Dragon of Venice was using his magic to check up on them and find out what he was up against.

Aldric told Simon to see to Valsephany, and the boy fled belowdecks. The ship rolled back and forth, and Simon was nearly hit by flying pottery and metal pans. His weak stomach was socking his ribs.

Inside, the sound of the storm was worse than seeing it. The wood around him creaked painfully under the strain. The thunder was muffled and weird-sounding, like the laughter of persons you would not want to meet.

Fenwick dashed from the galley and jumped onto Simon's back, shivering with fear. Surely the fox had gone through storms before; this one must have been stronger than most. Simon reached back to pat the animal's wet hide and continued on.

He crawled down into the hold of the ship where his father's horse was tethered. The horse grunted in greeting him, as if relieved.

Suddenly, a large wave must have thrown itself against the ship, because the locked door to the dead Dragon room flew open with a smashing blow, and the huge head of the medieval Dragon slammed its way into the cargo hold. The gigantic skull slid across the deck toward Simon. He turned and dived for safety, landing near the horse. The skull slammed against the stable fence behind him as if it were biting with vicious life.

Now all the Dragon bones and skulls tumbled from the chamber and scattered about the great Dragon's head.

Simon's eyes were locked open. He tried hard not to think the thing had come to life, that something was in here with him—

But the eyes in the Dragon's skull were moving.

It was too dark for Simon to get a good look, but something was rattling in there—and then he saw what it was. It was not the pupils of a Dragon's eye, it was the quivering, fearful muscles of a generously sized rat. Another rat was behind that one, and several more behind that.

It had been their home for a long time, that skull had been, and now the storm had knocked them loose.

The rats ran about, looking for somewhere safe from the booms and rattles.

Fenwick pounced at the panicked rats, but they were too quick for him, scattering under the hay, pittering into dark places on the shelves.

Simon was actually relieved. Rats were disgusting, but they were just rats. At least he knew now the Dragon was dead.

Until the skull moved *again*, the whole great big thing, and Simon's heart began shaking with new energy.

The skull moved aside, as Aldric pushed it away to enter.

"Are you all right down here?" he called.

It took Simon a moment to make his voice work.

Aldric came into the stable and sat beside him. There was nothing he could do for the ship; it would have to fight the storm on its own.

"Where's Alaythia?"

Aldric shook his head. "She's making sure her new paintings are safe, locking up that easel she made. She says she can handle it."

Simon frowned. "Shouldn't you be helping her?"

"I tried. She wouldn't let me. Don't get surly with me, boy."

Simon retreated into his heavy jacket, the hood flopping over onto his head. He pulled his knees to his chest, cowering against the wooden walls. He didn't like this storm, and he hated being afraid with his father staring him down. Aldric offered little hope.

"At least the devices are all working," he reported. "But I don't know if they'll hold up."

"There's nothing you can do?"

"Not a thing. They all run on magic, and I don't understand any of it. If they run down on us, there's no one who can fix them."

Simon swallowed hard.

"You're not going to be sick, are you?" Aldric asked carefully.

"I didn't plan on it," said Simon in his best low voice.

"You know, the sounds out there shouldn't frighten you. Why, when you were an infant I would put you in a dark room and play terrifying storm sounds for you, with growling and animal sparring thrown in for good measure, and you wouldn't even cry."

Simon looked at him like he was crazy. Playing these things for an infant?

"Your mother didn't allow that for long," he added.

Simon's interest picked up.

"I haven't seen a storm like this since your mother was with us," said Aldric.

The boy tried not to look too curious. Aldric, he had learned, didn't like to talk much about her.

"We were going from Norway to England," Aldric remembered, "and it was as if nothing in heaven nor earth wanted us to get there. Your mother was as strong as could be. She had you in her arms, worried sick about you, and still she was able to help me crew the ship. You were no more than six months old, wailing and screaming. As it happened, we were pushed back, and the old boat, seeking safety, took us to the nearest shore."

Aldric had a look that made Simon think there was more to the story.

"Is that . . . when she died?" he asked. "From the storm?"

Aldric looked grim. "No, not exactly," he finally said. "Your mother was taken by one of Them. One of the Dragons. The one in New York. She was lost to us in a fire. There's some poetic justice that you got to help in taking that thing down, I suppose." He pulled something from his coat pocket. "I have a picture of her," he said. "I imagine you'd like to see it."

It was a locket. Simon found it interesting that his father kept it with him. The photograph inside was old. It showed a beautiful, small-framed woman with long blond hair tied up neatly. She had on formal-looking clothes, perhaps a riding outfit, Simon guessed.

"Your mother was perfect, you know," said Aldric. "Perfect. Light hair, light complexion, light on her feet. A light heart. And she brought light wherever she went. An American, with their sense of ease. Her family owned a farm in England, and the horses she trained were the finest and bravest in the world. I got Valsephany from her. Your mother was sixteen then. Years after that, the horse grew sick, didn't want to work. . . . Didn't want to live, I suspect. A horse is a sensitive creature. Valsephany had seen too many of her friends die in battle, and she didn't have the guts for it anymore. I tried everything I could think of. I ended up coming back to your mother. Seems the horse had too strong an attachment to her. He'd grown up with her. They were inseparable. So your mother had to join me. It was that simple. She healed my horse, and I got a wife in the bargain."

He said these words with a brightening in his expression, which faded away after a moment. "She was taken from us in a flash of light."

Simon's mind went still.

There was a clattering as Alaythia pushed past the thrown-about junk at the door. She had a shining mood, even in the storm. "I saved them," she said, "the artwork's all put away."

Simon could not think of what to say. It was as if the storm had vanished. All he could hear in his head were his own thoughts, repeating over and over of how much he hated the wretched Serpent-things. He had never known what happened to his mother.

"You know, I think I'm going to be a big help around here," Alaythia commented, trying to break the mood. "I haven't told you this, but I've been having dreams about you. At least, I think they're about you. It's always the same dream. I'm in a dark place, like a cave, and it's coming down around me, collapsing, and a voice tells me, '*Lead them through the darkness,*' and I reach out and I pull someone's hand out of the dark, out of danger. I always wake up before I see who it is, but I'll bet anything it's you two. It's a prophecy. I'm sure of it now. It means I'm going to repay you for saving my life. The way I see it, I'm supposed to *protect* you."

Simon and Aldric gave each other skeptical looks. It was an odd statement, and neither wanted to have to rely on Alaythia to save them. Both of them let it go.

Simon huddled down under his hood and closed his eyes, trying to imagine his mother's voice.

Aldric said nothing more. The three sat in silence in the rocking, reeling ship, and after many hours, the storm passed, and they continued on to Italy.

They docked the ship in Venice.

Where mysteries waited to be solved.

Chapter Thirteen

THE MYSTERY OF THE MEDALLION

SIMON LOVED VENICE. IT was a city where the streets were made of water and people rode in boats instead of cars. All the buildings were old and fantastic-looking. Arching bridges, ancient and beautiful, stretched over the liquid streets.

In spite of all that, Simon couldn't help feeling a general sense of dread.

Something was very wrong here.

It wasn't just that Simon didn't speak the language and didn't know the customs. As he walked beside the canals, he heard the passing people chattering in Italian; it was a language that sort of hopped along, looking for a way to end. Everyone had an angry expression, as if accusing Simon and his companions of bargaining for something they didn't want to pay too much for. Simon thought there was something in the air that sizzled your skin and brushed invisibly on the hair of your arms, like a spider.

The creature responsible for all this could hide among the people. Simon found himself looking hard with a sickly suspicion at every face he saw. Clues were scarce.

They had only Alaythia's guess that the medallion came from here, nothing else.

Aldric took them to the largest newsstand in the city and paid for every newspaper on the racks.

"What are you doing?" asked Simon.

"Looking for things no one sees," said Aldric.

He took them to a dark café, where he laid out all the newspapers. They began going over them, looking for anything strange or bizarre that might have happened in Venice in the past few days. Anything that might indicate a Serpent was in the area.

They paid a man in the café to translate the headlines into English. He was a gaunt, old man with an eerie voice, though his eyes were kind and he did his best to help.

"'Brawl at local bar,'" he read to Simon.

"Not significant," said Aldric. "People are always brawling."

"'Priests leave the church in droves,'" he read to Alaythia from another article. "'Lose confidence in giving sermons.'"

"Could be something there," said Aldric. "When a great number of people lose faith, it usually points to a Serpent. Where was that?"

"The church is on the west side of the city," answered the translator, confused over exactly what Aldric was talking about.

Aldric stared at the photograph beside the article, squinting closely at a strange blur just behind the priests. The photo had caught someone in motion, passing by the church. "Interesting," said Aldric. "Something was there. Something that didn't want to be seen."

The translator looked at him like he was insane.

"There was another article about that area," Simon remembered, "about dogs that are losing their fur. Most of the dogs are completely bare, it said."

Aldric nodded. "Sounds like a Pyrothrax to me. You and I will start in that part of town at jewel and art shops, any place that might know about the medallions. Alaythia can go snooping about the church. Be careful. We'll meet back here."

Alaythia went off down the street alone, wearing a long blue cloak and hood that gave her an old-fashioned look. The cloak blew about her in the wind, her long hair lashing wildly. Simon watched her go with a pang of worry. Aldric said she could take care of herself, but it seemed to Simon that she had already gotten lost.

Aldric was in search of a jeweler's shop in the suspicious part of the city, looking for someone who might have seen the Dragon medallion, perhaps even the maker. Unfortunately, the first shop they went to gave them no help. The owner could not even tell them where else they might look, and he seemed somewhat spooked. Such a curious token they had found.

Later, as they were crossing a bridge, Simon began to notice a terrible stench coming from the water. The smell got stronger the closer they got to the western part of the city.

"That's the smell of a Dragon," said Aldric. "An overfed Dragon, left alone for too long."

"What are we going to do when we find him? We don't even know his deathspell."

Aldric nodded with a worried look. "*We* aren't going to do anything," he said, lifting a long black case he'd been carrying. "A weapon like this, I handle alone."

He was trying to look sure of himself, Simon thought. But nothing had ever worked to eliminate a Dragon except the ancient deathspells. Now they had no such magic to use.

Miserable, hunched-over, hairless dogs passed by, searching for hiding places, their eyes tainted white. The dogs looked pitiful and ashamed, their ribs sticking out of thin skins.

The water in the canal next to Simon had turned an odd greenish color, though he barely noticed it. His mind was fixed on how to eliminate a Dragon with no spells and no books. *What if this Dragon has powers we have never seen before?* He did not notice that people were staring at huge numbers of oddly colored fish that had gathered in the canal. The water was a thick, ugly green, but still you could see the sea life down there, swimming in patterns, creating giant figure-eights and circles within circles. The fish were upset at something. Something was driving them a bit mad, you could see it at once.

If you looked. Simon didn't, distracted by the noise of the people up ahead. It didn't matter that he didn't speak Italian; he could tell they were arguing. Aldric was looking across the street where beautiful women were crying, huddled alone in corners of the cracked-brick buildings. Sadness and depression had taken hold here strongly.

The next jeweler's shop was owned by a large man in a bad mood, like everyone else. He had a face like a huge plum that had sat in the sun too long but wasn't yet a prune. Purplish splotches were spread over his face. Over the years, he had tried many lotions and treatments to get rid of them, but nothing worked. He stared suspiciously at Aldric and Simon from a protective, bulletproof glass booth that enclosed him completely.

Aldric produced the medallion from his pocket. "Have you ever seen this?" he asked the jeweler, and the jeweler opened a slot in the big booth.

"I can't tell if you don't give it to me," he said glumly. "My eyes aren't that good since I moved to Venice."

Aldric reluctantly passed it to him. The jeweler squinted, and looked more prunish. Then he looked up nervously.

"This is very fine work."

"Did you make it?"

"This is the only shop that could have made it. That's how fine a work it is."

Aldric had played a hunch; now he controlled his excitement. "Who did you sell it to? Can you help us find him?"

"He wished to keep this a private matter," said the jeweler, rubbing a spot on his face.

"Well, that's to be expected," said Aldric. "What'll it cost me to learn his whereabouts?"

"You think anything is for sale?" grunted the jeweler.

"Let's put it this way," said Aldric, in such a way that Simon could tell his anger was about to show itself, "it had better be for sale."

The jeweler stared back, judging him. He was starting to sweat.

"You *know*, don't you?" said the jeweler, and his eyes flicked sideways, at an eel in a nearby aquarium. A strange pet, thought Simon.

"He left that for you, didn't he?" Aldric asked. "That eel. You've noticed he watches you through the eel's eyes?"

The jeweler's attitude quickly changed, and he leaned

forward. "There is a killer in Venice," he hissed. "He crawls into basements from the canals, he uses the waterways. He burns people away and pays the newspapers to hush it up. No one knows. He has powers. Ungodly powers."

Simon was riveted. "He wanted many medallions, as gifts, and he wanted them done very carefully, to very specific requirements," the jeweler told them quietly. "He said if each one wasn't a work of absolute beauty, I'd pay a painful price."

Aldric snatched the medallion back through the small door in the glass, asking hurriedly, "Just tell me, where is the man who bought this?"

Suddenly, the glass box the jeweler was sitting in began filling with murky green water. The doors had somehow locked, and the jeweler could not get out. Soon he was drowning in the glass tank, banging for release, looking much like the eel in the aquarium.

Aldric drew his sword and smashed open the glass, and the jeweler fell out, gasping for air, the water pouring from his booth.

"He lives underneath the city," he coughed.

"Under the city is nothing but water," said Aldric, trying to help him stand.

The jeweler choked. "That's where he lives. That's where he lives."

Simon felt a cold shadow and turned—but before he could yell to his father, a man clapped a hand over his mouth and grasped his arms. He struggled, trying to kick free, but the thug was too strong.

There were seven men. Six of them rushed at Aldric. Aldric's sword was up in a split second, but there were too many thugs, and one of them managed a punch to Aldric's stomach. Simon watched his father double over in pain. The thug who had hold of the boy laughed, saying something in Italian. Simon kicked him in the groin—and the Italian yelped.

Simon jumped free and ran across the watery floor to his father's side. The thugs were coming back at them, but then a voice, speaking in rapid Italian, stopped them.

The thugs turned. Their master had entered the shop.

To the Italians, the master was a big man, tanned from the sun, with a heavy brow, a large nose, and black-gray hair shaven short. His eyes were cold, like a sniper's. His dark green suit resembled the sludge in the canals. He had the look of a sleek international hit-man.

But to the St. Georges, he looked very different.

He was a tall, swaggering Dragonman with green and yellow skin, and his reptile face sagged with wrinkles. His clothes barely covered him. Simon could see that slugs were attached to his skin, living off the scum that thrived there. He bared his long yellow teeth, and Simon detected seaweed stuck inside his mouth.

Naturally, Venice would have a Water Dragon.

"I will deal with thissss one," said the Venetian Dragon.

Simon understood enough to be afraid.

The black weapon case had fallen away in the fight.

But Aldric still had his sword, and it flashed in the light as he raised it.

"Come forth and meet your destiny," he told the Venetian.

The Serpent breathed deeply, with a wheezing, sick sound. Either the air was making him sick or the thought of battle tired him out.

"A Knight from the time of mmmmmagic," he said, this time in heavily accented English. "How ssssadly out-of-date you are. Unfortunate that you would ssseek me out. I might never have believed there wassss one of you left out there."

His voice reeked of hatred.

"And now I will take my property back, pleassse . . . ," hissed the Dragon, staring at the medallion, still in Aldric's hand.

To Simon's surprise, Aldric began to move forward, the sword extended before him. His chance of destroying the Dragon was slim, but his bravery was unfaltering. "When you are faced with absolute evil," he said, "there is no choice but to oppose it, absolutely."

One of the thugs tried to attack Aldric from the side, but the Knight slammed him with the side of his sword, knocking him to the ground. Aldric continued his approach to the Venetian.

The Dragon tilted his head to one side. "You could run, and there'ssss a chance you'd live. I might not even bother to go after you. If you try to reach my heart, I'm afraid I'd have no choice but to feed you to the fire."

"I love a good fire," said Aldric.

"Then I won't give you the pleasure." The Dragon reached out a lean, slimy claw and called out a spell—and a greenish, garish rainstorm suddenly erupted indoors, blowing back at Aldric as he advanced. The thugs fell back behind the Venetian Dragon. They knew the dangers of being at the receiving end of Serpentine sorcery.

A green mist filled the shop. You couldn't see much of anything. Simon fell to the ground and got hold of the weapons case, but the gale swept him back against a counter. The jeweler crouched down with him, muttering Italian prayers.

The Dragonman called out another phrase and swept his slimy claw around the room. All of the jewels in the shop suddenly ripped from their settings and smashed out of the cases they were held in. Spiked diamonds whipped around in the wind like glittering flies, slashing into Aldric as he came forward.

His face was cut in ten places at once, and his fingers, gripped tightly to his sword, were sliced by soaring emeralds and jewels, as if the gems were tiny razor blades.

Simon heard his father yell in pain. The wind, and the rain, and the dozens of jewel tornadoes spinning about the place made it difficult to see, but the howl of agony was too much for Simon to stand. He pulled up his crossbow.

He had a choice. Fire his arrow into the storm, at the vague shape up ahead he thought was the Venice Dragon, or wait, and hope his father could survive on his own.

He chose to act.

Simon's arrow flew through the storm and got caught in a spinning eddy of ferocious gems. Simon could do nothing but watch. The silver arrow spun about in a frenzy of sparkling jewels and then somehow shot free, swooping across the shop and into a dark shape at the end of the room. There was a howl, and Simon saw the figure slump to the ground. Then he saw the figure raise a shining sword and rush for the door, shouting angrily.

The storm started to slacken. Some of the little tornadoes lost strength. Gems clattered to the floor, and the green mist that filled the shop began to flow outside. Now Simon could see a little better.

He did not like what he saw.

Chapter Fourteen

⚔

SUNNY WITH A CHANCE OF HURRICANES

THE WATER DRAGON OF Venice and his ugly henchmen were making a run for it.

Simon's father was yelling at them, brandishing his sword. He had been stabbed in the arm by a silver arrow, which could only have come from one place.

Simon had nailed his dad.

Aldric took the black weapon case, and begged Simon to stay put. Then he was gone.

From the doorway, Simon watched as the thugs ran down the brick street and the unnatural green storm rattled windows in buildings near the jewelry shop. Jewels still spun about in the air. People grabbed for the flying diamonds but found their hands were snipped and sliced by the buglike jewels.

Aldric snapped off the wooden part of the arrow in his arm and winced as the silver barb dug in deeper. In the confusion, he had given the Dragon a wound of its own, and he wanted the creature to move fast, hoping to weaken it further. The

Dragonman, clutching the steaming injury at his leg, snarled in rage at a street vendor who got in his way, knocking the man down. The Dragon was headed for water.

Looking up the street, Simon just caught sight of the Dragon plunging into the green waters of the canal. Its green-yellow tail sunk into the water with a slurping farewell. Aldric ran down the walkway, trying to follow the dark form in the canal beside him, but the chase was unfair. The Dragon, at home in the water, was moving far too fast.

Simon could see his father leaping onto a gondola and yelling to the rower to chase the beast. Simon ran to help, jumping into the boat and taking over the oars from the shocked Italian, who fell into the water. The boy got the gondola moving, using all his strength, but this boat was not like the ones back in Ebony Hollow.

Aldric pulled from his pocket a fist-sized silver gadget. To Simon's amazement, he fastened it onto the gondola, and the boat lifted just slightly off the water, wrapped in waves of magical heat. Then the gadget pushed them forward with a jolt. Simon nearly fell out. The boat floated and flew just above the canal, taking corners like a speedboat.

Simon took a deep breath. They were swooping through Venice, fast and low, like a seabird skimming the water. Buildings hummed past as the hovering gondola veered down the watery boulevards.

Simon could see the Dragon's shape just below them in the canal, moving very fast. Suddenly, the Dragonshape took a sharp turn and shot back *under* the gondola, as Aldric tried to reverse the boat. But the flyer-gadget soon gave out, sputtering, and dropped them back into the waterway.

"Bloody thing," cursed Aldric, banging it with his sword, "doesn't work like it used to."

As Simon rowed to keep the boat going, the greenish shape of the Beast slipped quickly under a group of gondolas coming the other way, and Simon could not get through the other boats easily. The St. Georges' gondola collided with the crowd of boats in the tight, narrow canal.

The traffic jam of trapped gondolas became a shouting match in English and Italian. Aldric watched helplessly as the Dragon of Venice, far ahead of the logjammed boats, crawled out of the slimy canal and spidered up a wall, disappearing into the window of a house beside the water.

Aldric was furious.

"You SHOT me!" he hollered at Simon. "What were you trying to do?"

"I was trying to hit the Dragon," the boy explained. "I couldn't see a thing in there!"

"Then why were you firing in the first place?"

"I thought you needed help!"

"You are supposed to follow orders!" shouted Aldric. "You are supposed to do what I tell you and only what I tell you!"

"What if you're not there to tell me? What if I can't hear you? If I don't think for myself, we could get into real trouble," protested Simon.

"What do you call this?!"

Simon looked down at his father's wound. Suddenly, Aldric spun around and aimed his crossbow at a man running past the windows of the building above them.

The man was the Venetian Dragon.

Aldric fired, striking the Dragon in its chest. The Dragon fell back against the wall.

Aldric hopped off the boat and onto the road, headed for the downed beast. He raced up the stairs of the building, smashing into the apartment where the Venetian had taken refuge. Running with the weapons case, Simon couldn't keep up. His father was up ahead, sword ready, but as he passed through the doorway, he was ambushed by the giant Venetian, who swung a fireplace poker down upon Aldric, knocking him to the floor. As Aldric brought up his sword, the heavy weapon came down again, clanging against the sword with force so strong it knocked the wind out of the Knight. He gasped for air, as the Dragon's clawed foot came down on his chest.

Simon notched an arrow to his crossbow. He had to do something!

But Aldric somehow wrenched his sword free, slicing the Dragon's foot as he pulled the blade loose. The Venetian screamed, and now the Dragon and the Knight were fighting in close quarters with a flurry of incredibly quick moves. Simon stood in awe.

Now the creature had fallen back to a window, as Aldric, exhausted, prepared to swing his sword again.

"Simon—the weapon case! Bring it up!" ordered Aldric.

Simon already had the case open. He pulled out a torch, glowing with bright yellow serpentfire, and tossed it to Aldric. The Venetian eyed the torch with fear.

The firelight gleamed in Aldric's eyes.

"Where's your fire?" he taunted the Dragon. "Out of water, out of strength?"

The Venetian sniped back in his hideous Dragon language.

The Dragon bowed his head, as if gathering strength, and outside, the storm began to rebuild its anger.

Lightning racked the green clouds behind the city. An *intense* magic was brewing.

But the dragon opened his eyes, smiling at Aldric, and let himself fall backward into the canal.

Aldric rushed for the window, Simon right behind him.

The Venetian Serpent dropped into the water backward, splashing into the green canal as his henchmen swarmed the street below. The wind picked up powerfully.

The Dragon's friends began storming the building, some climbing the vines on the wall.

"Get ready," said Aldric unhelpfully.

Simon felt anything but ready.

Hungry winds smashed along the canal, throwing boats aside. The winds roared between the buildings, howling down the watery avenues, curling the water with extreme power. The green-hued storm had built up a furious, horrific strength.

Simon was torn from the window by the power of it, dropping his sword to the street. He was swept down the block in the rage of winds before landing. He stared down helplessly. For a moment, it was like flying!

Meanwhile, Aldric was clinging to the window frame, as the water Dragon's henchmen tried to grab him from their wind-blasted perches on the wall. They couldn't reach him yet, but they were climbing.

The day had turned nightlike, the greenish pall filling the entire city. Lightning flashed behind the mist, and soon it was raining heavily.

Across the street, Simon was still caught in the winds, buffeted around amid the chaos, as people around him were thrown down and dragged on the street by the brackish hurricane, and boats smashed into windows.

Turning, Simon saw one of the evil men climbing the trellis wall pulling a pistol from his suit. Aldric was his target. Thinking fast, Simon raised his crossbow, fighting the wind.

Meanwhile, Aldric shoved over the trellis, sending all of the henchmen tumbling backward into the stormy canal. But Simon saw this happen too late. He fired his crossbow.

And struck his father *again!!*

He screamed when he saw it.

The arrow had slashed right into Aldric's leg.

And for no reason. Most of the Dragon's men were in no condition to fight now anyway. It took everything they had just to swim the rioting waters!

Aldric yelled, dropping the torch. It fell to the ground with a shower of sparks.

As Simon braved the blasting winds, running to his father, he rushed straight into Alaythia, who was fighting off two thugs of her own!

"You leave him!" she shouted to the men, defending Aldric. "Don't touch him!"

One of the thugs grabbed her by the neck and plunged her into the canal. Simon ran to her aid, but he had dropped his crossbow and sword—and if it hadn't been for the torch rolling down the street, he would have had nothing to fight with. He swung the torch threateningly, forcing the thug to let go and step back.

Alaythia thrashed underwater, trying to get free. She could see her attacker's face above the water as he held her throat, and suddenly she could read the rune medallion he wore. She could *read* the Dragon writing!

Alaythia read the medallion's words, "Loyal Slave to the Serpent," just as Simon forced the thug to release her. She burst from the water, gasping.

Simon hurled the torch at the first attacker.

"No, Simon—get away from it!" called Aldric.

The thug ducked as the torch hit the water. The torch fire swirled around in a ring and then exploded—as if the canal water were made of kerosene! The inferno whooshed down the canal in a wall of yellow fire that rose high and then quickly fell, lashing the street with drops of liquid fire.

The thugs ran.

Simon gasped.

He had set fire to Venice.

The flames swooped down the waterways, swiftly covering the city, but soon ran out of strength, breaking up into little puddles of fire that died out under the rain from the hurricane. The tiny embers drifted about like fairies, and Simon could swear he heard the little flames *hissing*, like animals of some kind.

He looked back at Alaythia, who was staring in absolute amazement.

She sat by the water, nearly breathless. "Are you all right?" cried Simon.

It took her a moment to tell him in plain English.

Behind them, the canals were in chaos, the fires dying. Above them, Aldric fell back into the apartment, completely worn out.

Chapter Fifteen

A Serpent's House

THE STORM WAS RUNNING out of energy. The mist, rain, and fire began to vanish as if none of it had ever happened, but the destruction it had left behind was undeniable.

For several long minutes, Simon was dumbfounded, while Aldric made his way down to the street.

He grabbed the extinguished torch floating in the canal and threw it in the case. "This is why we never use this fire," he moaned. "Too dangerous. If it weren't for the storm, you might've burned this city to the ground! You never touch this. Never!"

"You're walking," Simon gasped, trying to see his leg wound.

Aldric looked at Alaythia. "How is she doing?"

She sat against a wall, choking out water, shaken deeply by the attack. "I almost drowned," she said.

Aldric checked to make sure she was all right. "Gather yourself together," he said in a gravelly voice. "I might need you. This Venetian is special, to cause a storm like that. He's stronger than any I've seen in a long time. We've got to go after him—and we won't even have a weapon. The fire's far too risky to use."

He limped over to a little wall near the canal and examined his injured leg. He had pulled the arrow loose earlier. "You know, you're lucky neither of you was hurt. Doesn't anyone listen to me when I say 'stay out of the way'? What were you doing here?"

Alaythia tried to explain. "I came back to find you. I followed you, but you didn't hear me. I wanted to tell you I found some things out this afternoon."

Aldric winced as he dabbed his hurt leg with a piece of torn cloth. "I'd love to hear about it, but my son decided to impale me a few times, and the pain has me a bit distracted."

Simon felt awful. "Sorry. I didn't mean it."

"Twice. *Twice* you didn't mean it," murmured Aldric.

The boy could think of no response. He couldn't have felt more worthless. Everything his father feared about him was coming true. He was almost more dangerous than their enemy.

Even Alaythia could not defend him.

Aldric shook his head. "It's all right. Just take responsibility for your own failures and let's move on."

"The wind took my shot off course," Simon said, his eyes stinging. He fought hard against the tears.

"Am I going to get to talk?" asked Alaythia, mercifully pulling Aldric's attention away from Simon.

"After I clean up some of this trash," said Aldric, wandering away.

Alaythia looked at Simon. "Where's he going?"

They watched in curiosity as Aldric crossed to the canal and pulled at a heap of trash, some leftover clothing blown around in the storm. Then they both realized at once it was not a heap of trash, but a man. Aldric was pulling a person out of the canal, one of the henchmen who'd attacked them.

"Open your eyes, you coward," warned the Knight.

Aldric held him firm. The man struggled, kicking back.

"Dad, your leg," said Simon.

"I'm all right," said Aldric, shaking the thug by the collar. "But he won't be, if he doesn't tell us where the Dragon went off to."

The thug spoke some English. "I don't know anything!"

"How would you like a taste of steel?" said Aldric, pulling out his sword.

"I not want," said the thug. "But I have no clue where he go to."

Simon decided a bribe might be faster. And more peaceful. From his coat he pulled out a gem that he'd batted away from his face at the jeweler's shop.

"How about a diamond in exchange for what you know?" said Simon, flashing a sparkling oval in the man's face.

"Stay out of this," barked his father.

"Don't worry—I didn't steal it. It fell into my pocket," Simon explained. It was true, but it didn't sound very good.

The thug was delighted with the gem. "The master, he gave out word, if anything go wrong, we were to finish the job for him," he said, "and eliminate the Englishman. We were just following orders. All I know, we get paid from the mansion near the Santa Lucia church."

"That's what I've been trying to tell you," Alaythia interrupted. "Next to the church where all that supernatural stuff was happening, I found a huge mansion, and when I got close to it, my head started to hurt like you wouldn't believe. And I started remembering things, in flashes. About my apartment, about the fire. I remember you tried to warn me. I remember seeing something in the fire, an animal, a creature of some kind. I remembered all of this, and then I just got a terrible sense right here in my gut. Something's happening in that mansion. Something evil."

Aldric let go of the man. He plucked the diamond from Simon's hand and plugged it into the thug's mouth. They were starting to gather attention from onlookers. Simon and Alaythia followed Aldric in a quick getaway, but the thug stayed there, staring at his captured jewel. He was still looking at it when the police showed up and gave him the blame for the entire jewelry shop robbery.

Simon, Aldric, and Alaythia hurried down a narrow alley. "The mansion is where the Beast lives," said Aldric. "The whole operation starts from there."

"You're not going after that thing in your condition, are you?" worried Alaythia.

"What condition? I'll be fine."

Simon shook his head in disbelief. Alaythia badgered Aldric all the way back to the ship, insisting he get medical help. He ignored her, changing his tattered clothes and replenishing his weapons.

He ignored Alaythia's offer to make an herbal remedy, instead taking out a red elixir bottle, which he called a magician's salve. He spread the red gooey substance on his injuries, and, before Simon's eyes, they began fading away.

"That's amazing—what's it made of?" asked Alaythia.

"You wouldn't believe it if I told you," he answered. "It heals anything. But there isn't much left, and I don't fancy using it up on wounds my own son gave me."

"I'm sorry," said Simon. "I keep telling you, I'm better with a sword anyway."

As Aldric shuffled hurriedly around the cabin preparing supplies, Alaythia sat down and regarded the Dragon medallion, waiting for him to notice her.

Simon watched her grow frustrated. When Aldric finally settled down to lace up his boots, Alaythia tapped the medallion casually. "Turns out it doesn't say much at all."

Aldric looked at her sharply. "You can read it?"

She nodded.

"And when did this come about?"

"I nearly died back there," replied Alaythia. "I couldn't get any air. I came out of the water, and . . . things were just different. I'm not sure how. Brighter in a way, I guess. Anyway, I think I can understand the Dragon language. Parts of it, anyhow."

Simon watched Aldric take this in. "It's not unheard of. A near-death experience can sometimes bring about insights. Amplifications."

She looked at the medallion. "It must have helped this time. Some of this actually makes sense to me." She seemed to realize Aldric was itching to know what.

He practically shouted. "What does it say?"

"'The Mark of the Serpent of Venice,'" she read. "'Long May He Haunt the Waters.' Something, something, and then, 'Token of His Esteem.'"

Aldric looked less than thrilled. It was useless information. "Well, at least your understanding is growing."

Leaving the ship, they crossed town quickly and found their

way to the Dragon's lair.

The mansion lay across from an old church, near the canal. If there was any doubt that a Dragon was present, a careful glance at the surroundings ended that. The vines and gardens had gone out of control here, choking out sunlight by creeping over the mansion, covering even the windows. Simon looked down. All across the stone street were the brown carcasses of dead beetles.

There was no question.

The beast lived here.

"We're not going in there without a weapon, are we?" said Simon in disbelief. "We don't have the torches, and we don't have his deathspell!"

"That's why we have to go in," said Aldric.

"But that thing's too powerful!"

"Son, don't you observe anything?" Aldric grumbled. "The Dragon fled from us."

"I don't get it. I don't see why."

"Why do you think? Use your head."

"Well, I don't know—he probably figured, why get his hands dirty with something his lackeys could do for him."

"No," Aldric said, disappointed. "He fled because there was a risk. *He* doesn't know we don't have the deathspells. He was afraid of us, don't you see? And if we don't go in there, he'll know we don't have a weapon. He'll come after us, and he'll wipe us all out."

Slowly it dawned on Simon. "We're playing a game of poker," he said.

"By Jove, I think he's got it," Aldric said quietly. "We need a look at his lair. We may find out what evil he was planning with the White Dragon."

"But what do we do when we catch him?"

"We see how far we get on steel and courage," Aldric said thoughtfully.

The fear in his voice bothered Simon.

Aldric broke in through a side window and led the others in. There seemed to be no one at home. The place was dark and quiet. All he could hear was the rustling of old leaves from the trees outside, in the breeze left over from the storm.

Silently they moved through a side parlor to the front entry-way. The place was a ruin, haggard and falling apart, leaking water everywhere. Ivy had grown in through many a broken window, and dirt and slime slicked the floor. It was clear the place was deserted.

"We're too late," Aldric muttered. "The Dragon has moved on. We shouldn't have stopped to heal my wounds." He shot a peevish glance at Alaythia, who stared right back at him.

They found a set of stairs, down to the lower levels. The dim lights revealed that these halls were filled with water. The mansion had sunk into the canal over the years, and no one had done anything about it.

"This Dragon gets his power from water," Aldric told them. "That's why he was wheezing and sickly when we saw him on land. He breathes water."

"He didn't seem so sickly to me," whispered Simon.

Alaythia tried to see into the dark watery hall. "How do we know it isn't still here?" she whispered. "Waiting for us in the water?"

"We don't," said Aldric. He waded into the water at the base of the stairs. It came to his waist. "Come on," he urged. "We may find something of interest."

"Nothing I would want to see," whispered Simon, but no one heard him.

Aldric walked through the water in the hall. Slowly, Simon and Alaythia followed him into the mess. Dragon runes covered the peeling wallpaper. Alaythia was looking at them very strangely. She was about to say something, when the water seemed to touch her in a most unpleasant way. It got colder and rippled over her leg. It occurred to her it wasn't the water so much as it was something *in* the water. She sucked in her breath with fear. "I felt something," she gasped.

Simon felt it, too. Little waves underneath the surface, on his leg. Ripples that tickled cold and riveled past the skin. A little surprise was squirming underneath the water, or perhaps several surprises.

"Don't be afraid," Aldric said, "they're just eels."

He kept moving forward, so Simon and Alaythia had to nearly run in the water to keep up. No one wanted to be left in the dark with these things.

Simon felt ill. Alaythia's eyelids trembled. The light from the wall lamps shone upon the black water. Now Simon could see swarms of eels swirling around his legs. There were so many it was like walking through seaweed!

Alaythia and Simon moved in close behind Aldric. The eels were layers and layers deep, squirming into the light. The humans had riled them up. Now the water was splishing and puckering with noise as the eels quivered for position. They were green, black, and even white, and they were not in the least bit afraid of people.

"They're watching us," Aldric said, splashing onward through the water. "They're watching us for *him*. The Venice Dragon. Whatever they see, he sees."

Simon looked down into the eyes of several eels in the water near him. He shuddered, feeling as if the snake-fish were crawling right up his spine. Their eyes glittered with whiteness, with knowledge. They *were* watching.

"But if he can see through their eyes," wondered Simon, "can he give them orders?"

Aldric half turned to him. "What do you mean?"

"Maybe they're guarding the place."

Simon's remark sent a new chill through everyone. They were surrounded by eels. If they wanted to attack, they would be in a very good position.

"We'll move faster," said Aldric.

He did not need to say it again. Simon and Alaythia ran as best they could through the swamped hallway, behind Aldric. The eels tickled their feet and legs, and Simon was sure he felt the tongues of several licking above his ankles.

Aldric led Simon and Alaythia toward a doorway. Several eels poked their heads from the water, watching as they reached the end of the hall.

"Look," said Alaythia. She pointed up ahead through the doors, to a flooded study with expensive antiques, old desks, and bookcases half buried in water. The room was water-drenched, like the others, but there were no eels here. They seemed afraid, or perhaps too respectful, to enter.

"It's his den," said Aldric. "We may learn something here."

Chapter Sixteen

⚜

THINGS THAT GO SPLASH IN THE DARK

ALDRIC WENT IN, SPLASHING through the water. The eels were still, though it would be easy· for them to slither over the threshold and follow. Simon waded into the cold liquid of the den, glad to be getting farther away from the slithery spies in the hall. He noticed a greenish-black slime dripping from the walls and ceiling. It was soon splattering their faces and their clothes, splashing into the water.

"Dragonmuck," complained Aldric. "Common with water Dragons."

Some of the dripping ooze hit with a heavy sound. Simon could tell that some other objects were falling with it. In the low, flickering light, he began to see that the walls of the den were lined with jewels and precious metals of every kind. Pearls and diamonds were everywhere. Gobs of gold watches and rings and necklaces, piled and glued madly in place, were so heavy they were plunking down from the ceiling.

The Venetian seemed to have a thing for gems and trinkets.

Simon wondered if these items had been taken from victims.

Aldric caught some of the gems as they fell, and pocketed them.

"You're just going to take those?" asked Simon, incredulous.

"How do you think I got you into that school of yours?" answered Aldric, catching another windfall. "Spoils of war."

The Knight waded across the bilgy water to the old desk. Simon squeezed in to get a look at the desktop. All of it looked really rather ordinary. "Give me room to work, Simon," Aldric rumbled. "We want to be quick." Useless again, Simon backed away, picking up a little map scroll to keep his hands busy.

Alaythia was studying the papers pinned up nearby, the maps and charts that filled the wall. They were written in Dragonscript.

Aldric asked her what they meant.

"Well, I'm not sure," said Alaythia, peering at the water-speckled pages. "It's not as if I can just look at this and tell you— it says 'monthly business report of the . . .'" She gasped. " . . . 'Italy operations.'"

She looked up at Aldric, dazzled at herself. "I can read this. I can really read this."

Aldric stared back at her with less surprise. "It may come faster now. There are traces of old energy in you, Dragon magic— I've seen it before. When your blood pumps harder, you feel it more intensely. . . . It's kind of like snake venom."

"Don't mention snakes. Or eels. Or anything else that's creepy and crawly."

Simon barely noticed the discovery. He had roamed to a corner where weird relics were kept: swords and daggers engraved with runes, and iron sculptures that showed humans being eaten by Dragons. Nasty stuff.

Aldric was becoming annoyed with Alaythia's quietness.

She was examining the Dragon's wall of documents with increasing interest. "Fascinating," she said to herself, "absolutely fascinating."

"What?"

"It's very curious."

"What is? What does it say?" Aldric ordered, leaning closer, trying to understand the language.

"Well," said Alaythia thoughtfully, enjoying her new importance, "it seems to be a list of things that the Water Dragon controls in Venice, a list of criminal activity and how much money it all brings in. He hides his wealth in the jewel and pearl trade —that's his main business. And, of course, stolen Italian art relics."

"Art relics," repeated Aldric. "That's how he crossed paths with the White Dragon, I'd imagine." He glanced at the wall of paperwork. "I'd say this is what they were working on together. But what *is* it?"

Alaythia looked over the pages on the wall. The symbols were wet, and the ink ran down the wall eerily like blood. "I can't say for sure, but they were planning something very unpleasant for all of us," said Alaythia. "It's obvious he's insane; rambling like this, the wall is like a diary. I can't understand all of it, but it says something about secret operations, activities in motion, going on all over the world. It says orders are being given. Preparations are being made. It means something like that, anyway. And if you look down here at the bottom, there's a symbol . . ."

"I know that symbol," said Aldric ominously. "It's their symbol for death."

"No," said Alaythia. "It's their symbol for *mass* death."

You could have heard a pin drop. Simon was afraid to hear what she had to say.

"It means Tremendous Death. Actually, it's something worse—he's put together the word for massive death and the word for massive fire. It says 'Fire Eternal.'"

"Fire Eternal," Aldric whispered. "What does that mean?"

She put her finger on the symbol, unsure.

"It means a lot of people are going to die," said Alaythia. "Millions of people."

Aldric froze, his eyes locked on hers for a long moment.

"God help us. The Venetian is going to wipe out a city." He looked suddenly overwhelmed. "Or worse . . . "

He tore the watery banner from the wall and looked at it more closely, as if he could read it himself. He seemed pale, tiring, as if the weight of the paper were enormous. "We don't know when. And we don't know how."

Worry flooded the room. Their expressions filled with dread.

Then Simon wasn't listening anymore. He was staring at the map scroll in his hand. In the dark room, it was clear: Parts of the map were *glowing*.

"Simon?"

Without saying a word, Simon waded across the room to his father and unfurled the map for him to see. Rune-letters all over the continents were aglow, apparently agitated by Simon playing with the map.

Aldric and Alaythia moved together to look at it. It was an

incredible discovery: an old, yellowed map of the earth, covered in unusual lines and irregular grids. Though the words were unfamiliar, Alaythia could tell the markings for the countries were all insults of one kind or another. It was as if Dragons saw the entire human population on earth as a giant collection of insects, or as a disease, a scourge that had gone out of control. A plague.

"All I can tell from this," said Alaythia, "is that Dragons really, truly hate human beings."

"They hate to *need* us," Aldric added. "They feed on us, and feed on our pain, but they never could stand that there are so many of us."

"Is he planning to destroy us all? Is that what this is?" wondered Alaythia.

"I don't know," said Aldric, his voice unsteady. "How could he do it? The Venetian doesn't have that kind of power. None of them ever did, it's impossible. . . . " He looked at the mysterious map. "We'll have to figure it out. But this is *something*. A map of the world, from a Dragon's point of view. Not a bad place to start, if you want to know how he thinks." He shot a grim smile over to Simon. "A good find, son."

But Simon had no time to bask in his discovery—a group of eels had begun swimming into the den, out of the mouth of a large Dragon sculpture. The sound of their hissing, slithering frenzy alerted the humans.

Hurriedly, Simon shoved the map into his travel satchel.

Alaythia pulled him up onto the desktop.

The eel guardians swam closer. Their heads poked up, hissing snake-whispers; the sound was like a thousand rainsticks.

The eels were circling.

Aldric jumped to a chair and then to the threshold, leaping over the water.

"Follow me," he ordered Simon and Alaythia, and they did. But the eels moved after them with a chorus of splashing. Aldric pulled himself up to the light sconce in the hall, staying up out of the water. He then grabbed the next light sconce and moved along the hall like a monkey, swinging from lightpost to lightpost.

Simon had more difficulty. His arms were not as long or as muscular. Below him, the eels were jumping from the water, trying to shock him. They were electric!

The water buzzed with their current.

Simon pulled himself onward, frantic to escape.

Behind him, Alaythia was making surprising progress—but the sconces that held the lamps were starting to break from the weight of each person passing. Now the post on which Alaythia was clinging started to snap from the wall, nearly causing her to fall.

Simon grabbed her hand and helped her to the next post. The two of them were much slower than Aldric, who had almost gotten to the end of the hall.

"Move faster!" he shouted.

Simon could think of a half-dozen angry replies, but he kept them to himself. He slid along the wall, going from sconce to sconce, painfully tracing Aldric's path. As the electric eels leapt for him, his hand flailed for the next post—until finally it caught something. It was his father's hand. Aldric pulled him onward, across the hall, as the slimy animals snapped behind him.

Then he felt Alaythia's arms at his back, pushing him forward, helping him onward.

"Don't panic," said his father's calm voice. "Just come with me." Simon relaxed, trusting him, and he allowed Aldric to lead him out of the horrible, wet, murky place.

They had nearly reached the dry part of the mansion. But as they crossed into the parlor, the map dropped out of Simon's satchel. He reached back into the water for it, as Aldric yelled at him.

The eels boldly shot toward him, a frightening blur of speed and menace. Their electric skins sizzled in the water—and Simon felt a painful pulse as he dragged the map free. He felt a burning in his arm, and he blacked out for a moment.

He felt his body lifted by Aldric and pulled out of the mansion, into daylight.

The brightness around him began to make him feel warmer, and Simon opened his eyes to see they were on the street outside the Venetian's mansion. His hands still grasped the lightmap.

"You still can't seem to follow directions, can you?" his father said tiredly.

"We might need it," said Simon, pulling the map closer. "It was important."

"Important enough to risk your life?"

"Give him a moment," said Alaythia's soft voice, holding Simon in her arms. "Are you all right?" she asked. Simon hated being coddled like a child, but he was glad to have someone defending him.

Aldric came closer and put his hands on the boy's face. "Why do you do this? You like to torture your father?" he said. "I need you for this job. I need you alive. From here on out, don't do a *single thing* without asking me first."

Aldric looked at him sadly. "Try to stay calm. The sting will wear off," he said. "You'll be fine in a moment."

Simon rubbed his injured arm, letting go of the map, which fell into Aldric's hands.

As Alaythia saw to the boy, Aldric stared at the map in stunned silence.

"There's something here," he whispered.

"Maybe you could take some interest in *this* situation," pleaded Alaythia, as Simon moaned from the pain. She looked at his arm. "These are serious burns."

Aldric didn't take his eyes off the lightmap. "They'll heal up," he said distractedly.

Simon glared at his father.

"What is so important over there?" asked Alaythia.

"You tell me," Aldric said, holding out the map. "What is this land drawn in here? It's not a place I've ever seen on a map. . . . "

She glanced at the runes. "I don't know, those marks are strange—they're not like the other symbols."

Aldric kept tapping the map, changing its light-runes. "Odd little thing. It responds to touch." New markings were forming at his fingertips, at a place on the map near the western part of Russia.

"Wait, give it back. I can understand parts of that," Alaythia said, looking over. "Oh, look at this, it's like an encyclopedia." She took the map from him. "It's in an older form of writing or something, most of it's even harder to read than before. But this stuff here . . . it's some kind of notation about this strip of land. It says it is a place of Great Darkness."

Simon noticed a little white mouse crawling from the mansion's grounds onto his leg. The boy shuffled back, startled. He bumped into Alaythia, whose hands moved on the little map. New runes appeared, lit up brightly.

"Simon, watch what you're doing," said Aldric. "What've you got there?"

Simon held up the tiny fellow. "A mouse. I think."

"Stop being a child and pay attention to this."

Alaythia was caught up in reading the strange new words forming on the map. "I figured out what this place on the map is. It's a place called the Coast of the Dead."

Aldric look startled.

Simon patted the white mouse gently, whispering to it, "If you can survive in a place like that, I think you deserve to be saved." He smiled at the rodent.

Aldric and Alaythia were too busy studying the map to notice. "What else does it say?" Aldric asked.

"There are all kinds of marks here I don't understand, a history of the place," said Alaythia. "It says vault of treasures. Place of treasures, place of lies. Land of death and darkest darkness. It says it is where nightfall begins, or something like that, where a great Dragon died, and where Fioth St. George died fighting him . . . I can't figure out when . . . "

Simon looked to Aldric with curiosity.

"Fioth is an ancestor from medieval times," explained Aldric.

Alaythia kept reading, "'where he was rumored to be killed by a vengeful Dragon and buried in the snow with his armor, his weapons, and the Books of Saint George.'"

Aldric's eyes flashed with wonder. "*Book* of Saint George, you mean."

"No," she said. "Books. More than one. That part it says quite plainly."

Aldric was stunned. He sat back, thinking. "We were missing the books. . . . "

Simon moaned from pain, and Alaythia turned back to him, checking his arm burns. "Is it any better?" she asked. He nodded, embarrassed that he needed her. Pulling away a bit, he lifted the mouse into his shirt pocket.

Aldric was still contemplating the Dragonmap. Alaythia began to feel the eerieness of the mansion garden around them, and she turned to him with a shudder. "Can we just leave this place? I mean, what's the plan from here? Or do you even have a plan?"

As it turns out, he did.

After a pause, Aldric finally turned to them, his dazed expression still firmly in place.

"We go after those books," he said. "After the deathspell." He looked both worried and resigned. "We're going to the Coast of the Dead."

Chapter Seventeen

WE NEED A WEAPON

"FIRE ETERNAL." BACK AT the ship, Aldric kept muttering the words, shedding his armor and putting away weapons. "Don't you see what's happening here? Whatever the Venetian is planning, we have to stop it."

Simon tugged at his hair, confused. "But we're not tracking him down."

Aldric smiled. "Not yet. Not without a weapon."

He plucked the Dragonmap from Simon and handed it to Alaythia, who was hopelessly trying to fix a lamp that had dimmed, its magic old.

"The first thing we have to do is get the deathspell," Aldric explained. "The map says the last time the lost Book of Saint George was seen, it was on the Coast of the Dead in Russia. We have to start there."

"I know, I know. You're looking for the Venetian's death-spell," replied Alaythia. "But how can you be sure the lost Book of Saint George has his deathspell in it?"

Aldric frowned. "It's a start."

"It's kind of a stretch, though, isn't it?" Simon asked gingerly. "I mean, we're going to hunt down a book that hasn't been seen in hundreds of years?"

Aldric looked at them both, clearly feeling everyone was against him. "We need whatever hope we can get. We need that deathspell. We need a weapon. The fire is too dangerous, too unpredictable. The next time we use it, the inferno could be even worse. We can't follow the Venetian until we have something to fight him with."

Alaythia touched her forehead, where some cuts she had gotten during their escape stood out on her skin. Aldric dug out the red elixir, the magician's salve, and smoothed it over her injuries. "Let me use this, it works on anything," he said. "We need you in good condition. Hold still for a moment."

"It's nothing. What about Simon's arm?" said Alaythia.

Simon held it up. The electric burns were already fading. Alaythia stared. He didn't need the red elixir. He didn't need *any* medicine.

"I don't understand," said Simon.

"It's Saint George blood," said Aldric simply. "It heals itself. At least, most of the time it does. Depends how deep the wound goes. It can't work miracles. We're stronger than most. Faster. Harder to break," he went on.

"What are you saying—I have this, too? Have I always been this way?" wondered Simon.

"Simon," said Aldric in disbelief. "You've just healed yourself from electric shock, you fell out of a building in a storm and walked away from it without a broken bone. . . . What do you think?"

Simon's memory flashed back to dozens of falls from trees over the years, where he'd gotten up with nothing more than a dull ache. His bruises always healed within hours.

Aldric pulled some books off an old shelf. "We have certain qualities. Why do you think the Dragon fears us?"

"I thought you scared him off mainly on legend," Simon said.

"That, too. But it's our speed, our strength, our agility, that he fears. His magic is weaker against us than common people."

"I'm invincible," said Simon in amazement.

"Oh, don't get too full of yourself, young man. You can still be hurt. You can still be *eliminated*." Aldric's gaze went dark. "What's more, you'll be eliminated a lot faster if you keep disobeying me."

Simon blushed. "I'm trying to help."

"There'll be a time for that, when you understand the work. Until then, stay out of the way."

"Don't be such a billy goat," Alaythia chided him. "He's doing fine."

Aldric ignored her, heading for the desk, nearly stumbling on Fenwick. "Throw this useless animal overboard and get the horse ready for the cold."

Alaythia moved to pick up the fox.

"Not you," said Aldric. "Him." He indicated Simon. Then he handed Alaythia the books he'd collected. "You've got your hands full. You've got to figure out what we're up against on the Coast of the Dead. Use our books, along with the map. I don't want any surprises."

He clattered up the stairs, grumbling, "I've got to take a look around. That Thing may be watching us. It could move on us at any time."

He left Simon and Alaythia, looking worried. Simon's little white mouse crawled from his pocket and darted across the room, away from Fenwick.

"I almost think he likes the challenge of all this," Simon said.

Alaythia smiled sympathetically. "The Coast of the Dead. Sounds lovely, doesn't it?"

Simon tried to smile back. "Someone in a good mood named that place."

"And all we have to do is find that place and get the death-spell, before the Venetian burns some great city to the ground and begins an all-new reign of terror."

Simon nodded. He suddenly felt sick to his stomach.

An entire city was counting on them.

Not far away, the first rumblings of a great catastrophe were just starting to be felt.

The St. Georges did not know it, but they had more than the Venetian to deal with.

The city of Paris was under the spell of its very own wicked Serpent.

On one street corner, the air had turned cold as an Alaskan mountain, while the other corner remained swelteringly hot. Perfume in expensive stores had begun to stink of rot and decay. Perfect wine had turned into a foul and bitter drink that burned the tongue. Freshly baked bread suddenly crawled with maggots.

This quarrel with reality occurred around the clock. Paris at night was an active place. Some walkers noticed that as night fell, they felt quite uncomfortable when their feet hit the pavement. Men felt nothing but a slight tingling in their legs, while women could be heard hissing with pain wherever they went, as if the sidewalk were a stove, burning their feet. The Parisian Dragon was a lover of ladies, and its magic had a special influence on them.

All over town, lights flickered like those in a fun house.

The city had lost its joy. Once alive with parties and laughter, the City of Lights was now a shadow of itself. People glared at each other and barked insults with a special viciousness.

It was a mood nurtured by a Dragon.

Chapter Eighteen

THE DRAGON OF PARIS

THE DRAGON OF PARIS took great interest in reading about the destruction in Venice. The newspapers were clearly wrong, blaming unusual weather conditions, but reporters did the best they could with meager imaginations. The dragon knew the real cause.

The St. George Dragonkiller must have been quite a sight.

The Parisian Dragon hated the idea of such a confrontation. It was an unpleasant brush with death for a creature used to an immensely long and basically unthreatened lifetime.

There was a good chance the Knight knew where he was now if he'd gotten any information out of Venice. A fight would probably be unavoidable. It took all of the Parisian's power to cloak his hideout and keep his beetles from swarming.

The *Venice* Dragon had caused this new danger. He was radical, frightening, even to the Parisian Dragon. There was a good chance that the Serpent of Venice was completely insane. He wanted so much, so fast, it made everyone uncomfortable.

The Venetian had a great love for war and fighting; the Parisian did not.

Fighting required energy. The Parisian might have been vicious at times, but more than anything else, he was known for laziness.

At present, the Parisian Dragon was awaking to the smells of late-night bread baking in the café under his apartment. He loved the scent, but he had already gorged on his own midnight meal. He was a most interesting kind of Serpentine. Like the White Dragon, the Dragon of Paris loved art, but not in the same way. He liked to *consume* it.

Each and every Wednesday, he received a delivery from a group of men who stole art for him from the finest galleries and museums in Europe. The Parisian Dragon would then spend the afternoon slowly eating the paint, the canvas, the frame, and the art into oblivion. Some of the great painted treasures of our world had disappeared into the mouth of the Parisian.

The rest of the week, the thin, blue, yellow-speckled Pyrothrax would drink down gallons of paint. Paint—color—that was his passion. And things a Dragon has a passion for frequently end up in its jaws.

The Parisian had spindly arms with a thin overlay of hair, like a tarantula. Most of the time he wore an elegant robe, created by a top fashion designer. Several of these had been purchased for him and were hung in his closet. Nearly all of them were covered in splotches of paint.

Where the White Dragon had prized cleanliness, the Parisian Dragon was happiest in a filth of color. Its face and its neck, while naturally yellow-speckled, were often coated with red and green paint splotches, as were its teeth.

When the Parisian ate, he ate *vividly*. His thin little arms would lift a paint can up high and dump the contents directly into his mouth. The inside of his stomach looked like a work by Jackson Pollock. Nothing was more delicious to him than a great artistic effort. When his teeth burrowed through a Rembrandt, the painting tickled him. The more expensive and rare and beautiful the art, the better it felt on his insides.

The Parisian Dragon loved to laugh. He found delight in many things, but they were things that would cause most people to cry. His laughter sounded nothing like laughter, in fact. It was more like a wheezing, clicking, scraping noise. It sounded like the words "here, kitty, kitty, kitty, kitty," said very quickly in a hoarse tone of voice.

Eeer, ticky-ticky-ticky-ticky. Eeer, ticky-ticky-ticky-ticky.

It was a sound that made your skin crawl, and you could hear it every day if you listened closely at his apartment door during a depressing news telecast.

One thing that made his laughter disappear was the appearance of children. The Parisian Dragon hated children. He'd make them wet their pants when they walked by him. He'd make their balloons float away. He'd make their parents yell at them, so the children would cry. It made him feel good inside.

In his human disguise, he went by the name of Jacques Tyrannique, and he looked to all the world like a thin young man, with lady-hunting eyes and long, greasy, blond hair that went down to his shoulders and was swept back from his lightly bearded face.

The Parisian Dragon loved wine. His fire was so tainted with wine that when he burned buildings, the smoke would cause people to feel drunk.

His favorite thing to burn was schools.

He had expensive tastes, and made his money from threatening French businesses with arson if they didn't pay him, and by selling stolen art—when he could part with it. In the past, he had sold art to the White Dragon of Manhattan, though he spat on the pictures before sending them. He had never sold art to the Dragon of Venice. The Venice Dragon made money from art, but never took time to *enjoy* it. He was a pig, thought the Parisian.

Now the Venice Dragon had pulled him into a conflict he did not want to face.

He had never been called on to fight before. In medieval times, away from home, he had almost been discovered by a group of Knights, but he created the Inquisition, and that took their attention away from him. That was the closest he ever came to a struggle.

Life was good in Paris. If you are a hater of love, there is plenty to hate. But with the Knight tracking the Venetian, the city would no longer be safe for him, and he thought perhaps he had stayed here too long anyway. He needed a change of scenery. It made sense all around. Trouble was brewing.

He was impatient to find the Venice Dragon, somewhere out there, getting closer.

He had many questions for him.

Whatever the Venice Dragon was up to, the Parisian Dragon knew it was big. The world was changing—he could feel it, right under his feet. Every form of life was feeling it; it was working its way up the food chain. The humans would sense it soon.

At this moment, from his apartment above the café, he was staring out at the Eiffel Tower, twinkling with lights. Before he left, he just wanted to see the old town one last time. Roam around. Smell the air. Feel the insects writhing under him.

He had this strong sense that he should take advantage of every fleeting moment in life—not because he was going to die, but because everything on Earth would soon be very, very different.

Chapter Nineteen

ICY VENTURES

THE SHIP WITH No Name rode the sea toward the Coast of the Dead. The day was gray and silver, and the seabirds in the storm clouds trailed the boat mile after mile, watching. Simon stood on deck, staring up at the seabirds, his mouse crawling nervously on his shoulder, on his neck, as Aldric leaned on a crate nearby, studying an old book. They had been talking.

"I'm not sure I really understand," said Simon. "Just having two Dragons in the same *place* is dangerous?"

"Let's hope there's no reason to worry about it. When two Dragons meet, it is very deadly. Their magic runs wild, Simon. Nothing can control it. It's as if God himself wanted them isolated and alone." He looked at Simon. "We're lucky we got the White Dragon. If the Venetian was joining with him, as they encountered one another, their own magic would turn against them. One Dragon causes ripples in nature; bring two Dragons together, and it rips nature apart. The task of catching this one is not going to be simple. My fear is, that this 'Fire Eternal,' whatever that means, is only the beginning. The Venetian's plan could lead to terrors never before known in the world."

A shiver went down Simon's spine.

Alaythia came up on deck, map in hand, looking defeated. "I give up," she told Aldric. "I've told you everything I understand about this little map-thing, and my head hurts from trying to read the Dragon language. I think I need another near-death experience. You'll have to try to kill me off or something."

Aldric gave her a pale smile. "We'll do our best."

She didn't care for the joke. "I don't know what's waiting for us on the Coast of the Dead. It's as if you're just supposed to know, like it was a legend. . . . "

Aldric looked out to sea. "It *is* a legend. I never thought it was real until now." Simon listened, feeling unsteady. "There are many stories of people going to the Coast of the Dead. There are no stories of people coming back." He could see the fear in his father's eyes. "Everything that's come down to us . . . is legend. And what scares me is, to every legend, there is some truth."

"The Coast was the home of Dragonhunters long ago. It is where many Magicians of the old order were murdered. This was their treasury, the fortress that held all their secrets. A Dragon known as Daggerblood found the stronghold, killed the Knights, and from that moment, the land was cursed, hexed by our Magicians with their dying breath. Even the Dragon perished, his own fire turned on him." His next words gripped Simon the most. "It is a place both men and Dragons fear. Both have tried to steal its treasures, but nothing that enters there can live." He looked to the sea, worriedly. "It is a riot of uncontrolled magic, they say, that kills anything that comes near it. It is the greatest wasteland of dead Serpents there ever was, you understand. They came there, they died there, like flies in a web—but their bones still possess a dead magic. You put all of this in one place . . . makes for a bloody nightmare."

Simon and Alaythia stared at him, by now deeply frightened.

"There has to be another way," said Simon. "Why are we going there?"

"Because the legend is wrong," said Aldric. "Or there wouldn't be a legend."

He was unsure of himself, Simon could tell. They could be certain of nothing, except that their destination was feared by all living things that knew of it.

Simon tried to imagine a place with dragon magic completely out of control, and shuddered to realize he would soon see it for himself.

"The Coast of the Dead . . ."

Somewhere far from this quest for the Lost Spells, high in the sky, on a large and luxurious airplane, the most dangerous of Dragons, the one they called the Venetian, was enjoying life to the fullest. He was eating caviar, loving it as the delicious salty fish eggs squished apart in his teeth and turned to liquid.

It was hard to tell he was pleased. His breathing was sickly. Oxygen made him ill. It forced him to drink water like a fish.

In addition to that, his injuries from the Dragonhunter had been quite severe. He held his chest in pain every now and then. Even breathing hurt. He would make the Knight pay. He would give the Knight three wounds for each one he'd dealt out. Then he would destroy the pest, one way or another, when the time was right.

He wished he'd taken a private jet, but he wasn't sure what the Dragonhunter knew about him, and he couldn't arouse attention.

Nevertheless, his wheezing was getting him plenty of notice. The Venetian didn't know that. His large first-class seat could barely hold his body. He figured the other flyers staring were just marveling at his tallness and muscularity.

He did some staring of his own. The woman attendant serving him pricey wine was wearing the most wonderful little gold watch.

"Where did you get ssssuch a beautiful trinket?" he asked hoarsely in his Italian accent.

"It was a gift from my gramma. Are you feeling all right?" said the woman, alarmed by his breathing.

"Oh, *cara mia*, flying issssn't my thing," he answered. "I prefer the water."

"Next time, perhaps a ship might be a better idea."

"Yessss," rasped the Venetian, staring at her watch, "but I was in a terrible hurry."

Indeed he was. The plan he had hatched with the White Dragon was roaring ahead. He could see the world coming apart like a rock crushed in a mining press. He would make it all happen. It was as if the curtains were rising on a grand opera.

The airline woman smiled politely and moved away, checking her watch to see how much longer she'd have to listen to the awful breathing of the giant Venetian passenger.

By the time he arrived at his destination, he'd had the gold watch in his clammy hands, then in his salty mouth, and soon he'd slurped it down into his stomach, already brimming with gold and silver and rubies and diamonds. His body was filled with gems. They became a part of him. He glittered on the inside.

The airline woman, by the way, had gone missing.

Chapter Twenty

SECRETS

WHAT LAY BETWEEN THE Venetian and his plans, of course, was Aldric St. George and his son.

The Ship with No Name burrowed through the icy ocean with a creaking in its wooden bones that sounded like pure misery. It was nighttime, and the stars seemed to breathe down a cruel blast of chilly air.

But the sea was merciful tonight. Over the past few days, the ship had gone through storms that seemed to last for years. The chill got into Simon's lungs and into his bones, and chipping ice from the rigging had become a nearly constant chore. Simon shivered in the wind. The Coast of the Dead was well defended by the elements. The ship had not even come within sight of it yet.

In his off hours, Simon had learned a good deal about the Dragon of Venice. Alaythia had been reading from the Venetian's own notes on the Dragonmap, and the creature was the essence of evil. It boasted of drowning countless sailors in Venice over the years. It claimed to have stolen from the city's treasures for ages.

Now it seemed the Beast wanted more. It wanted to destroy millions of people, and perhaps, as soon as it could manage it, the entire world.

What disturbed Simon most was that the Dragonmap had begun behaving strangely. The European portion of it now rippled with waves of light. "The map shows you the flow of magic on the earth," Aldric had told him. "Something has thrown it into chaos, and it's spreading. . . . " They assumed it was the Venetian who had done this, but what it all meant was not yet clear. Simon knew only one thing for certain: They had to stop him.

He heard steps behind him, and Alaythia walked out of the darkness. "Come inside where it's warm," she said. "I've got some Celtic tea for you. Special recipe."

Simon took her up on the offer, but the hot drink seemed to have been made with melted cheese, old coffee grounds, moldy Hershey bars, and cajun spices. The steam from it smelled like Armageddon.

Aldric refused to drink any, lighting a pipe instead.

Alaythia pretended not to see his reaction. It seemed to Simon that she chose not to notice a lot of things.

For his part, Simon forced himself to drink the tea, to be polite. He looked down at his cup. He could swear there was cabbage floating in it.

He amused himself by watching Fenwick search around the galley, snapping at the little white mouse, chasing it. The two hadn't been getting along.

Aldric looked up from his book. He let the hunt go on for several minutes and then finally barked out loudly for Fenwick to go outside and take up watch. The fox bared its teeth, but finally crawled up onto the mast and stared out at the sea for danger.

Aldric looked at the mess the fox had made. "There are times, even after all these years, when I miss your mother," Aldric said to Simon. "She knew how to run a ship."

Simon turned to see Alaythia's reaction. She seemed hurt at first, but in a moment she looked like she might laugh it off.

Aldric settled back into his chair thoughtfully, his mind a thousand miles away. "This was never an easy way to live," he said. "But with a wife, it used to be tolerable. Of course, she had the powers on her side. A flick of the wrist, and anything you want could be found in the cupboard. No stopping in London for a packet of Earl Grey, or Bombay for a dash of curry. If you needed it, she could have it for you in an instant."

Simon was startled. "Wait a minute. You mean my mother was a Magician?"

Aldric looked away. "One of the best in the world. The name Maradine was known in the realm of Dragons. They hated her with every fiber of their existence, I can tell you that."

Simon felt tricked. "Why didn't you tell me Maradine was my mother?"

Alaythia leaned against the galley sink, listening.

Aldric sighed. "There's no sense dredging up the past. It's not my favorite topic of conversation."

"Well, what is?"

Aldric glared at the boy. "These are the rules of a time long past. A Knight is paired with a Magician, they protect each other all of their days. It's never wise for a Knight to fall in love with a Magician—there are too many risks. Your mother and I went against this, but we knew what we were doing. Look, I don't see how it profits you now to learn this."

Alaythia seemed especially interested. "All Magicians are women?"

"It so happens they are, yes," said Aldric, refilling his pipe, avoiding her eyes. "And when they fall in love, it becomes something they cannot hide from a Serpent. They become vulnerable. Emotion that strong is dangerous. A Serpent can sense these feelings a world away; it makes a Magician easy to find. It's like a beacon, you know. Maradine . . . was . . . " He made his voice firm again. "The White Dragon found us at sea, and set fire to the ship. She was the last of her kind."

Simon didn't really want to know more.

Aldric looked at Alaythia. "She was the last. The Magicians who could help draw the power out of you are long gone—whatever it is you're experiencing, it is nothing but the echo of old magic. It's some last bit of energy that rolled past you when you were young, like a fire that sparks to life for a brief moment before it goes out. You were touched by some special power—I don't know what—but it isn't going to last us long."

Simon watched as Alaythia considered this. "What if this power, whatever it is, runs out just when we need it?"

"Well, it wouldn't be the first time I've been let down by one thing or another," said Aldric.

Simon muttered back at him, "*You've* been let down?"

Suddenly there was a clattering, as if someone were tapping on the ship's wood from outside.

Then there came a muffled calling from the deck—the strange yowl of a fox.

Fenwick had spotted something.

Chapter Twenty-One

A Crash Course in Predators

ALDRIC RUSHED TO THE deck.

As Simon followed, he was met by the chilled ocean air. Above him lay a dazzle of stars in the black sky and Fenwick, high up in the mast. The fox was calling in alarm.

"What does he see?" asked Alaythia, pulling on a coat as she came up.

Aldric held his arm out to quiet her. Across the blackness of the night tide things were moving in on them. All Simon saw at first was a flash of white in the moonlight. They were moving fast, whatever they were. His eyes tried to get a fix on them, but the blanket of night hid the things from view.

Fenwick didn't need to see any more. He scurried down the mast and sped for the cabin, no doubt looking for his hiding place in the hold.

"It knows we're here," said Aldric, furious. "The Dragon. There's something on this ship. Something told him we were here."

He looked first at Alaythia, then his eyes swept the deck, searching for the cause. Simon could see him taking on his warrior focus, as intense as a chess player.

"Maybe we're just getting close to the lost book," Simon said, "We're getting close to the Coast of the Dead. You said it's protected—"

"We're not close enough for that. Something's here," the knight said. "Some kind of device. He's watching every move we make."

He snatched Simon's satchel and began throwing things out of it.

"What are you doing?" Simon asked.

"We have to hurry," said Aldric, and he grabbed hold of the Dragonmap. "This could be how he locates us."

"Don't throw that over, we may need it!" pleaded Simon.

"Whatever's out there is getting closer," said Alaythia.

Simon pulled at the map. "This is a spying device!" growled Aldric.

Suddenly, Simon realized it wasn't. He knew exactly where the spy was. "It's not this," he told Aldric. "It's in there!" He ran for the cabin of the ship.

Simon burst into the galley, only to find Fenwick rushing to get hold of the white mouse. The fox's paws finally stomped the mouse's tail, and Simon grabbed the little traitor.

Running topside, Simon flopped the slippery mouse into his father's hands. "I took it from Venice," he said. "It's a spy."

The mouse squirmed madly in Aldric's grip and bit into the man's hand. Aldric lost hold of the rodent and it spun over the rail, dropping off the ship. As it fell, it glowed with white light—and vanished before it hit the foam.

"Where are they?" whispered Alaythia, searching seaward for the shapes that were there a moment before.

Simon shivered as the wintry air got colder, and he peered out at the calm, dead ocean. He thought he caught sight of a slashing tail in the dark, but it was hard to tell, his imagination running wild.

He moved forward, his eyes frantically covering the half-frozen waters. All around, huge chunks of ice floated on the night ocean. As he moved for a better look, he almost slipped on the icy deck. His hands grabbed for the ship's rail, and his bare skin stuck tight to the metal.

Again he heard rumbling on the ship's stern.

"What was that?" he asked.

Aldric leaned over the side. "I'm not sure."

Simon pulled at his hands. They were not budging.

The rumbling hit the ship again. Now it seemed that whatever caused the sound was scraping the bottom of the boat.

"Stay where you are," said Aldric nervously, searching around the ship.

"I'm not going anywhere," answered Simon, his hands frozen to the rail.

The wind had died completely. No other ships could be seen on the waters. Only icebergs drifted about, great and small. It was a lonely picture.

"We're dead in the water," said Alaythia. "We've got to get the ship moving again. Let me tend to the rigging." Before Aldric could say a word, Alaythia was climbing to the sails. But she had no time left.

Suddenly the ship was struck again. Burring through the

moonlit sea was an ice-blue shape that looked something like a shark. As it scraped along the side of the ship, Simon realized that it was not the real thing, but an ice carving that looked and moved like a shark.

Its angry, sculpted face swam past them and sunk below water.

"What is it?" wondered Simon.

"Dragon magic," Aldric said.

More of the sharks began swimming toward the ship. Simon still couldn't move. He watched with fascination, but as the sharks battered the side of the ship, cracking and splintering off part of their bodies, Simon was nearly hit by flying shards of ice.

"Wretched magic!" cried Aldric. He loaded up his crossbow.

The icebergs nearby squealed with a frightful noise, as ice calved off the frigid masses. As the ice hit the water, it formed into new sharks. Soon the ocean was dotted with fast-moving ice sharks attacking the boat.

Again and again they rammed the ship, coming from every angle. Some of the ice sharks hit so hard they shattered completely, and tiny ice sharks were formed from the remnants of the bigger ones. The tiny sharks joined the larger in pummeling the Ship with No Name.

Aldric fired arrows but kept missing. The sharks were too fast.

"Get us going!" bellowed Aldric.

Alaythia swayed from the mast, trying to unfurl a sail as the ship shuddered from the attacks. "I'm trying!" she called.

"I can't do this alone!" Aldric yelled. "Simon, what the devil are you doing?"

Simon was trying not to lose his life. His hands wouldn't pull free from the rail. The sharks were leaping up out of the water, snapping at him. Every time the sharks hit the ship, ice splinters, sharp and savage, would cascade over the deck, cutting Simon's face.

"Simon, get below!" yelled Aldric from the other side of the ship. "It's too dangerous up here!!"

One of Aldric's arrows found its mark—and an ice shark was split in two! Now that same shark became *two* sharks, which swerved angrily for Aldric.

Simon had pulled one arm free, tearing the skin of his hand. He couldn't do that again. Quickly he pulled an arrow from the quiver at his side and held it to one of the torches mounted on the ship's railing. Then he moved the flaming arrow, to burn away the ice that held his hand.

Just at that moment, the two infuriated ice sharks leapt at Aldric's face. The first came within an inch of him. Before its nasty ice teeth could crush him, Simon fired his crossbow into the shark's nose. Its face shattered, and the force of the blow sent it reeling back into the water.

Simon had saved his father's life. But the joy of this vanished like vapor.

The second shark had hit the deck—shattering into dozens of tiny ice sharks snapping their icy jaws. They flopped about on deck, trying to get to Aldric's legs.

Simon stabbed at them with his sword. He batted them off the deck, smashing them into the water. One of the little fish-monsters sunk its teeth into his ankle. It was like getting caught in a vise grip studded with needles! The icy jaws clamped onto Simon's leg, forcing him to pull it free, painfully.

Above him he could see Alaythia fighting to free the sails and get them into position. Everything had gone wrong with the magic that ran the ship. Rigging was fouled up, machinery failed, and the wind had grown weak.

Simon kicked loose the vicious little ice-shark, but in doing so he slipped, sliding across the tilting deck to plunge directly into the ocean. He screamed from the cold.

Below him a huge ice-shark was just pulling itself out of the sea. He grabbed hold of its dorsal fin so it couldn't get its jaws around him. Now the shark was thrashing, trying to get at Simon.

Aldric was yelling for Simon to grab hold of a line he was throwing out. The rope missed Simon—and the boy went speeding through the water on the back of the shark, hanging on for dear life.

"Help me!" he shouted—but in the midst of his panic he felt a thrill, an exhilaration. He was holding on to a shark!

Other sharks were closing in around him. Simon gripped the icy fin. Then, just as the shark he was riding on swooped past the ship again, Simon leapt away, snatching onto Aldric's rope.

Aldric yanked him aboard as three sharks at once snapped at Simon's heels.

Simon laughed out of pure fear—tumbling onto the deck, into Aldric's arms. He could feel his father's heart beating in terror for him. Aldric looked into his eyes, made sure he was all right. Then he pulled loose and rushed for the rail to fight off the relentless sharks, who were still battering the ship.

High up on the mast, Alaythia closed her eyes, deep in concentration, and reached out to let loose the sails. She whispered to herself, a kind of prayer, a wish, a mantra, all in one.

Below her Simon lay on the icy wood, rubbing his freezing body. "Somebody do something!" he cried. "Can't this pathetic ship go faster?!"

And then it did.

The sails Alaythia struggled with now opened. The wind swept over the ocean and fell into the canvas like a stampede of horses. The deck lurched under Simon.

The ship gathered up all its strength and charged forward, shooting through the swarms of ice sharks up ahead and blasting past the ones beneath it. Soon it had put them all behind. It was speeding over the ocean like never before.

Simon was awed. Aldric moved in to check the shark bite on Simon's ankle. He waved his father off. "I'm all right."

"You'll have to be, for now." He called to Alaythia, still high in the rigging.

Her eyes remain closed, her body fixed to the mast like a wooden sculpture. She was nearly in a sleep state, terrified to open her eyes. "Are we through it?" she said. "I'm afraid to move."

"Yes. We're through it," called Aldric.

"We were grinding right through them," gasped Simon. "I think I saved your life back there."

Aldric raised an eyebrow. "That's your view of things, is it?"

"I *saved* your life," Simon said, resentfully. "You can't take this away from me."

"You endangered *yourself,*" said Aldric. "You put yourself at unnecessary risk. You have a *duty* to stay alive. You have a duty to follow my lead. I can take care of myself."

Simon was speechless—furious at his father for ignoring what he'd done.

"And we're not through this yet," said Aldric, turning to the horizon. "We're moving too fast. We're out of control."

It was true. The ship was cutting the ocean like scissors through silk. With incredible speed, it was rushing for land—a jagged ice formation up ahead.

Simon reached to brace himself.

Aldric shook his head with worry. "I was wrong. We *are* close to that godforsaken place. The ship's gone mad."

Simon reacted without a word. The ship's magic was beyond his understanding.

"We've got to get her down," said Aldric, heading for Alaythia.

"I don't need help," she said, hurrying down the ice-coated mast.

Simon felt a rush of fear for her as the ship tilted. Her feet slipped. She grabbed for a hold on the mast, barely escaping a fall.

Simon's heart shook. *"Help her,"* he told his father.

Aldric started up, but Simon knew it was too late. The ship was rushing for the glacial territory, and in the next breath it had slammed into the icy coastline.

Everyone rocked from the impact. The ship rammed into the ice, spitting off the frost in its sails, canvas clattering with windy rage. Simon was thrown sideways, away from his father. He slid across the deck, sweeping painfully over the ice, to hit the cabin door. It struck like a boxer's punch at his back.

Knocked breathless, he saw his father tumble over the railing. Alaythia fell from the mast, grabbing it again just before she would have hit the ground. Her scream shot across the snowy land.

Everything on the ship creaked and groaned, and then was silent.

Chapter Twenty-Two

GRAVEYARD OF DRAGONS

THE WIND DIED DOWN, whispering around the ship, taunting the survivors.

They had run aground.

Simon stood up weakly. The ship seemed mostly undamaged, from what he could see. His eyes met Alaythia's. She put her hand up, as if to say, *Don't worry, I'm okay,* and Simon moved to the side of the ship, looking for Aldric.

He was lying in the snow, just now lifting his head. He seemed to be all right.

Simon yelled down to him, rattled. "What do we do now?"

Tense with worry, Aldric gestured behind him. "Ransack the graveyard," he answered.

Simon and Alaythia looked up, surprised. On the coast was a blight of dead trees and a trail of skeletal remains, human-sized Dragons, each one encircled in a little tornado of ashes and embers, still burning.

They had found the graveyard of Dragons.

Aldric headed back to board the ship. It was lodged just out of the water. Now the damage could be seen clearly.

"We've got ourselves a wreck," Aldric complained as he boarded. Parts of the ship's deck had been cracked. The top of one mast had fallen.

"It could be worse," said Alaythia.

"You should've cut sail when you saw we were going too fast," said Aldric.

Alaythia looked at him sharply. "You can't possibly blame this on me. I was doing all I could."

"It's all I have left of her," Aldric answered, not meeting Alaythia's gaze.

Simon could feel the tension between Aldric and Alaythia, and decided to focus on the next step: "What do we do now? We haven't got a ship."

"The wood will heal itself," said Aldric, "but it could take a very long time."

Fenwick came out of hiding, running up and down the deck, highly disturbed.

"I know, I know," Aldric said, calling to the fox. "Quit complaining—I'm not happy about it, either. Put the cabin in order, and take care of Valsephany. We have other things to worry about now."

Simon looked at the landscape. "Looks almost peaceful," he said. "Just dead. Maybe the legends *were* wrong."

They would find out for themselves. They changed into dry clothes and gathered gear for an expedition. Alaythia stayed behind clearing debris and keeping watch, while Simon and Aldric forged into the icy region. As dawn broke, they discovered that the trail of Dragon bones led to a stone ruin. As Simon reached the top of a hill, he stared in awe at what lay hidden in the dim light: A castle in the snow. It had clearly been through some terrible times. Little was left of its crumbling towers. Ice had formed into unearthly shapes atop its decrepit walls.

In the courtyard, Aldric found a sword in the ice, marked with the Dragonhunter symbol. Simon and Aldric began digging there, searching for the Lost Book of Saint George.

They uncovered the armor and weapons of many Knights, but there was no trace of the people who lived in the fortress. "They were burned away," concluded Aldric. "The battle was here. The Dragon got through the outer defenses, and they resisted him 'til there was no one left to fight."

He pointed to a Serpentine form near a tower, the burned bones of the Daggerblood Dragon.

Aldric theorized the other dragon bones they'd seen had come from later visitors here. But there was something else bothering Simon. "I want to know about Alaythia, but you keep changing the subject—she went up in the mast, she did something, and the wind came out of nowhere. I mean, how do you explain that?"

"Let's get this done," said his father, as Alaythia came from the ship, bringing more digging tools.

"I'm not waiting out there alone," she said. "The animals are fine, and you don't have to worry, I got all my artwork put away."

Aldric kept digging. "Good. I was worried sick. You can help us now. I want to get out of here as fast as possible." But his shovel had just hit something hard.

Simon leaned down with Aldric. It was a grim treasure they had found. A human skeleton in armor stared out at them.

"Fioth St. George," said Aldric.

Alaythia came closer, intrigued. "How do you know?" she whispered.

Aldric cleared away more ice. "He carries the book."

In the arms of the skeletal Knight lay the Lost Book of Saint George. Aldric gingerly pulled the very old, leatherbound volume from his ancestor's clutches. It was slightly larger than an average Bible, and Aldric treated it with great care.

"Sorry, old fellow," said Aldric. Several Dragon-daggers lay embedded in the Knight's skull, still burning faintly with red dragonfire.

"*That* is hate." Simon stared somberly. "Why didn't the Dragon just burn the book after doing this?"

"The books can't be destroyed," said Aldric, moving away from the fallen Knight. "And the curse did its work: The Dragon never got out alive."

Simon watched as Aldric turned the pages. It was a white book, not the black one Simon was used to calling the Book of Saint George.

"There's a lesson to all this," muttered Aldric. "Back in the late medieval ages, there were two groups of Dragonhunters, those that followed Arthur St. George and those that followed Fioth St. George. They kept their work secret from the other so that if one group was destroyed, the other could fight on and not be discovered. But there were too many secrets. It would seem they worked from two different spellbooks. We didn't even know this book existed."

"Is it going to help us?" asked Alaythia.

"They're in here," Aldric said, satisfied. "The deathspells are in here."

And then he realized what he said, and his face fell into sadness.

Simon moved near him to see better. "No, this is—this is impossible," Simon stammered. His eyes ran down the long list of Serpents.

"Hundreds," said Aldric, his voice catching. It was like finding a new ocean after having just crossed one. "God help us. How many are still out there to this day?"

The wind and the shock froze out any more words for a moment. The Venice Dragon now seemed to be only the start of their worries. A spark in a vast bonfire. The danger before them was so infinite they could hardly bear to talk about it.

"What is . . . Whose deathspell is this?"

Simon pointed. At the bottom of the list was a group of words, fancily written in the human magician language. Like all magic writing, it was partly in Dragontongue, but the words did not match up with any particular Dragon.

"Not sure what that means," said Aldric. "Some old warning, perhaps. The important thing is, the book is undamaged. Let's just get it out of here."

"Why?" said Simon, his shoulders falling. "We can't get them all, just the three of us."

Aldric pocketed the book, looking at him. "We must."

It was the lowest they had ever been.

The threat of the Dead Coast was nothing compared to its secret.

With a sad fury, Aldric picked up the torch of blue dragonfire they had been using to light their work and tipped his arrow with it. He lit another with the dark red fire from the Dragon-daggers. Simon wondered what he was doing.

Angrily, he fired the first arrow into the body of the Daggerblood Dragon.

"I'm too late to kill you," snarled Aldric, and Simon was amazed at his wrath. "But I can burn you until there's no trace of you on this earth."

With a cry of desperation, he shot the red-fire arrow into the same spot on the Dragon's skeleton.

The two flames on the arrows came together and blew up with a calamitous blast. The skeleton was blown to bits. The exploded parts came down in pieces of burning bone. But immediately the fire turned into a quick, screaming inferno, and they were forced to run from it. Simon ran hard toward the ship, looking back to see the flames reaching across the winterscape.

Simon, Aldric, and Alaythia ran until they crossed a fallen fortress gate, and stopped to look back. The fire was still crawling toward them.

"When the fire of two Dragons crosses," Aldric said, breathing hard, "it unleashes immense power. I didn't know how bad it would be."

The flames would reach them soon. But Simon and Alaythia were already exhausted.

"Well, I promised you near-death experiences," said Aldric.

Alaythia groaned. "Feel free to break your promises."

They fled the fire, seeking safety. They found instead a wall of fog.

In the growing daylight, Simon watched, disturbed, as the fog expanded and blotted out the view of the ship, of the fire, of the dead fortress, and soon all traces of the landscape.

"Of course the Dragons left the book here," said Aldric. "No one ever comes here; no one ever leaves."

Simon and Aldric felt themselves grow dizzy. Alaythia said she felt it as well, a nausea taking over so strongly that she couldn't go far without help.

She stuck close to them, but it was clear no one knew which direction they were headed. There was nothing to guide them. They hiked in the snow for a long time, hearing horrible sounds in the fog, like wild predators killing their prey, snapping and tearing. Later they heard the cries and clanging of an old battle of Knights and Serpents, like an echo in history. Voices in the mist called out for them to run. They heeded the warning.

At last Aldric found the way to the waterline, and they followed it, heading back to the ship, but their path along the edge of the coast was now broken up by cracking ice. Simon looked down to see the white ground breaking up beneath him—and hundreds of snapping, piranha-like creatures furiously churning the water between the cracks. All Simon could see were their sharp, tiny, glittering jaws.

Hurriedly, Aldric led Simon and Alaythia to the ship, as the piranha-animals began eating at the ice around them, nearly chewing away the path.

The damaged ship launched, and its tattered sails carried them away from the small, frenzying creatures. Simon looked back to see the shapes of skeletal faces in the ghostly mist. The battered ship was making terrible creaking noises, but it had taken them from the Coast of the Dead. Simon's heart calmed; he felt his head clearing.

Within a few hours the sailboat, tilting unevenly in the water, limped to a misty harbor in Russia. Aldric told Simon to be on guard. He had noticed something. They had been followed for some time by a military vessel.

As Simon, Aldric, and Alaythia stepped off the boat to the pier, the soldiers from the vessel moved in. Aldric was dragging a huge black supply trunk, hoping to refill some of the ship's supplies. He yelled to the ship, "Lock up," and the cabin doors and windows locked soundly.

Soldiers swarmed around them. The men were barking questions already.

"Russian," said Simon, recognizing their language.

Aldric felt in his coat for the White Book of Saint George. Simon could see his nervousness.

The Russians came in and looked them over, as well as the supply trunk. They did not speak English very well, and they were very suspicious of these new arrivals. They ordered the St. Georges and Alaythia back to their station house in a nearby village.

Since more soldiers were arriving out of the snowy forest, Aldric decided to go without a fight for now.

Simon was very worried as the hostile Russians pulled them away. Suspicion was bred into the bone with these men; not just anyone could get past them. At the coastal station, they asked many questions, and if they didn't like the looks of you, off you'd go to a cold Siberian prison. Or so they threatened.

"You have nice digits," said one soldier to Alaythia. His English was bad. He meant to say she had a nice figure. Aldric was now clenching his fists, watching and clearly wishing he could get to his weapons.

There were many, many soldiers here, and they were large,

and it seemed to Simon they were angry, waiting for any excuse to strike them.

Just then, a smiling Russian, smooth and well-dressed, entered behind the hulking guards. He was clearly the boss. "It is our displeasure to detain you." He grinned. "Please enjoy a view of television while we review your case."

Literally. The Russians were trying to open Aldric's black steamer trunk marked with the Dragonhunter symbol. In the meantime, Simon glanced over at the TV news. He was astonished at the images he saw.

The news showed tremendous devastation, some kind of horrid storm destruction that ran throughout the French countryside. There were images of a beaten Paris, a smashed Berlin, a storm-struck Geneva—homes were leveled, people were crying, wandering aimlessly.

"That storm went through France, Germany, Poland . . . ," he said.

"I don't understand," said Alaythia.

"It is beginning. Whatever the Venetian is planning, this is the start of it all," Aldric said. "He's building toward his 'Fire Eternal.'"

The news showed coffins being prepared in the hundreds. Parts of Berlin looked as it had after World War II—broken buildings, shivering people. A world map showed the giant storm headed for the Russian plains.

"It's headed for Moscow," whispered Alaythia.

Aldric pondered this. "Why . . . ?"

The smiling Russian returned to them. "We have found cause for concern," he said. "I would like to see personally that you get to my superior. Please come with the guards. No cause for concern." His smile never left his face.

Aldric looked angry, sizing up the hulking men. One of them pushed up his sleeves, ready to fight, revealing a Dragon tattoo with runic writing. Simon looked at his father. He could see the tension leave him.

The grinning Russian escorted them all to an ancient, rickety train.

Aldric whispered to Simon with satisfaction, "These are the servants of a Serpent. There must be a Russian Dragon. They'll be taking us right to him."

Thank goodness, Simon thought miserably.

Aboard the train, the lead guard sat opposite them, smiling. In the train car was a large portrait of a hefty old general. He did not look like a Dragon. In photographs, they never do.

"General Pirakov, de facto chief of the military," Aldric told Simon. "Always nice when a Dragon is in command of a nuclear arsenal."

The thought gave Simon a chill.

There were two other guards aboard, toying with Aldric's black steamer trunk.

"Let me help you with that," said Aldric, and he played with a latch. A compartment opened. From inside, one of the guards pulled out a sword, staring at the red knob on its hilt, which was glowing.

"Enchanting little instrument, isn't it?" Aldric smiled. Staring at the hilt, the Russians' eyes glazed over, hypnotized. Their jaws went slack. Aldric calmly turned the sword toward the smiling official. He continued smiling, mesmerized, as Aldric shoved him into a sleeping compartment and closed it shut.

One of the guards grunted in satisfaction. "He drives us crazy with that smiling."

"Quiet," ordered Aldric. "Go to the end of the car." The guards obeyed. They would now do anything they were told.

Alaythia looked at Aldric, worried. "You realize we're going right into the path of that storm."

"That's the idea."

Simon swallowed hard.

The train to Moscow did not seem quite up to the job. The cold and storms of many winters had beaten it down. The loco-motive's giant steel head pressed on through the snow with a Russian stubbornness.

The journey was long. Simon stared out at the snow-coated mountains, and had hours to worry about the future.

As the train grew closer to Moscow, Simon took out the Dragonmap and was horrified to see the ripples of magic expand-ing. On the map the chaos now reached Europe, Russia, Africa, and parts of China. Whatever evil the Dragon of Venice had begun, it was now in rapid motion.

Next to Simon, Alaythia was feeling a slight pain in her head. The closer they got to the Dragon, the louder the high-pitch humming in her ears. She thought it was just her own fear build-ing, and she said nothing about it.

The storms raging across Europe had scraped around Moscow as well, and Simon could see from the window of the train intense devastation ringing the city. Houses had been thrown around, buildings collapsed. People stood on the rubble of their ruined homes and looked over the destruction in despair. The damage went on for miles and miles.

Even stranger, the blizzard conditions swirling around the

train kept stopping and starting, like a spigot turned on and off. Winter had gone mad.

Simon held back a shiver as a feeling of hopelessness ran its fingers over him.

"Strange forces of magic are being unleashed, and we're going to find out how," warned Aldric. "We can expect more of this."

He put on a brave face, but Simon thought Aldric had aged twenty years since this voyage began. How old *was* his father? It was hard to tell. At times, he seemed a slovenly old buzzard, but in battle, he wielded his sword lightning-fast.

Simon just hoped expertise with a sword would get them through this alive.

"Take us to the man you serve," Aldric ordered the guards when the train reached Moscow.

They all walked into the swirling snow, the guards pulling the steamer trunk. Simon tried to keep his balance over slippery ice. The adults and the two soldiers seemed to have no trouble. Why was it that he was always so clearly a kid, so clearly *not* the man in the group?

Alaythia helped him as he almost fell, managing to do so without embarrassing him.

After walking for some time, they turned down an avenue absolutely overrun with cats. Hundreds of them, a plague of cats.

Every kind of cat was present. Some darted from house to house, seeking food; others, most of them, sat idly in the street. People were wading through the flood of them, trying to go about their day.

Eerily, none of them made a sound. Not a sound.

It was quiet in the realm of the Russian Dragon.

Chapter Twenty-Three

THE RUSSIAN DRAGON

THE RUSSIAN RED DRAGON was a melancholy reptilian gentleman with red-brown fur and a wolflike face, four small eyes, two of which were always sleeping and all of which were set close together above his jutting, rounded snout. He had a set of fangs that could have intimidated Dracula, or even Stalin.

Over the light fur that covered his body he wore a heavy gray army coat with a thick white fur collar. He wore an army general's old Russian cap, for he was, when he pretended at being human, an old Russian general.

On his gray coat were medals. They meant nothing. They were for show.

Under his gray coat was a belly full of bones.

Inside his mind were many voices, constantly chattering—a side effect of his magic. The people he had sent to their deaths as an army commander remained with him in his head and uttered every word they had ever said while alive. Thus, he was forced to listen to radical ideas that angered him.

He covered the noise of the voices with Tchaikovsky symphonies, which he played on the old Gramophone in his living room, but the sound of chattering people contradicting him and contradicting each other was a never-ending headache.

He was often in a foul mood.

Only one thing lessened his sorrows.

The Russian Red Dragon loved cats.

He filled his home with cats.

He made magic that called them to his home.

And then, because he did not like their noise, he quieted them with magic.

Once in a while, he would eat them. He did it quickly. They felt no pain.

He taught his cats tricks, like fetching his slippers and clawing people to death.

The expression "There is more than one way to skin a cat" was not academic to him.

He made photographs of his cats. They hung on all his walls. Not just the photographs. Sometimes the cats, which paid the price for the Dragon's foul moods.

The cats would herd around his feet, warming him. This was pleasant for the Dragonman. He would watch black-and-white television (old recorded images of government meetings and interrogations), and the cats would lie on him, all over his body, warming his shoulders, arms, his belly, and his tail.

The cats had learned to tolerate fire. The Russian Dragon would sometimes be struck with a fit of coughing, which caused plumes of fire to shoot from his mouth. Other times, he would send fire out of his mouth in a kind of laugh when something amusing happened on his television.

He lived within sight of the capital, the Kremlin, those giant towers with turbanlike hats. He had a beautiful view from his large mansion home. He liked to keep the windows open, even in snowy winter, so his view was not blocked by a single thing. He was always plenty warm. He had fire in his belly and cats on his sleeves.

He liked being alone, living just with his cats and a couple of tireless women who did his cleaning. At the present, the tireless women had been sent away, for he had dangerous visitors coming. The Dragon of Venice, for starters.

It disturbed him.

The Venice Dragon was younger and more erratic. The old Russian hated the Venetian's flashy style. For a long time, he'd suspected the Venetian wanted to swallow his shiny medals. And the Venetian surely hated the Russian's dullness.

The Venetian had warned he was coming. He needn't have bothered. It was obvious.

When a Dragonman meets with another, their powers rake against each other. Their magic goes haywire and does what it wants. So, for the first time, the Russian Dragon was cold in his house. The fire inside him did not keep him warm. The walls kept shaking from irritating little earthquakes. The books in his library would flap around like birds and resettle in places he did not want them to be. Sometimes they would bleed black ink.

Flames slipped out of his body like convicts escaping a prison. Vague, fiery figures, men made of flames, danced around the rooms, burning things at will. They looked into places where they shouldn't be looking. They did not behave. They were like terrible children, and they chased the Russian's cats without mercy.

All of this was a worry for the Russian Dragon. To lose control of your own fire was frightening. Fire which had its own mind was a true danger.

"Get back into the fireplace," he yelled at one fire-figure, but the little character would hear nothing of it.

I am free, the crackling voice seemed to sing. It was like a voice from an old record or an old telephone. *You putrid worm. Today, I am a slave to no one.*

The Russian Dragon rolled his eyes in annoyance. He could hear the fire-figures jumping into his huge pretty bath and playing with fire, as children play with water. They would ruin the nice porcelain bathtub. It would burn and crack. Unforgivable, he thought.

How Dragons do love their baths. The Russian had his nicely lined with cat hair, just as he liked it.

"Get out of there!" he roared while sitting in his armchair. "You're making too much noise!"

You're making too much noise! mocked a fire-figure man, and the Russian thumped at his vest like a gorilla behind bars.

Show us some hospitality, came a chorus of crackling fiery voices. They echoed in the Russian's brain. *We are your guests now.*

The Russian put all of his energy into making the fires die out, and had just succeeded as his newest guests began to approach his room.

His teeth were aching. Growing old came with a good deal of pain.

Several blocks away, the Kremlin buildings towering ahead of them, the St. Georges and Alaythia followed the Russian guards.

Simon waded through the street cats, staring up at the ones who had found homes in the trees. The trees were bare, and all of them were bent in creepy, twisting ways.

Approaching the mansion, the Dragonhunters prepared their weapons.

"Open it," Aldric ordered the Russians, and they lifted the steamer trunk's lid. It was no ordinary suitcase. Inside were four torches of green serpentfire.

The guards stood blankly watching like toy soldiers.

Aldric began using one of the torches to set fire to his silver arrows. He gave a torch to Simon, who set his own arrows afire. Then they placed their fiery bolts into specially made quivers that were capped, to close the arrows in completely. The quivers had been made by Simon's mother, Maradine, long ago.

Simon slung his quiver over his shoulder, alongside his crossbow. Although the quiver was a safe holder for the arrows, it nonetheless gave off an unpleasant heat. Simon's skin began to itch from having the serpentfire so near him. It was as if the fire wanted out.

He noticed Alaythia looked worried about going in empty-handed.

Then Aldric lifted out three long silver shields. He gave one to Simon and another to Alaythia. "They'll protect you from the flames, should things get out of hand," he said. "This fire is stronger than the last we used. It will be far more dangerous."

As Aldric donned his armor, Simon and Alaythia looked over the rune-covered shields. They looked beaten and flimsy, considering the danger.

"One more thing," Aldric said, and he pulled from the trunk

a chestplate of armor for Simon, pulling off the boy's trench coat to fit him with it. It was heavy, but Simon was pleased with the added protection.

"I finished the adjustments to it. It was made for you, son, long ago," Aldric said gravely.

Simon's attention sparked at this. He had not been forgotten—he had been expected. In some way, it lightened his mood for the battle ahead.

Aldric looked at Alaythia. "I'm sorry the same can't be said for you," he told her, lifting out other pieces of armor. "This was forged for one of my fellow knights. It won't fit you, but it will keep you safe."

Alaythia let him tie the straps together, and he slapped her long cloak over the uncomfortable armor.

Aldric handed her the White Book of St. George.

"You'll need to guard that at all costs," he said.

"You won't have to say it twice."

"Good. The fire is fierce, but the armor is strong," Aldric cautioned them, "and filled with secrets. You may not be able to handle it. If anything goes wrong, throw down the armor and leave it behind."

Alaythia and Simon stared back at him nervously.

"Let's be going," said Aldric.

They trekked closer to the mansion, Aldric keeping the Russian guards up front.

"Call your master," said Aldric when they reached the great doors of the mansion. Then he, Simon, and Alaythia took cover behind a statue.

The Russian soldiers took turns rapping the brass snake-head door knocker, until it suddenly came to life. "What do you want with the General today?" it said, with a vicious voice.

"We have much to discuss," said the first soldier.

"I doubt he has much to say to you, unintelligent drone," said the brass head. "Who is seeing to the General's business if you are here and not working at his labors?"

"We are seeing to his business by coming here," said the second soldier. "We need to see him."

"He will see no one now," said the brass figure. "He has urgent business this day."

Aldric glared at the second soldier, urging him on.

The second man tried once more. "I insist you let us in."

The brass face angered. "You insist? *You* do not give orders to the General. No one is allowed in today. And impertinent tres-passers will be prosecuted."

Trapdoors on either side of the doorway opened beneath the guards, and they fell into a deep darkness. Cats deluged the trap-door, diving down from all directions.

"Feed, my lovelies," said the brass head, and the trapdoors slammed shut.

"Hurry," said Aldric, and he smashed his shield into the front entry, slashing the knocker's head off the door.

The great doors opened. Cats leaked out of the open doorway. There were hundreds roaming the interior of the home. Simon, Alaythia, and Aldric came into a great hallway with multiple stairways leading up.

"They're here," whispered Alaythia, and now Simon could see the beetles up the staircase—blue, yellow, brown and green ones swirling the banister, weaving together.

Aldric climbed the stairs, Simon and Alaythia close behind, crackling beetles under their shoes.

Simon heard strange noises from the second floor.

Eeer, tikky, tikky, tikky. Eeer, tikky, tikky, tikky.

At the top of the steps was a hall, and then a wide room with many chairs and couches, a large chamber made into a cozy living space, all of it filled with cats.

And something else.

Quickly, Aldric shoved Simon to one side, behind the doorway. Alaythia dashed to the other side.

There were three Dragons in the room ahead.

Three.

In his huge armchair, the Russian Red Dragon was looking lazily at his two unusual guests. Across from him was the Parisian Dragon, making that odd noise—*eer, tikk, tikk, eer, tikk, tikk*—and near him, the creature who had asked for the meeting: the Dragon of Venice. They were *not* in conflict. They showed *no* signs of aggression. Simon looked to Aldric. He was dumbfounded.

"*Mon Dieu*, my aching jaws . . ." complained the Parisian Dragon, turning to look at the door, "the Knight may have found us out."

"Don't be sssuch a withering worm," sneered the Venetian. "Not every little thing is because of the Dragonhunter. You are sssafe, for the time being."

"This is right," nodded the Russian. "If he comes near us, he will never get past the doors without our sensing it. If it's the Coast of the Dead you worry about, my men are always watching the area, at a safe distance. If the Knight survives it somehow, they will shoot him down. The only worry is we may not get to burn him to death ourselves."

Aldric eased up at the door and said in a voice Simon could barely hear, "Wait for the right time. . . . "

In the room, the Dragons sat together as the cats at their feet pawed at stray beetles.

"*Oui*, I am sure you are right," the Parisian Dragon was saying, "it's just nerves. *Tik, tik, tik.* Our gathering has brought strange feelings upon us, has it not? It is hard to tell anymore whether this is this or that is that. *Tik, tik, tik.* Our magic is like a woman who does not like to be awakened early: spiteful and confused. There is much to fear in our coming together."

The Russian grunted. "The fires concern me greatly, Venetian."

"*Oui, monsieur*, and me as well," said the Parisian, "it gives one the chills, no?"

Even the Venetian looked uncomfortable. "Yesss, it issss unfortunate."

Peeking around the door, Simon saw the occupants of the room as they truly were: Dragonmen. His ability to see through Serpentine magic had grown considerably since the last encounter. Near the reddish, wolflike Russian were two reptilian forms: one was blue-yellow and sickly thin; the other, tall, green, and water-drenched. The Parisian and the Venetian. They were speaking English.

The Russian, stroking a cat, leaned forward in his chair. "You say this is merely 'unfortunate'?" he growled. "I think it is worse than that. Our fire is not listening to us, comrade. You've witnessed it yourself. We have no control over what it does, and all because we are together. This is grave danger of the highest order!"

Simon put his ear closer to the wall. *They feared their own fire?*

The Parisian nearly trembled. *"Eeer, eer.* Think what would become of us if the firelings wanted more. What if they were set loose?"

"We shhhhould be ssssensssitive to the dangersss here," said the Venetian. "But let usss not overestimate the risksss. I control my fire, Russki, you should be able to control yourssss."

"Watch your tongue, comrade," said the Russian, his teeth bared. "This is my house you're speaking in, not yours."

Simon readied his crossbow. Through the crack in the door, he had a clear shot at the Russian's chest. Aldric remained still. From the other side of the entryway, Alaythia glimpsed the meeting as a discussion of men: a tall, scarred-face Italian, a hefty, tired old Russian general, and a thin French intellectual with sleek, designer, robelike clothing.

"I am not sure the massster would appreciate your tone of voice," said the Venetian.

"You serve a master, not me," said the Russian. "I haven't agreed to anything yet."

Aldric's eyes narrowed. "A master?" he whispered.

The Venetian's eyes burned with indignation. "If you wish, you can perissssh with the rest of our enemies. But that hardly seemsss sssensible."

"We came to hear a plan, no? *Eeer, tikk, tikk, tikk,"* said the Parisian, calming the others down. "So let us hear it, *Monsieur Brakkesh."*

The Venice Dragon was about to answer, when suddenly a shot flared across the room. The cats screeched and scattered. The Venetian was hit in the chest with a flaming arrow.

Simon clenched his fist proudly. *Direct hit.*

"What are you doing?" Aldric looked furious.

"I had the shot. I took it," said Simon, knowing instantly he'd done something terribly wrong.

The Venice Dragon roared, fists clenched, arms bristling with muscle.

The arrow's flames spread all over him as he painfully shook them off, like an angry dog flinging bathwater. The fire scattered into what appeared to be puddles of flames.

The other Dragons rose to their feet, ready to kill.

Chapter Twenty-Four

THE FURY OF FIRE

T HE VENETIAN CLAWED OUT the arrow and came thundering across the long room.

"We can't run," said Aldric. "Rush them!"

In a move that shocked Simon as much as the Dragons, Aldric rushed forward into the room, firing his crossbow.

Two bolts left the bow. Both hit the Venetian. The infuriated Dragon fell back just a few steps.

The other two Serpents were stalking Aldric.

Simon had followed him in, but now he stood before the hideous things in gut-wrenching terror. Alaythia came in, shield raised, apparently to protect him. The Dragons snarled at them both.

Alaythia felt her lungs go empty as the Dragons dropped their cloaking magic, and she saw them in their true reptilian forms.

The Russian opened his fist, and a sudden wind threw Alaythia back against the wall with brute magical force. He tried the same for Simon, but the boy slid back only a few feet, willing himself not to move.

Aldric threw down the crossbow, lifting his shield and sword.

In panic, Simon shot at the Russian Dragon. The arrow hit its arm. The wolfish creature howled, and the voices in his head echoed the pain.

Lowering the bow, Simon raised his shield instinctively. To his shock, the *shield* fired arrows as well. Some device inside it shot smaller, dartlike arrows. Three of them sank directly into the Parisian, who screeched with rage.

Then its eyes fixed on Simon.

It was coming for him now.

The Russian joined in the assault. Both of them rushed at the boy as the Venetian clawed at Aldric. Their howling was deafening. No matter how bizarre and eccentric they might have seemed, the predators were stunning when on the attack. They were not a bit human anymore, and all Simon could register in his brain was the rush of two massive, snarling *animals*.

And they were wickedly fast.

Aldric had his sword up, and slashed into the Venice Beast— which screamed in rage as the fireblade cut into his shoulder. But the creature shook off the pain and gnashed back at the Knight's shield.

Alaythia was being thrown about by magic, as if by gale winds, and she tumbled onto the beetles at the stairs.

Meanwhile, the Paris reptile never lost his speed, and its bony arms whipped around the boy's shoulders, pulling him down. Simon struggled free, but his shield clattered away. Now he was trapped by the French one, and the Russian one was close behind.

Aldric avoided the Venetian's snarling face and jabbed with his sword, the blade flickering with serpentfire. But he could not disguise his fear for his son.

The Venetian saw this. "*Yes—take the weaker one,*" the Venetian hissed, "*and the Knight will lose all heart for fighting.*"

The Dragon of Paris snapped at Simon, who fell back against a wall.

Tikka-tikka-tikka-tikka . . .

The boy thrust his crossbow up to protect his face, and the Dragon's jaws clamped onto the bow, struggling to get it loose. Simon tried to use the weapon, but he couldn't get his fingers into position.

The boy stared in horror at the Dragon's wild eyes. Liquid fire, like blue paint, dribbled from the Parisian's mouth. It steamed when it hit the floor.

"Dad . . . " Simon tried breathlessly to call for help.

The Dragon pulled his teeth from the crossbow, saying something to Simon in French, a string of insults. Simon kicked him and pushed himself back, free.

The Dragon spit tiny gobs of blue light at the boy, which splatted the wall when he dodged them.

The Dragon was preparing his fire.

Tikk, tikk, tikk, tikk.

Alaythia screamed, crawling to get to Simon, but she was being dragged away across the floor by Serpent magic. Her fingers scratched the floor as the wind pulled her back.

The Parisian opened his jaws, and they were filled with blue flame.

The Venetian spat at him in Dragonspeak, stopping him with a warning.

Aldric's eyes lit up. He spotted a weakness now.

He swung his fiery sword back and forth. "Afraid of the flame?" he taunted them.

An intense quiet burned for a second. The Dragons shifted on their clawed feet, wanting to strike. Staring at the boy, the Parisian kept his jaws wide, the flames there awaiting escape. Simon stayed still, back against the wall, wondering if he could reach his shield on the floor.

"They won't hurt you, Simon," said Aldric, eyes on the Venetian, "they're afraid."

The Russian Dragon turned to him and bared his teeth, a steam drifting out eerily. He leaned back his long snaky neck and prepared to sling fire.

Aldric smiled. His plan was working.

"No. Do not raise fire againssst them," said the raspy Venetian, "it cannot be controlled."

"I want him dead," the Russian howled.

The Paris Dragon inched closer to Simon. "I want *him* dead," he whispered. *"I want him gone. Eeer, eeer, eeer . . . "*

Alaythia was crawling back into the room. She could feel the Russian Dragon's magic ebbing away, his reptilian mind distracted with Aldric.

"He will die with the ressst," wheezed the Venetian to the Parisian. "But if you attack now, your fire will go mad with rage. We might be burned along with him."

"We don't know that, comrade," the Russian interjected, slashing a razorclaw at Aldric. "Now is our chance. Three of us against him."

Aldric smiled at the Venetian, who glared back, sorely wanting to rip him to shreds.

"Three of ussss here *creates* the danger," the Venetian said, as close to pleading as he could ever get. "Our magic growsss unpredictable. Ragemagic will occur—"

Aldric lashed out with his sword, once, twice—testing the Venetian's will. He laughed defiantly. The Russian saw this and snarled.

"NO ONE MOVE," barked the Venetian.

The Russian remained unsure. His furry head tilted this way and that, the rage inside of it quarreling with its own logic. He was close to Aldric. One good fiery blow, and the Knight would be dust. . . .

"*Eeer, tikky, tikky.* I *hate* children," hissed the Paris Dragon, teeth bared at Simon.

Simon's heart, already on overload, hammered harder.

"You've alwayssss been careful, Tyrannique," the Venice Dragon said. "Don't lose your head now."

"You'll all lose your heads," threatened Aldric, "one way or another."

As he spoke, Alaythia had picked up her shield and raised it, tapping the rune inside—which sent arrowdarts flying straight into the Parisian, who screeched in fury.

And let loose his fire.

At the same time, the Russian spat fire at Aldric—a thick jet of pure red flame. The fire swept over Aldric's shield, spilling onto the Venice Dragon, who roared and screamed with pain.

Across the room, Simon threw himself out of the way of the Parisian's dragonfire. The fire was blue and yellow—just like the Parisian's skin—and when it hit the ground, it spread out in every dazzling shade of blue and gold imaginable. The flames looked like paint that had learned how to flicker.

The Parisian Dragon blew several quick blasts, but Alaythia had rolled over to Simon, using her shield to protect them both from the flames. Simon could not believe the heat. One of his sleeves had been torn, and the hair on his arms was singed away, loosing a sickly smell.

He watched as the blue and yellow fire grew, stretching over the floor, reaching toward Aldric and the red fire near the Russian. When the two rivers of flame met, a screeching of many voices came forth.

"Ragemagic!" cried the Venetian.

From out of the pooling flames figures rose—built of fire—four from the blue and yellow inferno, four from the red. The firelings screeched madly, full of hate for each other.

Aldric ran across the flames to Simon. The flame-figures parted; some flew to the wall, watching with gleeful insanity, without any eyes.

"We've got to get out of here," said Aldric, pulling Simon and Alaythia away. But three blue firelings flew to the door with a screeching cackle, blocking the way out.

The Dragons were in turmoil, too—they had fled to the back of the room.

"Death to the Knight," the Venetian howled. "Rage upon him!"

The firelings snickered with an evil delight.

The fire had burned nearly all of the floor around Simon and the others. Parts of it began to cave in, revealing a long pit beneath it.

Suddenly, the floor gave way—and dropped Simon and

Alaythia into the deep, dark pit. Aldric was still clinging to the wood shards remaining on the floor, dangling over the abyss.

The Russian's eyes widened and he laughed. "I see you've found my bear pit."

Aldric's grip weakened as the fire flashed around his hands. The firelings stood over him with joyous anticipation.

"I throw starving bears into the pit and watch them fight," purred the Russian, "savaging each other . . . or wolves, dogs, people, whatever you like."

"Let the firelings have it today," said the Venetian, and he shouted to the fire-figures, "Dare not fight amongst yoursss-selves. . . . We leave you these mortals to feast on."

We'll take the mortals, crackled a voice in the Dragons' heads, *and we'll take the palace, too. . . .*

The Russian Dragon's face curled into dismay.

"Let it pass, *Monsieur,*" whispered the Parisian. "Let them take it and we'll go without a fight."

One of the red firelings jabbed a long hand at Aldric's chest. Scorched, the Knight screamed and let go, falling into the dark pit.

Simon was relieved to have him there. The pit was a giant wooden arena piled high with wolf skulls, bear skulls, and carrion of unknown origin.

The firelings crouched on the edge of the pit, laughing.

Behind them, the Venetian smiled to see Aldric hit the ground, and something caught his eye. Alaythia had her hand on her coat pocket, on a shape hidden within. She was protecting the White Book. Suddenly, Simon saw it rip from the coat and fly into the air, as the Venetian called the Book to his hands. He'd found it.

Aldric yelled in rage.

"Eat them, comrades," said the Russian to the firelings, and he stared down at the pit, saying something in Russian.

The Paris Dragon laughed and replied to him in French.

Simon's eyes widened. He caught the words. A strange phrase. But there were other concerns at that second, as the firelings had begun crawling down toward them in the pit.

The fire figures crawled on all fours, down the sides of the pit, like men imitating spiders. Their obscure faces were grinning behind their flames.

Simon had never been so scared.

Aldric lifted up his shield—all of their tools had collapsed into the pit.

"What good is a sshield against fire?" sneered the Venice Dragon above. "I leave you to your ssssscreams, Knight of the Old Order. Keep your weaponsss. They will do no good against the firelings . . . "

. . . which were, at this moment, yearning to torch human flesh. Above the crawling shapes, Simon saw the Dragons turn and scatter, rushing away through the smoke like cockroaches from light. Gone.

"GET YOUR SHIELD!" Aldric bellowed. Simon plucked his shield from the ground, holding it up as the firelings leapt down upon them.

Simon could see Alaythia react to something, as if a gnat were whispering in her ear. It was the firelings. Only she could hear them. *Mortal morsels, mortal morsels,* they chuckled in her head. *Don't you like to play with fire?*

"Stand together," Aldric ordered. Everyone stood with their

backs together, shields out, as the fiery men moved around them, enjoying the game.

They're mine, said a blue fireling.

You can't have them all, said a red one.

I'll fight you for them, muttered some others. *You can eat their ashes.*

"I hear them," she said in a way that terrified Simon even more. "I hear them in my head."

The firelings laughed uproariously.

Aldric seemed to be out of ideas. The pit was deep, and it was made of wood, with ugly oak carvings of bears and wolves and deer built into the walls, all the way up its steep sides. Everything would burn, all too well.

Surrounding the Dragonhunters, the firelings began to scrape their fingernails over the shields. They pushed and shoved at each other as well, blue against red, hissing and crackling in hideous competition.

Huddling down in the darkness behind the shields, Simon could see nothing except the ceiling.

It was just then that Simon saw there was a skylight dome above him.

And this gave him an idea.

The mansion was burning to nothing. The fires had torched the walls and were reaching the ceiling rapidly. The entire structure was ready to collapse.

Simon reracked his crossbow.

"What are you doing?" Aldric asked nervously. "Simon?"

Simon was concentrating too hard to answer. He lifted his bow, and shot—directly into the thin glass supporting beam of the skylight. With a tinkling crash, the pretty glasswork shattered as the ceiling broke apart.

A thick, heavy collection of snow from the roof tumbled in upon them.

The firelings screeched in surprise. Some yelped and scurried from the unexpected snowfall. For the others, it was just enough of a shock to distract them from their prey.

Aldric plunged his sword into a blue fireling. The firespawn howled, as the flames of Aldric's sword swept toward his heart. *GREEN FLAME! GREEN FLAME!* he screamed in Alaythia's ears.

The green Dragonflames covered the fireling in an instant. Aldric slashed at another creature, breaking him in two. Its body turned into separate patches of fire, hitting the floor and evaporating into nothing.

The other firelings were in disarray, aghast at the human's power.

He controls the living fire! Alaythia heard them scream. But right in front of Simon's eyes, the green flames grew into firelings as well, voracious and ready to eat the others. Aldric had quickly lost control of his own fire.

No war, no war, twittered the redlings.

Whipped into pandemonium, the firelings flew up out of the pit, scrambling to escape each other, leaving behind a trail of flame. Crying for freedom, they scattered to the winds.

But the wooden pit remained a cauldron of flames, and increasingly, of deadly smoke. Now the entire mansion was coming down on top of them as well.

"What did you do that for?" yelled Aldric, throwing off his coat to stamp out the flames.

"What was I supposed to do?" shouted Simon helplessly. He thought he'd saved them.

"You've brought down the entire building, you've given oxygen to the fire!"

"He was only trying to help," Alaythia said.

"He would help if he would *listen*. Take up your shields."

"Why?"

Aldric picked her shield up and shoved it into her hands. "Because we're getting out of here. Gather your weapons. Simon, open your coat—show me your armor."

Confused, Simon did so.

"Alaythia," ordered Aldric. "Hands on his shoulders."

Not understanding, Alaythia blinked at him, unmoving.

"The armor," Aldric explained, "you may have the power now to use it as it's intended." He pointed to some runes at the top of Simon's shoulder. "Read that."

"Well, what is it intended *for*?" asked Simon.

And suddenly the answer was clear. As Alaythia read the runes aloud, tapping them, Simon shot up into the air, his body weightless. *He was flying.*

"Oh my gaww . . . ," he stammered. He began spinning in air, violently.

"You're fanning the flames," yelled Aldric. "Lean back so that it lifts you!"

Simon tried with no success, flipping completely over.

He stayed in the exact same place, only upside down, facing the flames.

With fire spreading everywhere, Alaythia read the runes on Aldric's armor, and the Knight rose into the air, expertly gliding up to take Simon's hand. He pulled him upright, guiding him straight out through the roof.

Below, Simon saw as Alaythia struggled a little with her shield, rising slowly from the burning mansion like a ghost, her cloak and dress trailing her.

As they rose out of the blazing mansion, Simon could see no sign of the dragons. He saw only a stray fireling still playing in the flames, rolling around in them, laughing, and throwing fire all about. It turned to them and, snickering, threw a long trail of flame toward them.

Reaching them through the smoke and darkness, Alaythia grabbed hold of Simon and Aldric and pulled them out into the cool, snowy weather of the city.

Escaping, Simon saw the darkness of smoke part out of the way; they rose above it; he let go of Alaythia's hand, floating in the air above the world for a long moment.

He had never been up so high. They were far higher than the Lighthouse beacon. He felt himself grow light-headed. He could see the lights of Moscow twinkling in the gloomy, blue-gray daylight.

They flew across the mansion compound, high and graceful, in an aimless path.

Aldric pulled down on Simon's arm, lowering them gently to the street.

Alaythia swooped in beside them, tossing up snow.

Simon fell over on top of his shield.

He still felt giddy and joyful from his flight; it was like waking slowly from a dream.

"Fire . . . ," Alaythia said in a daze, staring as the light in the mansion flared stronger. The snowfall was trying to beat it back, but the fire was merciless.

"I used to love fire," said Simon thoughtlessly.

Aldric turned to him with absolute disgust in his eyes. "What."

"I didn't know . . . ," Simon said, unable to find the right words.

"Fire is a killer," rumbled Aldric. "It is ruthless. Murderous. Never say that again. Ever."

The flames flicked out of the mansion and reached in long, thin lines out across the streets to other buildings.

Serpentfire loves to grow.

Simon and Aldric watched in horror as the fire spread to the houses nearby, the flames reaching out like the tentacles of an octopus.

Then Simon felt many eyes at his back.

He spun around.

They were now joined by swarms of cats creeping toward them on the snow. They knew who had burned their home. Staring down, Simon saw the felines arch their backs angrily, claws out, fur on end. *Tiny jets of fire burst from their jaws.* Aldric and Simon backed away, pulling Alaythia, who could hardly move.

They ran, and Simon looked back to see the cats unable to follow, cut off by the fire they had shot into the alley. But ahead of him, a red fireling was just diving into the bricks of another building, spreading flames. The Dragons were nowhere to be seen—gone into hiding—but fires were now breaking out everywhere.

"Another city burned by Pyrothrax," sighed Aldric.

Chapter Twenty-Five

Elements of Destruction

LATER, THEIR FACES BLACKENED from soot, the three Dragonhunters drank hot tea in a burned-out restaurant they had tried to save. Only the building's supporting steel beams were left standing. The walls were burned away. The restaurant owner had set up some tables inside, and was serving borscht soup and tea heated on an enormous cast-iron stove.

Simon, Aldric, and Alaythia sat solemnly, at a table half buried in ashes and snowfall.

The Russian tea warmed Simon down deep. No wonder Russians could endure their terrible weather. Their tea was magic.

They were still reeling from their discovery. What was once unthinkable was now an undeniable reality: The three Dragons were coming together in partnership.

Aldric tapped his hand on the table, pondering it, "forming an alliance . . . an alliance . . . " It spooked Simon. The Serpents were serving an unknown master. And the situation for the

Dragonhunters was getting worse and worse.

"The storms were just because they were in the same place," said Simon. "The Venice Dragon was going to each territory, right? Bringing the Serpents together, one by one . . . "

"But to do what? What are they joining up *for*?" wondered Alaythia.

The mystery animated their thoughts for a long moment.

"We'll figure it out. We'll find them," she said. "We'll have to follow the storms and supernatural activities—that's where they'll be."

Aldric gave a heavy sigh.

"I don't know what to do," he said with a weary tone. "I'm not sure where I can send you that would be safe, but I'm not entirely confident that working together is the best idea, given the state of things."

His remarks weighted Simon down. The boy sat as still as a statue. But Alaythia was furious.

"What are you trying to say? After all we've done, you'd rather go it alone?" Simon could hear the hurt in her voice.

Aldric responded coldly. "Well, let's list those accomplishments. Besides helping to burn a Moscow neighborhood into tiny bits of ash, you two have repeatedly blown our cover. You have refused to follow my lead, over and over again. You have lost the deathspells that were our only chance at killing the Serpents, making our entire journey so far a complete and utter waste."

"We fought those things," Alaythia said. "We fought them off, all of us together."

"We did the best we could," was all Simon could offer.

Aldric rubbed his eyes. "You're too easy on yourself," he murmured.

"I can see why you'd attack me," said Alaythia, "but Simon's just a kid. Leave him out of it. He's never a burden, and he's done an incredible job of keeping up with you. You're always criticizing him."

"Leave it to me to decide what's a burden and what isn't," said Aldric, drinking his tea.

Simon was stung by the insult. Did Aldric think of him as nothing more than an iron weight?

Alaythia got up and crossed the room, where newspapers from around the world were left out by the café owner for weary firefighters. She idly picked one up and sat down at another table, away from Aldric.

She slapped open *The New York Times*, and Simon watched the ash flurry around her shoulders in the breeze. He felt closer to her than to Aldric right now.

Aldric looked up, with perhaps a touch of regret, then poured more brown tea into his cup. "I should've got vodka," he said. "I wonder if they have any left."

Very quietly, Simon said to his father, "You're just going to let her sit there?"

"Drink your tea," he told Simon, "and stay out of the affairs of grown people."

You're not acting like grown people, the boy thought.

Alaythia was turning the pages in *The New York Times* when her eyes snagged on something almost impossible to believe, a headline that read: "Gifted Art Curator Dies in Mysterious Fire. Brilliant Woman Will Be Missed."

She sat back, stunned. It was some kind of mistake, surely. She fluttered the pages, checking the date. It was many days old.

They thought she was dead! Well, of course they thought she was dead. She'd left New York without a word to anyone, after the fire. She looked back at the article, which told of her genius for finding new talent.

And, in the midst of her haywire thoughts, she heard Aldric's voice behind her, arguing with Simon. "She has to know what a mess she's made of things," he was saying. "It's the only way you'll ever help me to fight them again—you have to realize that I'm right, and trust me."

Simon protested. "Who knows where we'd be now without her?"

"I know one thing," Aldric said. "We'd have the deathspells now."

Silence. Alaythia turned to him. "I went with you . . . because I had an obligation to protect you. The dream I had said I *must* protect you."

Aldric looked at her with a tired gaze. "You've already fulfilled your dream. You pulled us out of the burning palace. Isn't that what the dream said? *'Lead them through the darkness.'* Well, you've done it. You're all paid up."

Alaythia stared back. Simon could see a change come over her eyes.

"All right. Fine. If that's the way you feel, we'll just part ways," she said, holding up the newspaper. "As far as I know, I've never been *burdensome* in any relationship, so let's not start here. I'm going back to the world I know. I'm going back where people respect me." She tossed down the newspaper and headed for the exit.

But she stopped at the door and said, "You know, it wasn't lost on me that out there on that icy sea, the first place you looked for betrayal . . . was at me." Then she went out, pushing through ashes and snow.

Stunned, Simon let his eyes fall to the newspaper. He looked at Aldric. "She's heading back to New York," he said. "Aren't you going to stop her?"

Aldric said nothing, and downed the last of his tea.

Simon couldn't believe it. He couldn't move; he was in a kind of suffocating grief.

In a blink, it was over.

Alaythia had left them.

Chapter Twenty-Six

❧

TWO AGAINST THE WORLD

BY THE TIME SIMON fully appreciated what had happened and dashed after her, Alaythia was out of sight. She was simply not there.

"You let her go," Simon said, bewildered. "You just let her walk out. I can't believe you."

They were now trekking through the snows of a lonely Russian street, at night.

"Whatever strength she has," said Aldric, "it would take years to hone into something useful and reliable."

"I'm not talking about that," Simon blurted out. "She actually cared about you. Who do you think will ever care about someone like you? You're . . . impossible."

He couldn't believe he was saying it; the words just spilled out of his mouth.

Aldric said coldly, "This is not a chess match. She made mistakes that rendered our work useless. We have no way of stopping them. No deathspells. All we have left is the unpredictable living fire. We're *lost*. Do you understand this affects every human being in the entire world?"

But Simon had walked off ahead in frustration, not even turning as he raved on, "You just can't stand relying on somebody else. Why did you bring me if you didn't want me here? I would've been just fine in Ebony Hollow. There are, you know, lots of things you took me away from. There are certain girls' names I never even got to know. You wouldn't understand any of this."

"I have one obligation," Aldric said evenly, "and that is to end the reign of the Serpents on this earth, before they kill us all. That woman could cost us our lives."

"'That woman'?" Simon repeated in anger. "She's an actual human being with a name."

Simon knew the argument would go too far, so he kept walking, avoiding Aldric's response.

"I had to get rid of her, Simon," Aldric said, leveling with him. "Staying with us, she was in danger. We all were. At least this way she'll be safe."

"So you go and make this decision without telling me. What *I* thought didn't matter."

"Watch yourself," Aldric bristled. "You might at least make a show of respecting me."

Simon wouldn't turn around.

He walked on, and stood waiting at a seedy hotel he knew his father would want for the night. *Cheapskate.*

In the hotel room, tempers had cooled to a civil silence.

Aldric sat at the table alone. Simon watched the snow at the window.

Aldric coughed. "Well, you're getting better with the bow, I'll say that. I knew I was right to keep you working at it. Even though it was the wrong thing to do, you hit that glass ceiling-beam dead on."

"I'm still better with the sword. You should give me a chance to prove it. If you'd stop treating me like I was fine china and let me *do* something."

Aldric looked at his son across the room, and although it was dark, Simon thought his eyes had misted up as he said, "I can't let anything happen to you." But Simon wasn't sure.

"Well, if that's the best I'm going to get out of you, I guess I'll have to take it."

Aldric groused, "What do you want from me? I said I'm sorry."

"You *never* said you were sorry." Simon looked away from him, tiredly, to the window and the falling snow. "Looks like we're past the worst of it."

"We're not past anything," mumbled Aldric. "Dragons uniting. This hasn't happened for thousands of years. I'm not sure how it even got this far. It will make things nearly impossible for us. The power of Dragons united would be terrifying. We've got to break their alliance. We'll have to watch the signs and figure out where they've gone. Time is of the essence. And we've nothing to go on."

"There is *one* thing to go on . . . " Simon said quietly.

"What's that? Did you say something?"

Simon took the seat near him. "The Paris one. Before he vanished, he said something. He said it in French."

"You know I don't speak French. My brother had the gift

for languages, not me."

"He said the Dragons could leave us there without a worry. He said all that stands between us and the Fire Eternal is 'a visit to Peking.' I've been thinking about it all day. . . . "

Suddenly, Aldric was out of his chair, dragging their steamer trunk through the door of the old hotel. Simon wasn't sure if his father was pleased with his knowledge of French or not, but they were once again on the move.

"We're late. We're late figuring this out, and we don't have any time left. These Serpents have been joining forces one by one," Aldric said. "Whatever they're planning, they must be seeking out the last Dragon they need to join them. In China."

"China . . . ," whispered Simon, marveling at the idea.

He hoped it was warmer there.

Chapter Twenty-Seven

THE LAIR OF THE PEKING BEAST

THE CHINESE CAPITAL WAS too far to get to easily by land or sea, and time was ticking away cruelly. Aldric hired a private plane for the voyage, paying with the gems he'd taken from Venice. The ship would have to be left behind, but in its remote dock it was in no danger, and there was plenty of food aboard for the animals.

The airplane left from Moscow, a fast, small jet that belonged to a group of gypsies who rented it out to make money. The crew was a joyous, singing, eccentric group that included guitar-playing girls and a grandmother who had brought a rocking chair aboard. The jet flew erratically across the ragged gray clouds, leaving Simon terrified.

He tried to get some sleep in the back of the airplane, hidden behind a beaded curtain, though the music and partying never really ended, continuing all day and into the night. There was always some part of the crew awake enough to sing. Frustrated, he pulled out some of the English-language newspapers he'd taken from Moscow, which held further evidence of the work of the Dragons.

Whatever the creatures were uniting *for*, the effects were already apparent: whales beaching themselves worldwide; rat populations out of control; mass infestations of insects from one end of the globe to the other—people were being swarmed by thousands of wasps, while crops everywhere had been gobbled by locusts. Tensions between countries had suddenly risen tremendously, with former allies now seeking war. There were cases of plague in some areas, entire cities ground to a halt, hospitals overrun with the dying. No matter where they were, people were weak and sickened, losing their hair, complaining of sleeplessness. Trees were dying by the thousands, entire forests gone barren, flowers wilted, great vasts fields of them.

Simon felt overwhelmed. The road ahead seemed hopeless. Two people alone could not defeat a union of the three most powerful Serpents on earth.

He began to wonder if there was another way to deal with the beasts. Was there ever a way to negotiate with them? To make a truce?

The only bright light he could see was that it seemed possible there might be reasonable Dragons among those listed in the White Book. If the humans could make some kind of bluff, perhaps the Serpents would fear a fight and would agree to a draw. At this point, Simon would settle for just going back to the way things used to be.

Aldric had been silent for a long time, and when he finally spoke, he surprised Simon. "You suppose she'll be all right out there? Alaythia?"

Simon gave a sigh. "I don't know. What's the point of think-ing about it now?"

Aldric answered his own question. "She's probably roaming around New York trying to find her own apartment. A bit rattly, that lady is."

Simon thought about it. "So she's different. So are we. She's a . . . there's just something *good* about her," said Simon. "And I definitely thought she was pretty, didn't you?" he prompted.

Aldric looked out the window. "I shouldn't have brought it up," he said. "More trouble than she's worth."

Resentment burned in Simon. "Well, don't blame me for pushing her out," he said, moving away from the rear of the jet, and back toward the gypsy party behind the curtain. "You just can't handle anything normal in your life. I spent so much time thinking about what you would be like . . . and you are so much *less* than anything I pictured."

There. It all came out, and Simon was done with talking.

So was Aldric, for he said nothing. He made a half-turn, look-ing out the window, in a daze.

Not knowing what to do, Simon went out past the beaded curtain and left his father alone.

Sitting in the shaking, shuddering plane, Simon took out the Dragonmap and traced his finger over its glowing runes. Now all over the world, the waves of Dragon magic were rippling, spread-ing; covering Europe, Africa, North America, South America, Asia. The map was a visual record of chaos itself.

And something occurred to him.

Aldric came out from behind the curtain to say something or other, but Simon was fixated on the little map. It looked very different to him now.

"Underneath all of this chaos, there are all of these rings drawn in here," he said. "It's showing something new—it isn't the world as it is, it's the world as it will be. I think these are rings of fire. Burning away the earth."

He looked up at Aldric and saw grim recognition in his eyes.

Simon didn't want to finish his thought, but he did.

"This is a Doomsday Plan."

Aldric's face told Simon he was probably right. The Dragons somehow aimed at destroying civilization completely.

The jet noise soon overtook his thoughts.

It would be a miracle if they got out of this airplane alive.

Eventually, however, the jet shook and rocked its way to a landing in the Chinese countryside. The crew waved good-bye to Simon and Aldric, promising to wait for their return. Simon hardly believed them. They were too drunk to remember any-thing, least of all a promise. The only thing that tied them to the land was the possibility of a good time, which they quickly went to work on. Chinese shepherds had already joined them in drink.

"Alcohol is a Dragon's vice," said Aldric. "You must never be tempted by it."

They set out on foot until they found a truck headed to the city, and secretly hopped aboard. They would travel to Beijing half buried in piles of wheat.

As the truck rumbled along old roads, headed to the massive metropolis, Simon pondered what the Dragons had said.

"They used the city's old name," said Simon. "Peking. You think it's an old Dragon?"

"There's almost no other kind, Simon. Dragons are rarely born—since Dragons hate each other's company, it's hard to make new ones. This Serpent is likely two or three hundred years old."

Simon's mind reeled at the idea of living so long.

"He will know a lot of tricks," said Aldric.

Simon had never seen such large crowds in the streets. Nothing existed in Beijing unless it was part of a crowd. Huge masses of people, in buses, and cars, and trucks, and bicycles, all moved past him.

Crowds of factories spewed black smoke into the sky, blotting out the sun.

Stray cats passed Simon's legs, and he shuddered, gripping the sword under his long coat. He was ready for anything.

His eyes were crowded with wonders. But this was not a time for sight-seeing.

The city was an impatient gray wonderland that wore its ugliness well; there is a point at which industry and gloominess become nearly artistic in their own way. But the shield of gray smoke hid a vile secret.

"This city was once home to many great sorcerers, all of them fine hunters," said Aldric. "The great Red Mandarin, the Phantasia Imperial, they're all gone now. We are on our own."

But it took the Knight and his son only a few hours, even in so vast a city, to locate the Dragon of Peking.

There was simply no mistaking it. His part of the city was overwhelmed with supernatural events.

Simon and Aldric first noticed a one-block area of rainfall; a thick, dirty, oily substance falling on car windows, greasing the sidewalk, and dripping off umbrellas in fat, slimy droplets. People ran for cover as the rain of black oil spattered their faces and spun off the rolling bicycles.

The oily rain made Simon's skin go numb, until Aldric pulled him under a metal roof. The smell was like burnt chocolate, and it stung the nostrils, but after a time the rain stopped.

And the birds came out.

Simon saw them at a distance and thought at first they were just large black birds, but as several of the dark shapes fluttered closer, he began to realize they were all vultures. The birds were looking for death, looking for the harvest the rain had brought.

Their eyes were small and black, mindless and doll-like. Their bodies were huge, with a wingspan of five feet or more. Their beaks were long and sharp, their claws ready for business. More and more came, plummeting out of the clouds.

It seemed that people on the street had seen this before, and learned to live with it. The birds swooped down on people's heads and were swatted away with umbrellas or newspapers.

The people in the neighborhood were themselves an interesting lot. Having lived so close to the Dragon for so long without knowing it, they had grown sick and distorted from prolonged exposure to the effects of magic. Many of the people were misshapen, sometimes with one overly large, lumpy arm, or an assortment of too many fingers or too many eyes. It was an unnerving sensation to see them rushing about, in the shadows under the rooftops, fearing more rain.

Somehow Aldric found a young Chinese man from Boston who could speak English. He could help track down the source of all this strange misery. Through him Aldric began questioning a woman in the crowd, and Simon saw that as she gestured and moved, the people around her moved also. He kept studying her, until he spied a thick piece of flesh that connected her to a man next to her. She was a Siamese twin, he realized. Then he noted that the man on the other side of her was also linked to her, and that there were two or three people who seemed stuck to his arms as well. The entire crowd was linked together!

Gasping, Simon showed his father. "Yes," the woman said in Chinese, "slowly, day by day, walking on this street, we have grown together. Now we are all one person, a face in the crowd forever. . . . "

Evidently the Dragon's magic had become dangerously out of control over time.

But where exactly was the beast?

There were no beetles and insects to trace, so Aldric reasoned the Dragon lay underground. As he and Simon parted from their translator and searched the area, they came upon a strange-looking streethole cover, large, square, and marked with Chinese letters. It had the appearance of a doorway built into the ground.

Aldric immediately tore it open, and down they went.

They found themselves in an ancient crypt beneath Beijing, standing in a wet, dripping tunnel, poorly lit by dim electric lights. But the St. Georges knew what lay ahead. The smell gave it away.

They began walking forward.

"They'll be together now," worried Simon. "We'll have to take them all on at once."

"I will take them on, Simon," his father said seriously.

"What do you mean? What will I do? I came to help."

"You will stand guard here. Have your crossbow ready and your arrows at your side. If anything comes down this way, it means I've failed. Shoot it."

"You can't do this alone!"

"I can, and I will," said Aldric.

"I knew this would happen. You're too afraid for me to let me fight. I came to help you."

"You will help. From here."

"Don't leave me—"

"Our record so far isn't very good," said Aldric. "We've gone up against three Serpents, and each one has gotten away and gotten stronger. Maybe I have less of an edge when you're with me. Maybe you're unlucky. It doesn't matter. We've got to stop these things, or the world will know it."

"I can do more than you think." Simon burned with anger.

Aldric calmed himself. "I have work to do in this place. There's no use for immature boys here. Just stand firm and do what's called for, if you're needed. But you are staying here. And I am going in."

He turned and walked into the darkness. Simon watched him leave, and gripped his sword as if it would protect him from the blackness itself.

Chapter Twenty-Eight

THE BLACK DRAGON

ALDRIC WAS GONE, OUT of the light. Simon could not even hear his footsteps. Only the dripping of water echoed through the tunnel.

Time moved slowly. Simon lost track of how long he stood there, but after a while he became aware of a kind of whistling noise behind him.

He turned. Nothing came at him.

Perhaps this was worth investigating. He stepped forward, and saw that the tunnel did not end behind him as he had thought, but rather turned at a sharp angle, and kept going. The whistling came from somewhere back there.

He walked on, reaching a hole in the tunnel wall just large enough for him to fit through. Through the hole he could see a birdcage with a small canary inside. The canary was twittering softly.

He crawled into the hole. His crossbow was tight in his hands.

The birdcage sat on a table, and now he could see beyond it

to a quite nicely arranged kitchen. The stove held a soup pot that was burbling quietly.

He watched as a small, dark, stooped figure limped into the kitchen, leaning on a cane. The figure went to the pot, poured a tiny cup of soup, and picked up the cup and saucer with a shaky, elderly grip.

As the figure shuffled away, its hands were shaking so much that it dropped the saucer and cup, which shattered on the floor. It regarded the mess sadly.

Simon could see that it had the reptilian skin of a Dragonman, but it was black, with heavy black eyebrows, a long, drooping mustache, and a mane of braided black hair that stretched down its back. It had the narrow eyes of the Chinese, protected by tiny eyeglasses on the end of its smallish nose.

At the loss of the cup, it made a hurt little sound of regret.

Turning, the creature went back to the stove, pouring a new cup of soup. The soup smelled delicious. The warm spices tickled Simon's nose.

The little figure grunted happily, anticipating eating.

Simon skirted behind the rocky, half-shattered pillar to see more safely.

The second cup was dropped as well.

This time the black figure whimpered more loudly. It reached out its small, furry, hands, trying to sweep the ruined cups away by magic. The china pieces shivered a bit but were not swept away.

Then the diminutive creature looked up and saw Simon.

It shuffled back in fear.

In *fear*.

Simon was caught off guard, but he came out from behind the rocky wall with his crossbow aimed. He was actually able to keep his own hands from shaking.

For a second, the two just looked at each other.

Then the Black Dragon smiled.

"Would you like some soup?"

Simon just stared.

"I've never seen one quite like you. Usually when I get beggar children in here," creaked the kindly voice, "they are Chinese. I help them same as I'll help you. Are you hungry?"

"I didn't come here to eat," said Simon. He hoped his voice sounded firm.

The Black Dragon looked perplexed. "What did you come here for?"

"I would think that's obvious," said Simon.

The little Dragonman leaned forward now and squinted, lifting his eyeglasses to see the boy. "Ahh," he said, seeing the crossbow. "My eyes are not what they used to be. You've come here on a mission. I thought all of your kind was gone."

"You were mistaken."

"I see that now."

Simon did not even notice that the creature spoke passably good English.

The Dragon let his hands fall to his potbelly. "Would it be possible for me to eat a little something before you do whatever it is you came to do?" he asked.

"I don't think that's a good idea," Simon responded. "I've heard you can't be trusted."

"From who?"

"My father, for one."

"Your father, who is who?"

"Aldric St. George."

"Does he know me?"

"I don't think so, no."

"Then why does he have such a bleak opinion of me?"

"A Dragon is a Dragon."

The Dragonman's eyes went wide at this remark, and he clucked his tongue. "Would it be possible for me to take a seat before I tell you the error of this thinking?"

"No. Don't move."

"You trust me so little that I cannot rest my aged legs?"

"I don't trust you at all."

"Please can I be seated? My bones are very old."

"I should bury this arrow in you right now," said Simon, wondering why he didn't.

"You wouldn't give a moment's thought to destroying a creature that has lived for over two hundred years?"

"I seem to be giving it some thought," said Simon.

"You came here alone?"

"My father is somewhere behind me. He'll find his way here soon."

"Your father, Aldric St. George. And you are who St. George?"

"Simon St. George."

The little creature smiled. "Simon, have you seen many Dragons in your short life?"

"I've seen enough of them."

"I wonder if you—" The Dragon interrupted himself. "Simon,

I am going to sit down." He shuffled over a few paces, pulled out a small chair, and sat with a weary sigh.

Simon watched him tensely.

"I wonder if you have seen enough Dragons," the creature went on, "to decide what you think of *all* Dragons. How many have you known?"

Simon thought about it. "Four, I suppose."

"Four. And from that you know them all? I wonder if it is possible to say that all men are evil from knowing only four? What if the four men you met were criminals? Wouldn't that be a mistake on your part?"

"We aren't talking about men."

"No, but can you say, for example, that all Chinese are evil? All Americans are evil? All Dutchmen are evil?"

"No."

"Can you say that any species is altogether evil? Can you say that, Simon?"

"What do you mean?"

"Well, do you think all dogs are evil? Or all birds?"

"No."

"Of course not. Not even all snakes are evil. Some are very beneficial. Do you agree?"

"I suppose," said Simon.

"Then if no creature on earth, neither man nor beast, can be said to be totally evil, doesn't it stand to reason that perhaps not all Dragons are evil, too?"

Simon said nothing, and the Dragonman went on, "Could it be, perhaps, that you have seen only the worst of us?"

"The worst of you are pretty awful," said Simon.

The creature turned sorrowful. "On that you are absolutely right. That is why many of us are fighting back against the evil ones."

"Many of you?" Simon's curiosity swelled.

"Certainly," said the Peking Dragon. "There is a whole world of Light Dragons who are working to stop the spread of evil."

"That's very interesting, because I've never seen one."

"Of course not. We're in hiding. It simply shows how well we've concealed ourselves, that you know nothing of us."

The boy considered this. "Why do you have to hide?"

"May I take my pipe? It eases the pain in my throat from talking so much."

"No, stay where you are," said Simon, but the little figure frowned, then reached over to a table and picked up his long, long pipe.

"We must hide, or the evil forces would hunt us down and destroy us. You see, we have *two* enemies: you hunters, like your father lost in the labyrinth behind me . . . " Simon was surprised he had figured that out. " . . . and the Dark Dragons as well."

"You haven't done much to stop the Dark Ones," countered Simon.

"You don't know. You don't know," muttered the Black Dragon tiredly. "We have done much. The world would be much more tattered and pained if we had not. I told you, we work in secret. No one knows what we do. There was a time recently when the world nearly chewed itself up in warfare, and . . . May I have a stool for my feet?"

Simon moved in closer, knocking a stool toward him, without really thinking.

The Dragonman put his feet on the stool and continued. "The world would have gone to war with itself with a violence never seen before. The dark Dragons have built up so much hate upon hate in human minds that people were ready to bring death to themselves on a tremendous scale. My magic, and the magic of others like me, saved the earth from a terrible fate."

"From here? From this little place, you did all this?"

"Yes, and from many places like it. May I have some soup before it gets cold?"

Simon got the soup for him without even noticing that he'd done it, as the friendly creature went on. "Deep in the earth, we work. It is not a nice way to live, but we do it. We do it for the good of all things." The Peking Dragon sipped the soup, satisfied. "You should have some," he told Simon. "It will give you pleasant daydreams. A long time ago, I had tea that came from the tears of a whale. Quite exquisite daydreams from that. This was ages ago, when it was safe to go outside. People were not afraid of unusual creatures, like me, walking among them."

Simon found that he was now sitting beside the little animal, drinking his own cup of soup. Everything about this tiny individual seemed frail, brittle, and peaceful. The Dragon, no more than five and a half feet tall, was not in any way like the others he'd seen.

"If all you say is true," said Simon, "there are a lot of things left to explain. I overheard a conversation between three Dragons who said they were coming here to find you. They said you were the last link in their plans to destroy every human city on earth."

The Black Dragon shuddered. "I was foolish to think they would not find me."

"Why do they want you?"

"They are coming to kill me," said the Dragonman. "They are coming because I am the most powerful of the Light Dragons, and with me out of the way, the dark forces will have the upper hand."

Simon could not help but feel pity and fear for the Black Dragon; the evil that was coming for it seemed vast. Undefeatable.

It was like trying to battle the wind.

"I am very old," said the Black Dragon. "My magic is strong, but it is hard to shape. It does as it wishes. I carry it wherever I go, and wherever I go, it hurts people. I know those who live above me are made to suffer from it, but I cannot end their suffering no matter how hard I try. The powers I *can* control are concentrated on keeping the Dark Ones from gaining more strength."

The Black Dragon exhaled blue smoke that drifted all about the room. "These side effects of my magic will call the other Dragons to me. They will take my life in terrible ways. I would prefer it if you were to kill me."

Simon looked into his eyes. Destroying this Dragon would not be easy.

"I'm not sure . . . what I'm going to do," he said.

All of a sudden, with a flutter of wings, the tiny canary flew from its open cage and alighted on the Dragon's shoulder, startling Simon. The old Dragon smiled at it sadly.

"If only my body were strong enough to leave this place, I would go," said the Black Dragon. "I am comfortable here. I find this tomb to be a perfect place for me, though it causes problems for the people in the city above. I wish more than anything I could be on my old boat. It sits in a harbor waiting for me, but I could never get to it."

"We could get you out, perhaps," said Simon quietly.

"You and your father?" scoffed the creature. "He would burn me to a crisp. His quiver of arrows would be empty in half a second's time. From what you've told me, he is obsessed with destroying us."

"No, he's a good man."

"To humans, he is good. But he made up his mind about the race of Dragons long ago. Nothing will change that. I sense it. And you know it. I am trapped between him, and the forces of darkness. It is only a matter of time before one or the other comes in here and sends me to my death."

"I can save your life."

"Why should you pity me?"

"I don't know," said Simon, searchingly. "But I don't want you to die. I haven't decided about you yet, I guess."

"If you helped me to leave here," said the Black Dragon, growing hopeful, "I could show you the world of the Light Dragons. I could take you to see them. You would see the work we do for the good of all."

"You would trust me?" said Simon, his eyes narrowing.

"In return for your trust." The creature nodded. "And for one other reason: my own self-preservation. Sooner or later, your father will hunt me down. If you come back to him and show him proof, proof that the spells of the Light Dragons are made to serve the natural order, then perhaps he'd give up his quest and spare my life."

Somewhere back in the darkness of the tunnels, Simon heard his father approach, the drain water sloshing under his feet.

"Let me speak to him," whispered Simon.

"If he knows of me, he will terminate me," pleaded the Dragon, "you know he will."

Simon felt a desperation building in his head, a choice needing to be made.

The Black Dragon closed his eyes. "I will not fight him. If my time is now, it is now."

Simon heard Aldric coming nearer.

"I can use my magic to get us to the street above," the Dragon said hurriedly, "but I cannot go much further."

The clang of his father's armor echoed behind them. The Knight pulled himself through the hole in the tunnel wall, tearing down decayed bricks as he came. Simon saw him now the way the Dragons must see him: a fierce and relentless warrior.

Aldric's gaze was fixed on the Dragon. Nothing would stop him.

"No—he's not what you think!"cried Simon.

But Aldric had already launched a fiery arrow, which struck the Black Dragon in its side. The creature's roar of pain shook the room.

"Father!" called Simon.

Aldric had notched another arrow instantly. He raised his crossbow.

"USE YOUR MAGIC!" screamed Simon. The Black Creature closed its eyes, and a warm blur engulfed him and Simon as well. A wall of black-red fire flew up between Aldric and Simon, and the boy ran with the Black Dragon through a secret passage and

up a stairway. Aldric could not see them, and they vanished from
the tomb before he could react.

The Knight was in turmoil. His son was gone. He had rushed
the room, and all he had seen was the ferocious Black Dragon
preparing to swallow Simon. He had acted as quickly as possible.
But he was not fast enough.

Simon was gone.

In the streets of Beijing, the Black Dragon and Simon St.
George came out from the underground labyrinth on a bustling
corner near old pagodas. The Black Dragon seemed, to all those
who saw him, as nothing more than an elderly Chinese man
wrapped in scarves, an old Oriental coat and robe, and wearing a
traditional hat. His yellow canary twittered on his shoulder.

"We must move quickly," said the Black Dragon. "I need rest.
We will need a bicycle cab to get us to my ship."

Simon could hardly believe what he was doing, but he got
them a cab, and the cyclist pulled them away into the ocean of
people. The crowd closed in around them, forward and behind,
and Simon could no longer tell where he was. There was no
going back. No time to explain things to Aldric.

Simon was leaving his father behind.

He had no idea if what he was doing was right.

"Be calmed," said the wounded Dragon, rubbing the slash in
his stomach from the arrow's point. "It will all turn out for the
best."

His soothing voice was all Simon had to cling to.

He was on his own.

Chapter Twenty-Nine

A CHINESE DRAGON'S SAILING SHIP

THE BLACK DRAGON CONTROLLED the pain he must have been feeling from his wounds, hardly making a sound as he and Simon finally made their way to a port. Simon watched the Black Dragon closely. But he saw nothing to fear in its eyes.

The creature was delighted at seeing his ship again. Simon wondered how long it had been since the creature had been out of his cave.

The large junk bobbed before them in the water with a humble dignity. It was very old, its sides worn, with a look of obvious abandonment.

"Isn't it beautiful?" said the old Dragon, leaning on Simon's arm to help him walk. "We must get aboard at once."

Up close, the junk was no prettier than it was from a distance. Dust. Rust. Rot. The one saving grace of the dilapidated ship was a faded, painted Dragon on the sides of the cabin.

"What are we going to do now?" asked Simon. "I can't leave

my father long. He'll never forgive me. He's probably worrying himself into a coma."

"He is well," said the Dragon, closing his eyes. "I see him now in my chambers. He is afraid for you; he fears he has failed you. But if we do our work quickly, we will find him in good health when we return."

"I wish," the Dragon added, collapsing onto an old chair on deck, "that I myself should be in such good health." He rubbed his side, and Simon saw what looked to be liquid fire dripping from the wound Aldric had made. Thin strands of burning water slipped through the Black Dragon's fingers and fell to the deck with a hiss.

"Fireblood," he explained weakly. "Your father is quite skilled. Serpentfire-tipped arrows are a fearsome weapon. Fetch some water, there."

Simon turned, finding a bucket full of rainwater. He tossed the water onto the small flames the blood had made on the deck.

"Forgive me," said the old creature. "I should be able to put out my own fireblood, but I am saving my energies. I am not well."

Simon came closer, to see the wound.

"It looks bad." The boy winced. "Can you survive it?"

"I don't know for how long. I hope we can make our journey before my strength leaves me."

A sobering thought lifted itself in Simon's head, of being alone on the sea without his father *or* the Dragonman. What happened to a Dragon when it was dying, anyway? What if its magic burst out of it, and it wasn't safe to be near it? He remembered the death of the White Dragon.

The Black Dragon coughed. "The wound is worse than I thought. The arrow pierced my solar magensis."

"What's that?"

"It is not my heart, but the heart of my magic. It is the organ which generates magic, feeding off the sun. Dark Dragons feed off the moon. It means, Simon, that my time is very short, and that my magic will be more erratical than ever. It could be dangerous to be near me."

"I'll stay," said Simon. "If there's anything I can do to help you, tell me."

"My own life is of sad little importance," said the Black Dragon, "but if we do not get to the Light Dragons and warn them of the danger ahead, the world will be ripped apart by the Dark Draconians' power."

Simon felt desperate. "I left my father behind for you. Don't let it be for nothing. Tell me how to help you. Would this . . . " He rummaged in his satchel for the red elixir bottle, the magician's salve. "Would this do any good?"

The Dragon tilted his head, startled.

"It may. It may," he said.

Simon poured the viscous fluid onto the wound, which glowed like embers as it repaired itself.

The Dragon seemed astonished at Simon's generosity. "That will seal and hold the fireblood in. My strength will return to me."

Simon leaned back against the cabin, worried.

The Dragon kept looking at him in disbelief, as if he were a puzzle of some kind.

"You have done me a kindness," said the Dragon. "All I have for you is a path through great danger."

Simon pulled his crossbow into his arms, still wary. "What does that mean?"

The Black Dragon looked seaward. "Our path is set. We will find our way together. Where the Light Dragons are meeting. Across the world . . ."

"Across the world?"

"To London, boy . . . to London . . ."

The Dragonman closed his eyes. A great ruckus sounded as the sails on the junk burst to life. They swung into place. The wind laid its hands on them. The ship had set sail by the Black Dragon's magic.

Simon looked around in amazement. The junk was seaworthy. The old vessel still worked!

He put his face toward the wind, closing his eyes. Praying for luck.

He took a deep breath. He'd done it. He'd proven . . . useful.

The junk rolled over the waves, pressing toward the city of London, an ocean away.

Deep in the heart of the Black Dragon's home, Aldric was examining everything he could find about the old creature. Perhaps there was a clue as to where they had gone. As he paged through yellowed scrolls of Chinese writing, and books that breathed as he held them, Aldric's mind focused on one problem only: getting his son back.

He wasn't even concerned about the world anymore, or the location of the wicked Serpents. He just wanted his son. If the world ended tomorrow, at least they would be together.

The Black Dragon's magic had lingered behind. Flickering ash drifted around the room. Beetles crackled under Aldric's feet as he explored the chambers. In one room he found an aviary, where black canaries twittered in cages and never saw the sun.

Deeper in, he found a small, beautifully carved wooden table that held wine chalices and dirty plates. Many guests had dined and drunk with the old Dragon. Not long ago.

And then he saw something that gave his heart a chill.

All around the base of the ceremonial table were medallions.

Medallions from other Dragons.

Dozens and dozens of them.

He could see the mark of the Water Dragon of Venice, of the Russian Dragon, of the Dragon of Paris—they had all been here. They had spoken with this Peking Black Dragon, and they had left tribute. Tokens of friendship. Many tokens.

How many more Serpents were a part of this? Evil was flooding the earth. His boy was out there with a creature of profound darkness.

When Simon awoke, it was night. Stars gleamed in the black velvet canopy above him. The face of the Black Dragon was staring down at him. It was dark, but for just an instant Simon thought the Dragon had an expression of distaste, of disgust . . .

But it was just an instant, and he might have been mistaken.

"You should eat," said the Black Dragon politely, and he handed the boy a plate of noodles. Simon took it gladly.

"I am feeling better, for the moment," said the Black Dragon. "It pleases me to see I can still manage some of my own magic. I heated the plate myself." He paused. "You are supposed to be impressed."

Simon gave it a try. The food was good.

The Black Dragon dined with him, feeding his canary bits of noodles. At the reptile's clawed feet, beetles roamed about.

The Dragon explained that it couldn't be helped; even gentle Dragons drew insects to them. At sea the effect was less severe than on land. Tonight, only a small cloud of butterflies managed to trail the ship, fluttering above its white wake. Moonlight glittered on the blue winged insects.

Simon's thoughts were still of his father. He tried to shake the notion that he had betrayed him. It felt terrible to leave him behind, no matter what the reason. Maybe in the end, Aldric would see Simon's actions as brave. It took courage to act against a father's wishes.

It was possible, he had begun to think, that the Black Dragon had helped him find that courage. Perhaps there was something in the soup. The pipe smoke was strange, as well; perhaps the smoke had burned his eyes and made him see things differently.

The Dragon was smoking the pipe now. Nothing was strange about it here. *I'm just thinking like my father*, Simon realized. *Distrusting everything.*

"How old are your years, son?" said the Chinese Dragon.

"I'm thirteen. No. Fourteen," he realized, startled. "Fourteen today. Not that anyone cares . . . " He had forgotten his own birthday. He wondered how that was possible, but days had been passing like wild horses lately. He hadn't been thinking about himself.

"Is that so? Fourteen years of age? You do not look so old as this."

Simon nodded unhappily.

The Dragonman went on, "And your father takes you into battle at such an age? Does he not realize the dangers of a Serpentine?"

"He realizes it. He doesn't trust anyone else to protect me."

"If I had a son . . . I would not send him out in battle. I would protect him from warfare no matter what the cost. No matter what his age."

Simon looked at the Dragon.

"I suppose I should not speak. What do I know of these things? I am old; that does not make me wise. I will tell you, though, that I regret having no children," said the Dragon.

"Maybe one day with a Light Dragon, you'll have a child."

The Pyrothrax looked at him oddly, maybe just sadly—Simon wasn't sure.

"Perhaps," he said, finally. "Perhaps there are as many wonders that lie ahead as there are terrors."

Simon considered this for a moment and said, "None of those terrors will come from you, I hope."

The Dragon lowered his head and peered over his tiny eyeglasses. "Still you do not trust me?"

"Let's just say I'm not sure I trust you."

The Dragon frowned. "Sadly, I must say it is perhaps for the best. My magic is untrustworthy. Terrors, yes, may come our way. But I shall work against that."

Simon nodded, satisfied for now.

Birds flew by in the night, lit up by the moon glow. Simon noticed that as the sea birds gathered near, they were chased off by black vultures like those in Beijing. At night, against the torn-silk clouds and the stars and the white-skimmed black ocean, the dreary flyers looked almost pretty. They stayed together, eyeing the ship with their glassy eyes glinting from the moon. Simon watched the vultures winging after the ship for miles and miles.

The shapes unnerved Simon, and he stayed awake nearly all night.

Chapter Thirty

SEPARATE JOURNEYS

I T WAS JUST BEFORE dawn.

Sunlight was licking at the edges of the horizon.

Ahead, on deck, in the dim light of morning, a Knight on horseback drifted past the ship.

Simon squinted.

The Knight was made of smoke.

Jolted, the boy looked to the Black Dragon, who was sleeping on deck, his curled pipe still in his mouth. As the smoke left his pipe, it was making shapes, dozens and dozens of them, and all around Simon the smokeshapes enlarged and drifted.

Other Knights, and other horses, formed from the pipe smoke. They were huge and fearsome, and moved slowly, heavily, gliding away onto the sea, to break apart in the wind.

Simon realized the smoke was sculpted from the dreams of the Dragon.

Curious, he crept to the sleeping creature, who was talking in his sleep. He appeared to be having a nightmare.

"No, no," he moaned groggily, "Do not kill me, Knight. . . . Let me live . . . "

The Dragon stirred restlessly, his eyelids quivering. He muttered on, in Chinese, as the canary on his shoulder hopped about, disturbed.

Simon took the pipe from the Dragon's mouth and set it safely aside. He picked up the woolen blanket that had fallen from the Dragon's chair and laid it gently on the old creature. The Dragon relaxed, slipping into a more comfortable slumber.

Pleased with his work, Simon stepped back to let him sleep a bit longer.

The pipe unfurled the last of its smoke, which took the shape of a tiny junk that slipped lazily out over the ocean, expanding and growing until it was almost as large as life, and in the smoky hues, Simon could see the outline of a boy and the Dragon himself on its deck. The pleasant image drifted away above the tides, until a flock of seabirds and the breeze passed through it, making it into a stringy mist.

The boy had seen the creature's inner heart and found only fear there.

Thus, for better or worse, Simon came to put his faith in a Dragon.

This was something his father would never have allowed. The Black Dragon was not to be trusted. Simon was too generous and innocent a person to understand the dark ways of the world. Aldric told himself he should have seen that.

He stood in the Dragon's den and felt rage take over. He kicked violently against the table and yelled out in anger. As it cracked and echoed in the chamber, Aldric heard the patter of running feet.

A man was fleeing the tunnels, and Aldric chased him down. He threw him against the wall and drew his sword to his throat.

"Who are you?" Aldric cried.

"No pain, please, no pain," he answered. "I serve the old man who lives here. I brought feed for his birds. He was to be gone."

"Gone where?" Aldric prepared to use the sword. "Your life depends on it."

"He is . . . good. Good to me . . ."

In his desperation, Aldric grew furious. "He has my son— where is he now?"

"England," said the terrified servant. "He would not hurt anyone. He's been forced to this. It's beyond anyone's control. He serves a powerful master. The only thing anyone can hope for now is to find a good master, and hope to live through it."

The Asian man told Aldric where he could find his son in London. Aldric lowered his sword. The servant went on, out of breath: "Your time will be brief with the boy. Your time, and the time of all of us who are human, is ending. The Dragons are remaking the land."

The man had no fight left in his eyes, as if brainwashed by his time with the Dragon. "They are united now, one effort. One mission. It is all but done. Serve them and you have hope. My master is a good one. All of you who have raged against them have lost now."

Aldric began walking away.

"They will now dominate all mankind as they have always wanted," the servant said after him.

Aldric kept his stride.

"All that is left for us is to enjoy the days we have left, the freedom we now cling to." His voice echoed down the tunnel as Aldric headed out. "Go to your son. May you find him before the End Time."

Aldric left the underground chamber and made his way through the city, numb with worry. In the countryside, he found his jet and ordered a course for Russia. It was the longest flight of his life.

Hours and hours later, he returned to the Ship with No Name, long awaiting his arrival. Fenwick the fox lifted its head, rushing to him with joy.

It took a moment for Aldric to feel the ship was secure enough to launch as he went to a wood console at the front of the ship and set the lever forward. He placed his hand on a metal engraving of a world map, his finger on London, and the magic that was left in the ship calculated his desired destination.

Patting Fenwick, Aldric felt the ship surge to life, then moved to a floorboard, opening a hidden cabinet where his brother's sword and other weapons lay waiting.

"A bit unwieldy for one man," he said to himself, looking over the devices. "But I'll need anything I can get. . . . "

The weapons here would augment the ones he always relied on. The Knight now stood ready for battle. He took his ship from Russian waters and left with all speed to London. The Ship with No Name had never sailed so fast. Maradine's magic, woven into the lines and threaded into the sails, labored hard.

Aldric arrived just hours after the Black Dragon.

Chapter Thirty-One

FRIENDSHIP WITH A DRAGON

DISGUISED AS A DOTTERING old Chinese man by the name of Ming Song, the Black Dragon led Simon through the streets of London. It was dark by the time they arrived at the building where the gathering of the Light Dragons was to occur.

Before they left the ship, the Dragon had given Simon a very fine suit to wear that fit him fairly well, and he had cleaned up considerably.

The Chinese man led him to an immense white palace where an exhibit of modern art was under way. Well-dressed people moved in and out of a spacious gallery.

"A museum?" asked Simon.

"Private gallery," said the Dragon. "The opening allows us cover for the arrival of so many. It is hoped no one will notice the Light Dragons slipping in to London."

The ground shifted under their feet, rolling like a wave. A heavy earthquake. Simon looked at the Dragon in horror.

The Dragon was calm. "Inescapable side effect. The Light Dragons are meeting beneath us. We enter here. . . ."

Art lovers roamed throughout the gallery. One woman near Simon was complaining that there were too many people here, rude people, such as that tall gentlemen with the ruddy face and a slight problem breathing—he seemed awfully uptight, she said. And the slim Frenchman—she was more than a bit perturbed to catch him nibbling at one of the paintings; at least, she thought that's what he was doing. He turned around with such a handsome, innocent smile, perhaps she was imagining things. And then there was the Russian general. A plump man, he dressed drably, so it was hard to tell if he had any money to spend on art. But the nerve of someone bringing cats to a gallery. . . . She was saying all this, and Simon only dimly heard, for he was now quite distracted.

He had noticed a familiar kind of painting. It was a collection of abstract scraps, and he realized it was Alaythia's, which someone must have salvaged from her New York apartment. He turned, and was surprised again. In a flowing evening gown, Alaythia was there, standing before a huge white painting. Simon ran to her.

"Alaythia?"

She stood, unmoving, eyes fixed to the painting. Spiritless.

"They caught me in Russia," she said, as though half asleep. "As soon as I left you, their men found me. They've got me chained here somehow. . . . The painting has an enchantment to it. I can't seem to get away from it. I just find it endlessly fascinating. Isn't that so strange?"

In his confusion, Simon felt a sudden urge to pull her away, get her out.

"My proudest moment," she droned on. "They're displaying my work in a gallery. Too bad it's only in this evil place. They were all in the art world, you know. The Venetian, the White, the Parisian, they all knew each other. It was only a matter of time before they brought in others."

Simon struggled to understand, as she looked blankly away. He stepped in front of her. "What is happening?"

"Your father . . . he won't be happy with this."

"No," said the Black Dragon, who had joined them, "he most certainly will not be happy." With that he looked quite uncomfortable, and behind him, Simon finally saw the other gallery guests. He saw them for what they were.

Dragons.

He had walked into a gallery of Dragons. Simon almost lost his breath. The Water Dragon of Venice stood with the Parisian Dragon; the Russian Dragon, in a muddle of cats, stood beside them.

The sinister beasts closed in on him, walking slowly through the crowd.

"Do forgive me," the Black Dragon told a shocked Simon, "but they would have killed me if I failed to bring you."

The boy's eyes widened with terror. "This was a trap . . . ?"

"A thousand sorrys," said the Black Dragon, and he did seem to mean it, "but my fear of you is greater than you know. My fear of your father greater still."

"You lied to me," Simon said. "Everything, from the beginning, it was all a lie . . . ?"

"I am afraid, boy-child, that there are no Light Dragons. There is no such thing. Though I did enjoy your company," he replied. "And you did heal my wounds, for which I am grateful."

"The least I could do," hissed Simon, his teeth gritted.

The Black Dragon looked apologetic. "You are more than just a human. Your life has . . . value."

"Not to me," grumbled the French one.

"What do you want?" asked Alaythia, the spell she was under slowly being broken by the sound of Simon's voice. She was desperately looking for an escape route.

"What we want is the boy," said the Russian, "and his hateful father."

"That's what this is all about," said Simon. "You want my father. And you know he'll come for me."

"*Très astute.* Clever boy," said the Parisian. "Smart as your father. You would be dangerous if you were allowed to grow older."

"What are your plans for him?"

"I should think that obviousssss," smiled the Venice Water Dragon. "We've been trying to get at him for agessss. Now we have you as well. We can destroy the last of the Dragonhuntersss all at once."

"Don't fear," said the Black Dragon, "I will see to it you feel no pain."

The Paris Dragon glared. "Nonsense," he said. "He will feel great pain."

Simon and Alaythia were surrounded. Simon could feel his weapons under his long coat, but getting to them would be impossible. He couldn't move that fast. The creatures would burn him in an instant.

"We have tried to remove your father for many yearssss," said the Dragon of Venice, moving closer, steadily closer, "and never had any luck. Now we know his weaknessss is his child. He will come for you, and when he doesss, we will capture him. From there, death will come ssslowly, not all at once. Where's the fun in that, after all?"

"Not likely. He's beaten you before," said Simon bravely.

"Oh, but not all of us together, little child," the Venice Water Dragon said with a sickly cough.

"He won't fall into your trap," said Simon. "And when he gets here, he will bring your plans crashing down on you."

"The skinmonkey's brave," said the Russian coldly. "How sad that his bravery will win him nothing."

"There was nothing I could do, Simon," said the Black Dragon, "I cannot defy the master now—he has far too much power."

"The Masquerade is over," said the Parisian, and the Dragons let go of their disguising magic.

The Dragons were now revealed.

Alaythia just stood there, wanting to faint. *Please faint,* she told herself, *faint so you don't have to look.*

The sight of the creatures sent the crowd running from the room with shrieks of terror.

Simon took the chance to whip out his crossbow.

The Dragonmen stopped their approach.

"Don't touch her," Simon said.

"Oh, no," said a voice. "We have plans for her. . . . "

Alaythia and Simon knew the voice.

Everyone turned—and it seemed to Simon that the Venetian cowered a bit from the new presence. And it was clear why he was cowering. From out of the chaos, behind the other Dragons, with great authority, strode the Man in White. He was dressed in a white suit and white cloak. Beneath his feet hordes of white lizards crawled, and high above his head white bats swarmed.

To Simon's eyes, he became the White Dragon, undisguised and very much alive.

The Master.

"We have been having a wonderful time with you," said the White Dragon. "But all good things must come to an end."

Now you have to faint, Alaythia told herself, but still she did not.

Simon did not think he could stand the horror a moment longer when suddenly the huge gallery windows behind the Dragons shattered gloriously and in crashed Aldric St. George, riding his furious steed Valsephany.

The horse was outfitted with a special harness—a new weapon Simon hadn't seen before—with little pipes attached, pointed forward. The pipes fired arrows automatically. The bolts blasted out at once as Aldric rushed the gallery. But he couldn't aim anywhere except straight ahead, and most of the arrows fell short, slamming into the floor. Simon gasped as several stabbed near him. The Venetian caught one of the arrows in his jaws and spat it away.

Aldric swung his sword down first on the Paris Dragon, but the blue-yellow Serpent shot back away from him, scurrying to the wall.

Aldric galloped to the end of the gallery, where Simon and Alaythia cowered. "Are you all right?" he asked quickly.

"We'll live," said Simon.

Alaythia looked relieved. Hearing Aldric's voice had erased all traces of the spell she was under.

Aldric paced the horse in front of them to keep the Dragonmen back.

The White Dragon stepped in front of the others.

"Welcome to my humble home," he said. "It's open to the public tonight, but you seem to have scared most everyone off."

"You live," Aldric said with astonishment.

"I have risen from the ashes," the White Dragon said, and smiled.

"Then I shall have the pleasure of killing you twice."

"You never really gained anything, Dragonhunter. My death was an imitation, of course. A bit of drama, a flash of fire, and the illusion was complete. A risk, to be sure, but I needed to buy myself some time to put my plan in motion. You should have realized it. When a Serpent dies, his ashes turn red to the touch. The clues were all there. You hadn't even finished saying my deathspell."

"I thought I was unusually lucky," said Aldric, "and you unusually weak."

Venemon laughed, the skin of his long white throat shuddering. "You should have studied the lore more carefully . . . but then you had only half the story."

He pulled from his white cloak the Lost Book of Saint George.

The room was filled with madness now from the conflicting Dragon-magic. All of the paintings showed images of faces suddenly forming under the paint, and the faces were screaming. Pieces of glass from the shattered window were floating about, or ticking on the floor like nervous claws. Earthquakes rumbled under their feet.

"I am sure you are expecting," said the White Dragon, "a most climactic showdown." His white reptilian feet tapped the floor with a nervous arrogance while he continued, "But I am sorry to disappoint. There will be no fight to the death. This is not a battleground. It's a trap."

He chanted a quick spell. The other dragons' hoarse and cloudy voices laughed in the background. The top of the gallery became a smooth, pearly mist.

The humans looked up in horror.

The white mist descended on them; the ceiling of fog simply fell, like a great ivory curtain. Valsephany gave a neighing cry. Aldric tried to control the horse.

As it fell, the huge curtain became solid, turning into bars of white iron. Simon and the others were now in a huge white prison cell that quickly sunk into the ground, below the gallery, into an all-white dungeon. Alaythia had managed not to faint. Instead she was struck by falling debris from the quaking room, and fell unconscious.

It would seem they'd been captured.

The game was up.

Chapter Thirty-Two

UNWELCOME GUESTS

THE DRAGONMEN WERE NOWHERE in sight.

No one spoke for a while. There is a certain level of shock involved with failing to save the world and being captured against your will.

Wind whistled through the white dungeon. The prison was huge; it had been made to contain other enemies of the White Dragon, of which there were many, and whose bones now littered the floor.

The white-iron dungeon lay under the Great White Palace, and the Great White Palace lay in the heart of London. It was not hidden away, but protected by magic, which kept people from asking questions. No one knew the Dragonhunters were being held there. No one would hear their calls.

Alaythia remained sleeping. Simon checked to see she was unharmed.

Valsephany neighed, shivering from the chilled dungeon air. Aldric was still atop the horse, letting it wander within the dungeon so it might feel warmer.

"She's sort of beautiful when she's not talking," said Simon, putting his coat over Alaythia. "Don't you think so?"

Aldric sighed. "Will you let me deal with our little mistake here?"

"Mistake? I'd call this a failure."

His father gave him a most unappealing glance. "We aren't finished yet," he said, "despite your best efforts."

Simon looked up with a touch of anger. "What I did," said Simon, "I did for everybody here. I was doing what I could to keep the world out of their claws."

"By joining with them?"

"I didn't know the Black Dragon was with them!"

"You *should* have known. What have I been telling you since we began? The Dragon is the source of all that is rotten in the world. It can never be trusted."

"I didn't believe that. Nothing is completely evil. No race, no species, no thing on earth is totally filled with darkness."

"Idiocy. You could see the good in anything."

"Yeah, everything. Everything but you."

The horse stamped its foot, discomforted with the fighting. It quieted them.

Alaythia awoke, and regarded the argument with annoyance. "Are we working on a way out yet?"

Aldric swung his sword against the white cage. Metal rang against metal. But the cage stood firm.

"They've made something that can withstand our steel," said Aldric. "Our weapons are useless. And there are many magics weighing down on us at once. It's making us weak. It's making our bones brittle. They're going to break us, in every way possible."

Simon could sense it as well, as if gravity itself were getting heavier. He could feel himself growing tired and the bones of his body almost seeming to shrink inside him. "How long can we survive it?"

Aldric dismounted and looked him in the eye. "Not sure. Days, perhaps. I have to say I've never felt the effect of their magic so strongly. There must be many of them."

He was quite right.

Somewhere above them, in the Great White Hall, a gathering of Dragons was taking place. Nothing like it had been seen on earth in centuries. The White Dragon had sent out word that all the Pyrothraxes were to come together. He had personally journeyed to the homes of most of them and convinced them he could be trusted. He had invited them to his grand ancestral home in England, and he had laid down its protective magic so that all could enter. He was about to reap the rewards of all his work.

The Dragonmen were finding their places in the immense hall above the dungeon. The huge, echoing ceilings weaved their voices together so that the noise was like a terrible music.

It was an amazing sight.

To begin with, everything in the palace was the color white. The white walls were supported with the sculpted beams of a Gothic cathedral, like a great animal's rib cage. It was like being in the belly of the White Dragon himself. Which was exactly his intention. Guests of the White Dragon had only two purposes: either to be eaten and served to him, or to be beaten so that they would serve *for* him.

Huge chairs had been set out for each of the reptilians. The White Dragon had placed his chair at the end of the hall, before an altar that held a long banquet table. Piles of medallions lay at the foot of his chair.

And then there were the Serpents.

Counted together, the creatures appeared to number about a hundred. In fact, there were many more who remained invisible, still distrusting the others. Of the ones that could be seen, many had to be seen just to be believed.

The Red Dragon of Russia and the Blue-Gold Dragon of Paris looked quite different now, in their ceremonial armor. The Russian had brought three prized cats, who gnawed on the bones of something unknown, and the Parisian had painted a wonderful but somewhat terrifying abstract collection of red and yellow splotches over his chestplate for decoration. These Creatures were joined by the other French Dragon (of Calais), who smelled of cheese that had spoiled centuries ago, and the other Russian Dragon, a Bear Dragon of Siberia, who was as gray as stone, with a personality to match.

Unable to endure the breathing of air for long periods of time, Brakkesh, the Water Dragon of Venice, had come encased in a giant water tank that moved about on wheels. He looked out on everyone from the murky green water in his glass bubble, munching seaweed. One could dimly hear his favorite opera music playing inside his tank.

And there were others. The Sand Dragon, Mistral, whose leather-skinned reptile children surrounded him, fanning him with palm leaves to cool him from his own, always-smoldering red heart under his skin. White robes covered his head and his body. His children were dressed just like their father; they were proud to be following in his footsteps. Their mother, of course, was nowhere to be found. They had eaten her up years before.

The Tiger Dragon, Issindra, was a female Serpent from jungle-land India, whose title derived from her tiger-striped hide. Issindra was beautiful. Even humans might have thought so. But her habit of scorching those who fell in love with her kept most suitors away. At the moment, she was whispering in the ears of the Parisian Dragon, and he was liking what he heard. When another female, the Fox Dragon of Quebec, looked in the direction of the Parisian and purred, Issindra became jealous, growling and wishing she could shoot a hot stream of flame at her rival's face. She couldn't, of course, it was too dangerous, so all were spared the sight of her fire. Issindra's fire was tiger-striped like she was: Red-black stripes ribboned the flames whenever they flew from her mouth. Quite beautiful.

Watching the Tiger Dragon with equal jealousy was the Spanish Lasher Dragon, who had numerous slim, whiplike tails jutting from her back. Her arms were like two bullwhips, and they were usually set afire. Her snout and her mouth were covered in tiny, hanging whips, and scars where the whips had cut her. When she was agitated or upset, she would slither and slash her whips around angrily. The other Pyrothraxes kept a good distance from her.

The guest list went on. There was the heavy, baggy-skinned Elephantine Dragon, who had gray, sagging skin, a long elephant's trunk, and huge ivory tusks. Even heavier was the Nine-Ton Dragon, an obese Belgian monstrosity so fat she could barely move, and was bed-ridden for life. There were the diminutive

Midget Dragons, who had come from Romania and who were unhappy that their morsel-sized bodies had been seated next to the Nine-Ton Dragon; seated next to them were their exact opposites, the towering, slim African Tall Dragons, whose long black hair was coiled into braids of astonishing workmanship; there was the Spider Dragon of Brazil, who had a strange feature at the top of her head, something that looked like a giant spider turned on its back, with its eight legs opening and closing grotesquely.

Mind you, these were not the most fearsome in the group. Those creatures remained invisibly safe and watchful, expecting to be double-crossed by their own kind.

Only the Black Dragon held himself apart. He sat without speaking, looking at the little canary in his hand, his dearest companion and the closest thing he had to family.

The chattering, arguing Pyrothraxes all quieted as the White Dragon finally entered and took his chair.

"This is an historic moment," he began, "and one which will never be forgotten. The raw talent in this room numbs the mind. Never have so gifted a group been gathered together for so significant a purpose."

The response from the crowd was a rumble of skeptical approval.

It was heard, down below, in the white dungeon.

It sounded like a million rattlesnakes, a million tapping spiders, a million growling wolves. If it was possible for a noise to be *scaly*, this was it. The entire palace shook from the presence of so much evil.

"Incredible," mumbled Aldric. "How many of them are there?"

"More than I want to see," said Simon. His lack of faith in

himself frightened him. His father's fear frightened him. He felt hopeless.

Alaythia felt a different anxiety. Her growing power had come with a price. The Dragons were now able to *talk* to her inside of her head, something they could not do to the St. Georges. She could hear the low rumble of their voices, taunting her, telling her she should have fled when she had the chance, trying to wear her down. There were more than she had ever dreamed. She had been ignoring the sound for some time, and now she decided to challenge it directly.

Just by concentrating, she pushed the noise out of her head and slammed the doors of her mind. With effort, she'd done it. She surprised even herself.

She simply wasn't going to be afraid.

"They're going to kill us," she said plainly. "That much is clear. I hate to think how. My vote is that we break out of here, and take some of them down with us."

Simon and Aldric looked at her incredulously. Their artist had become a warrior.

"How do you suppose we get out of here?" asked Aldric doubtfully.

"Well, the first order of business is to snap you out of this trance you're in," said Alaythia. "The two of you look like fish in a basket, waiting to be cleaned and gutted."

"I'm just being realistic about our chances," said Aldric.

"Enough of that," said Alaythia. "We're not exactly useless, Simon and me. I'm not going to hand myself over to these things to be burned, or swallowed up, or whatever it is they plan to do."

"What they plan is more terrible than you can imagine," said

Aldric. He'd pieced the plan together by now. "They're planning to unleash the Serpent Queen."

Simon felt like someone had punched him in the stomach.

"They've been at each other's throats for centuries, ever since the Serpent Queen was banished to the shadows. Ever since the Great Egyptian Sorcerers sentenced her to a dark sleep in the core of the earth. Now . . . the White Dragon has hatched a scheme to get all the Dragonmen to unite for their queen. They think they can revive her, with all their magic combined."

"And you think they can do it?" asked Simon quietly. He already knew the answer.

"Yes," said Aldric. "And if they succeed, their strength will be beyond anything we can hope to fight. They will rule the earth. Right now, they have one difficulty, and we have one advantage: Their powers react and chafe against one another. Bring two Dragons together, and their magic becomes hard to control. Bring this many vile Serpents into one place, and there is bound to be chaos on a grand scale."

Aldric was right. Simply by having this many Dragonmen collected in the White Palace, the world had begun to react in unnatural ways. The rippling in reality fanned out from London, where there was a calm in the eye of the magic storm: mere earthquakes and foul weather, and a wicked yellow fog that swallowed up the sky.

But in Oslo, Norway, people were already reporting vast rat populations infesting the city, so many they were like a flood in the streets. In Holland, butcher-shop animals, already quite dead, rattled and moved around; fish flopped off of the chopping block. In Ireland, snakes by the hundreds slithered out of the ground and emerged from people's chimneys and sinks and toilets, and any opening into the world a home might have. In Germany, bats by the millions ripped over the sky and glided low through Berlin, squealing ferociously.

Massive earthquakes hit cities throughout the Northern Hemisphere.

Some people caught fire randomly and quickly burned beyond recognition.

Across the world, storm winds began to blow, then would suddenly stop completely, and start again.

Dragon magic was everywhere at once.

In Paris, lightning rattled nearly every building, and flames shot from the ground mercilessly.

As far off as Australia, millions of people felt weak, angry, and depressed. The clouds made vague and angry shapes: wolves and lions and evil, humanlike faces.

A giant eye made of clouds peered down over the quaking skyline of New York.

Shapes of Dragons could be seen in storm clouds across America.

"All of this," continued Aldric, "happens because the Dragons cannot live together. But if the Queen of Serpents is raised from the shadow world, the Dragons will live in harmony. Her magic will unite theirs. The danger to humankind has never been greater."

No one needed to say this. They knew it in their bones.

All the world was depending on them.

Chapter Thirty-Three

HEROES IN NEED OF HEROES

IMON LET OUT A heavy breath. The White Dragon was more resourceful than anyone had expected.

"Well," sighed Alaythia, "we can't just give up. There must be some way out of here. I know I've made my share of mistakes, but I have been working to repair what's been lost."

She pulled from her pocket an old scrap of canvas, and on the back of it were all the deathspells they had lost.

"Where did you get that . . . ?" Simon asked, astonished.

"I drew it from memory," said Alaythia, "each and every one."

Simon took a closer look. The runes looked exactly like the book's, right down to the unnamed spell at the bottom.

Aldric looked at her with new respect.

"We have the spells," Simon said. "We can destroy them with this."

Aldric did not share his enthusiasm. "Listen to them up there.

We can't possibly get that close to them. There are too many."

"It's a start," said Simon, and he took the canvas scrap from her thankfully, rolling it up like a scroll.

"That isn't going to do it alone," said Aldric.

Simon looked at him. "There are other ways. They have another weakness."

"What is that?"

"They hate each other."

Aldric watched him, waiting to hear more.

"They don't trust each other. Everything the White Dragon is doing depends on all of them working together. We have to work on their natural hatred for their own kind. We have to make them believe this is all a plot he's come up with to kill them."

Alaythia immediately saw his logic. "All we have to do is get the word out."

Simon stood and faced his father. "We don't need the death-spells."

Aldric looked doubtful. But there was no more time to discuss it.

The White Dragon entered the dungeon.

"Uncomfortable, I hope," he said, regarding the cage with pride. "I designed it to reflect my own artwork."

Alaythia saw him as the man in white, and couldn't believe she'd ever had warm feelings for him.

"Aren't you missing your honorable guests?" asked Aldric.

"You," said the White Dragon, "are the guests of honor today. I have waited a good long time to have you here. Without you, there would be no grand celebration, as I'm sure you realize. You see . . . when I discovered the boy, I had a vision: If the

Dragonhunter has one secret, perhaps he has many. I let it be known in the world of Dragons that a Knight with a new and terrible weapon was stalking them mercilessly. Everywhere you went, you made my lie more believable. Now the Dragons are uniting, largely because they fear this weapon I've told them about. Such silly superstition. It's a shame you won't see my plans fulfilled. You will be long dead by the time the Serpent Queen has risen."

"You turn my stomach, Venemon."

"Oh, that pains me. All I want in this world is to be loved by humankind," he said, and snickered.

"How did you know I would come here?" said Aldric. "I might've tried to round up new forces, new allies, before I attacked."

The White Dragon sneered. "And leave your boy in the meantime? Not likely. What's more, in recent days, you have become all too easy to find. Love is like the scent of a wounded animal to us. Your emotions give you away."

Aldric looked to Simon.

"Oh, not the boy," said the Dragon. "Your feelings for the woman. And hers for you."

Simon and Alaythia were taken aback. Aldric lowered his eyes. Because Alaythia truly was a magician, the Dragons could sense Alaythia and Aldric's growing feelings anywhere in the world.

"If need be, we would have arranged for you and Alaythia to find each other," said the Dragon. "And tracking you then would have been a simple matter. A Knight and a Magician? In love? It'd be so easy, there'd be no fun in it."

Simon could see Alaythia was feeling guilty.

"How do you think we found her in Moscow?" the Dragon snorted to Aldric.

"Are you so low that you would stoop to harming women and children?" he replied.

"I didn't bring the child into this," scowled the Dragonman, and Aldric looked ashamed. "I left him alive. I was baiting you. As for the woman, I have never had difficulty dispensing with the female of the species."

The White Dragon pulled his long neck up, peering down at Alaythia.

She kept a brave face, but moved just slightly back, away from the reptilian. "What use am I to you?"

"Aldric hasn't told you?" The White Serpent tilted his head playfully. "You hold a most distinguished place in our proceedings. You should be overjoyed."

In the pit of her stomach, Alaythia felt a slow, growing disgust. "You want to marry me."

"Marry you?" The Dragon laughed. "No, you will be swallowed up in far finer flames than my own. I find you delicate and ravishing, of course, but such exquisiteness deserves special attention. You are to be a sacrifice to the Dragon Queen herself."

Alaythia's worry and nausea scraped within her.

"I have already taken a bride," the beast said pensively, "God rest her soul."

Simon knew whom he meant. His mother had been taken by this monster because in its own sick brain it thought it loved her. What a disgusting idea these creatures had of love. He understood his father's hatred of them now completely.

Aldric eyed Simon, doing his best to look soothing. "There will be a time for revenge," he said quietly. "Don't go off without thinking."

"Do you understand what it means for a Dragon to love?" said the White Serpent. Simon didn't look at him. "It means that the Dragon must cast the woman in flames. You see, Dragons can feel human emotion, so at the instant of the woman's death, the Dragon knows what it feels like to vanish in flames. The Dragon *shares* the experience with his bride. It is a beautiful thing.

"Your mother," he went on, "was no different. I saw all of her memories, all of her feelings. She is gone, but her dreams, her hopes, everything that she was, passed over my eyes to look over, like volumes in a library. Wouldn't you like to have seen her mind? Wouldn't you like to see what I saw?"

Simon watched the creature move his head back and forth beyond the bars, trying to catch his eye.

"Don't you want to know what she thought of you? What she thought of your father?"

"Leave him alone," said Aldric.

"I can see why you wouldn't. I've seen her memories, child-boy," said the White Dragon. "She grew to hate you like a weight around her neck. And your father was no better—"

Aldric moved toward him threateningly, but the Serpent went on. "Your father loathed you, I could see it in her mind's eye—he couldn't stand what you'd done to their happy existence. Before you, they lived well. Seeing the world, doing as they wished. But you made them poor. You made travel difficult. You made him feel guilty for not loving you, and for that, he hated you even more."

Simon felt like he was drowning; the Serpent's words were killing him.

"Watch yourself—" said Aldric.

"Oh, let's have it all out now, shall we?" the Serpent taunted, turning back to Simon. "I took the Knight's wife, and he was left with you, Simon-boy, a sniveling baby. A grown man doesn't want such burdens. You know this, surely. When he left you at that school, he went off to celebrate."

"They're all lies, Simon," said his father, looking nervous.

The Dragon smiled. "The Knight is not worthy of you, boy."

"He will be. When he avenges himself on you," said Simon.

"And I *will* have my revenge," said Aldric, "for ending the life of my wife, and my brother."

The Dragon's neck recoiled. "We have both lost brothers. I hated mine, but his spies did find the boy and pass on the information, I'll say that for him. So I seek vengeance as well, Knight."

Behind him, rolling into the dungeon, was the Dragon of Venice, encased in his traveling water tank. "Kill them now, Venemon," he hissed. "To keep them any longer is foolish risk."

The White Dragon shot him a withering look. "I make the decisions, Brakkesh. Any more questioning of the plan, and I'll torch you to ashdust, regardless of the fire risk." A slight white glow in his throat removed all doubt. The Venetian pulled back inside his watery chamber, retreating.

The Dragonhunters watched this exchange very carefully.

Suddenly, Simon felt a tugging, and looked down to see the Dragonmap fly from the satchel he carried, straight into the White Dragon's claws. The creature lifted the map.

"You played your part perfectly." He smiled at Simon. "We

lost track of you here and there, but when you were sighted in Beijing, it all fell into place. Rather than another messy battle—one the Black Dragon was far too feeble to win—I thought, why not bring him here? Make the Dragonhunter a gift to the others. Break him down. With all of us working against him, he could hardly escape. I thank you, boy, for helping me."

Simon could not bring himself to speak.

"He wanted me as a father, Aldric," said the White Dragon. "Me. I can see it inside him. The Man in White seemed like the right kind of father to him when I came to his school. And it's true: I would've made a wonderful father." Simon looked away from Aldric, embarrassed he'd ever felt that way.

Venemon grinned. "I knew you'd end up in my grasp sooner or later."

"Don't fear him," Aldric said to Simon. "We'll have our time."

Simon was under control. It was Alaythia who was on edge, stinging with anger.

The White Dragon leaned close to the bars, whispering to her. "Now, the last Dragonhunter will die, along with the last magician. You will give light to the world, my sweet, your flesh, your skin, and your bones."

And with that, a torrent of shimmering heat waves rushed up his body, as he revealed his true self to her for the first time. The white-haired man who had stood before her now flickered into the shape Aldric and Simon had known all along: a white-skinned reptilian beast the size of a man, but with all the fearsome aspects of a Dragon.

The Venetian laughed.

Alaythia screamed.

Moments later she was dragged out by the White Creature, the bars of the cage vanishing for her and quickly re-forming, slamming shut, as she was brought up the stairs to the Great Hall. She was bound with heavy ropes to the long white table.

When she turned to see a court full of hideous Dragons, she screamed again.

Then she tightened her eyes shut, trying to breathe. She would find a way out of this. And she was not going to rely on a Knight in shining armor.

Chapter Thirty-Four

THE HONOR OF DRAGONS

BELOW THE GREAT HALL, alone in the dungeon, Aldric lifted Simon's sword from the stone floor and slowly passed it to him.

Simon's hands closed around the hilt. The heart inside it beat firm and steady.

"You are more than I ever deserved," said the Knight with no trace of doubt. "Nothing that creature said was true. I know you don't understand the sacrifice I made in leaving you, but we have to see our way out of this together now. There's no room for error."

The responsibility made Simon's sword feel heavier.

"Use your sword," he told Simon. "But follow my instincts. Not yours. Work with me, not against me. Try to believe in me."

I do, thought Simon, but a new arrival, outside the cage, kept him from speaking.

"You," said Simon, turning, surprised at seeing him.

Ming Song, the old Black Dragon, kept his eyes lowered.

"Honorable St. George family," he said. "It is my duty to send the Knight to the Great Hall, where he will be witness to the ceremony for the Serpent Queen."

Simon glared at the Black Dragon. "I never should have trusted you. You're all liars."

The Black Dragon turned his head away, not able to stand Simon's fierce gaze. "I had no choice in the matter," he answered. "It is with some regret I tell you this."

"I'll teach you a thing or two about regret," said Aldric.

The Black Dragon ignored the Knight. "The Queen of Serpents awaits us all," he said.

Aldric swung his sword at the bars in anger, but suddenly white iron chains came out of the floor and clasped his arms and legs. Then Aldric was pulled upward, flying toward the ceiling of the cage, which opened for him.

"They are sending him to his death," the Black Dragon said to Simon, bowing his head.

Simon called out, watching helplessly as Aldric ascended to the upper floor and the ceiling slammed shut.

Aldric landed in the Great Hall in front of the White Dragon. The Knight stood in chains before his enemies. Alaythia looked to him worriedly.

Below in the prison, Simon tried to climb the bars, terrified, listening desperately for what would happen. The crowd was quieting. He could hear only what Aldric was seeing: The White Dragon stood over Alaythia, full of confidence and power.

"Tonight, comrades and brothers, we look upon the future," said the White Serpent.

The reptilians rustled with interest.

"For too long, we have been needless enemies," he went on, "our powers at odds with each other because of what the humans did to our Great Queen. In this very hall, even as we are gathered together in goodwill, our magic quarrels against our mingling."

Indeed, the hall was slowly filling with beetles. They seemed to have been generated out of nothing. Beetles of every color went rolling over each other, crawling over the toes of the Dragons. Earthquakes continued to shake the palace. Lightning moved over the Dragons, fitfully biting at their snouts and necks.

"All of this will end soon. The great tragedy that befell the Serpent Queen has too long defined us," the White Dragon bellowed across the hall, "and we have been too distrustful to realize it. With the union of our strengths, we will bury our differences and seek a new life under a common queen."

The reptilians began murmuring approval.

Simon heard the serpent's words from the dungeon, his mind on his father. *We are going to die,* he thought, *because I wanted to prove you wrong.*

The Knight was plagued with his own worries.

His hopeful eyes fell to Alaythia. And beyond her he saw the Lost Book, useless to him now, under the clawed foot of the White Serpent.

Venemon, showing his white fangs with pride, continued to address the crowd: "With the rebirth of our Serpent Queen, our power will be infinite. We will begin with a fire built on magic, built here in this palace, by all of us in unity, a fire that will reach out and grow, minute by minute, hour by hour, to encompass the entire world. This fire will swallow cities and towns, lakes and bridges, mountains and valleys. It will be an inferno the likes of which we have never been capable of in the past."

Simon listened with growing horror.

"Flames the size of skyscrapers will rush across the continents, dancing over the oceans, burning away all of that wretched, degenerate pestilence called humanity. No more will we have to fear that our beautiful, graceful fires will be erased by the human animal. No more will we have to worry that our artful flames are only a temporary and always-dying creation. Fire will live forever now. We will live in a heavenly landscape of fire."

The creatures erupted into a growling, screeching cheer, a disorganized howl of total jubilance. All doubts were blotted out. All skepticism whisked away. They were overjoyed with the White Dragon's vision of a new world. Fire Eternal.

"We will go, then, in fire, to each of our territories, and they will become kingdoms we rule under the Serpent Queen. We will never be dominated by man again."

Simon felt his knees weaken at the thought of such a future.

"Few humans will survive," Venemon sneered. "There will be just enough to enslave for our domestic needs. They will serve us as the inferior, weak creatures that they are. They will count themselves lucky for every day they survive to scrape the muck from our claws, or polish our teeth, or bathe us with wine, which they will toil to make for us. And when they get old, we will find them useful as nourishment for our stomachs."

Below them, the hissing of their sickly laughter pulled Simon deeper into misery. In the white, carved-wood hallway beside the prison, the Black Dragon tapped nervously at the floor with his feet. Simon thought he seemed alarmed at Venemon's words.

"Such a triumphant age must begin fittingly," said the White

Dragon, "with the death of a great hero of mankind, and a great enemy of Draconians. We have all waited for this moment. I have already destroyed his great weapon, and now we will fear the flash of the Knight's sword no more. The last of the Dragon-hunters stands before us."

He turned to Aldric. "As you can see, he is held and weakened by metal we have constructed, a symbol of what we can do together. The union of Dragon magic is no myth."

"I wish I had taken a thousand more of you down!" cried Aldric.

Simon's heart rose.

The White Dragon pressed his white claw down on the man's chest, pushing him against the wall, grinning wildly. "Sir Aldric St. George, I hereby sentence you to death by fire."

And then the most amazing thing happened.

Simon couldn't believe it.

In awe, he stared as the Black Dragon opened the door to his cage. He was releasing him from the cell. The beast had a mournful look in his eyes. "Run, boy. I cannot bear to see your agony."

He didn't have to say it twice.

Simon ran past him, his sword in hand.

The White Dragon was addressing his army. "Let us make the last Knight the first to die in the flames of the Dragon Queen's mouth. Let us join our magic in the chant of the Unum Draconum, the legendary spell that will release our Imperial Majesty from her slumber."

The White Dragon began chanting a strange language, and the others joined in, a rambling, rumbling mass of words and gnashing teeth.

Simon was running down the long corridors, chasing the sound.

In the Great Hall, Alaythia opened her eyes, waiting fearfully for Aldric's death. But he remained defiant.

"The enemy of the Dragon IS the Dragon!" bellowed Aldric. "It has always been so, and it shall always be so!"

As Simon ran down the white stairs of the meeting room, he could hear his father's brilliant ploy:

"The White Dragon has led you into a trap," Aldric told the Serpents, "and my presence here has been the bait. He is going to eliminate you once and for all!"

The White Serpent turned on him with a snarl. The crowd of Dragons whispered with hostility. The chant began to fall apart.

"Are you so blind that you don't see it? Ask yourself why he hasn't shown you this Great Weapon that I'm supposed to have. It doesn't exist!" said Aldric. "Reviving the Serpent Queen is a fantasy. It can never happen—because the White Dragon wants to be lord and master himself!"

The Venetian growled. Mistral, the Sand Dragon, was provoked. He stared down the White Dragon with a venomous glare. "Is this true?"

"Of course it's true," Aldric answered. "The chant is a diversion. Once your mind is on this all-mighty Serpent Queen, the Great White Liar will throw a flood of fire on all of you." Aldric laughed savagely, looking at the Venetian. "He's so arrogant he had to tell me about it. He's proud of his work. You're all going to die. He has you right where he wants you!"

The words rang true for at least one Dragon. The Venetian clanged in his water tank, furious. This set off Issindra, who screeched over the crowd with anger for ever believing in unity.

Aldric turned to the group. He'd saved the best for last. "He's already told the Venetian—he doesn't fear the fire going wild! He's going to kill you."

The creatures went wild.

"He is a human!" shouted the White Dragon. "Don't believe a word he says!"

"Don't believe it, then," Aldric echoed him. "Go to your deaths quietly."

The Venetian called out, and Mistral howled with a burst of sound that set the others into a frenzy of furious cries, feeling betrayed by the White Dragon, knowing their fear of each other had always been true.

"Madness! Do not listen to him!" the White Dragon thundered. "We have come here to unify our sorcery—"

He could see the group was losing faith in him.

Enraged, he spun around and snapped at Aldric's chains, breaking them in two. "I'll tear you to ribbons myself," he snarled.

Simon burst into the room just in time to see the White Dragon dive with his sharp jaws for Aldric's chest. Simon let loose a silver arrow from his crossbow that slammed into the Dragon's snout, forcing him away from Aldric.

The Dragons were now fighting fiercely among themselves, each accusing the other of treachery.

Simon drew his sword and rushed for the White Dragon. There was no time to think—his father would be mincemeat at a moment's hesitation. . . .

SLASH! Simon whipped his sword at the White Dragon,

driving him back, mostly from surprise. Then the boy turned and cut open the last chains left on his father's wrists.

"Go!" Simon yelled.

Aldric grabbed for his own sword, slung around Simon's shoulder. "Vengeance is an ugly thing," he growled, swinging his sword at the white beast. "It makes a man a devil."

The White Dragon fell back against the wall, stunned for the moment. He pulled a sword from the palace wall, smiling with a gleam in his eye, and flew into a punishing attack against Aldric. "I shall take my time with you," he said with a snicker. "We'll do this the old-fashioned way."

All the while, the Venetian was moving toward Venemon.

"Simon, free Alaythia," shouted Aldric, dodging the White Dragon's sword.

Simon leapt upon the table and slashed at Alaythia's binds.

Eeer, tik, tik, tik—suddenly the Parisian rose up behind Simon and pulled him to the ground, snarling in rage.

Alaythia took Simon's fallen sword and swung it at the wretched Dragonman, but his back was armored and the blows glanced off.

Across from this pandemonium, the White Dragon and Aldric were locked in conflict, swords clashing. Now the Russian Red Dragon moved in toward the White, preparing to crush him in his heavy arms. But the White Dragon threw a claw at his rival and forced him back by magic. "First the human," he growled, "then I'll deal with you."

The Russian was blown back into the thicket of Serpents.

But still the Venetian moved toward Venemon.

As the swordfight continued, as Simon and Alaythia both

fought off the Parisian with swords and battle-axes taken right from the palace walls, something even more horrifying began to happen.

The palace grounds began to rumble.

In a moment the hall changed under them; the entire floor was becoming *invisible,* so that now beneath them in the heat of battle all you could see was a long, dark tunnel, a cave that led straight into the darkness of the earth.

A huge batwing shape, lying with its back down, was levitating out of the darkness into the white light of the palace. Many of the Serpents stopped their quarreling to stare down at this gargantuan, monstrous figure.

The Queen of Serpents was rising.

Chapter Thirty-Five

THE QUEEN OF SERPENTS

As the fighting continued, Simon became slowly aware that the entire floor had turned invisible, and that something was coming toward them. . . .

Aldric did not see it for another moment, and then the rising shape could not be ignored. The White Dragon's eyes shot downward as well.

The Queen was floating upward.

At first it was nothing more than blackness, the dark shape of a massive Dragon from the Old Times, the long neck, the long tail, the massive body, the vast, sharp wingspan. And then—the shape began to move, and fire filled its body. It was made of fire.

Even its eyes were of fire.

The Dragonmen themselves were horrified.

It was awakening. Rebirthing. It would reign over them all.

The flame-riddled head shifted, and Simon felt its yellow, unnatural eyes land on him. They were lifeless and electrically terrifying.

The red flames of its body flickered and roared and move-ment began to animate the creature, slowly. Gradually, it was lifted up toward the invisible floor.

Simon scrambled past the shocked Paris Dragon.

As he crossed, Alaythia reached for his shoulder—her hand brushed the runes of his armor—*and he flew into the air*. He soared across the hall, so intent on his goal that his movement was as graceful as a dream. He rocketed toward his target.

As he flew, Simon could feel Alaythia's magic flowing out-ward.

She was deep in meditation, her magic pushing back against the rising Dragon. The Dragon Queen, still waking from her centuries-old sleep, was sluggish and not prepared for battle.

Alaythia tried sending it to sleep, but her abilities were far too weak. It was an immense creature, and it would not go back easily.

Simon flew toward his fallen crossbow. The Russian saw his move, and strode after him. The Parisian turned back to Alaythia. She grabbed a lance and landed a strike at its shoulder. This gave her time to snatch up the Lost Book from the floor. Across the shaking hall, Aldric still clashed with the White Dragon, taking vicious blows.

Dodging the Russian, Simon snatched up his crossbow in mid-flight and rose again, high into the air.

Then, a desperate idea came to him. He ran the palm of his hand against the silver arrow's sharpened tip. His blood ran over the barb.

He looked down at the floor, at the deathspell scroll Alaythia had made.

It was fluttering like something alive, scraping the floor, and Simon soared after it.

He stabbed it onto his arrow.

Then he hovered over the great gash in the floor. He aimed for the heart of the Queen and chanted the deathspell that had no name. The last one in the Book. It sounded almost like a prayer.

The arrow fell through the invisible floor. It disappeared into the fire at the creature's chest and slashed into the Dragon's heart. The Dragon roared in anger.

Simon fell back to the floor, as the heated wind from below racked his armor, ruining its power for flight.

Alaythia renewed her chant, and the Queen of Serpents was launched back down into the depths of the earth. The darkness seemed to pull it down as if it were an infinitely heavy weight. Its roaring rumbled farther and farther away, a world-quaking growl filled with star-shattering screams, a roaring of absolute ferocity. The Queen was being buried again.

The White Dragon screeched in fury, seeing the massive creature slip back down. He looked to Simon with pitch-black hatred. And then he did something very foolish.

He opened his jaws and spat fire.

It shot over the room in two quick, lean flares. But Simon dived behind the Venetian Dragon, who was hit. Enraged, ripping from the roiling water of his tank—the Venetian crashed loose and fired back with a blast of green-black flames. At once the fire took the shape of a dozen, crazed fire-figures, flying toward the White Dragon.

In response, the White Dragon rolled out more flame.

The white fire took the form of vicious man-creatures with gnashing fangs. The green firelings met the white, swooping toward one another in the air, locked in combat.

The sight of fire set off a chain reaction as other Dragonmen threw fire at their enemies. Soon the palace was a sprawling inferno of firelings in every hue, attacking everything in sight.

"Ragemagic!" Simon heard someone call. "Don't throw your fire!"

The floor before Simon became solid again, but the battle of the Dragons raged on—fire was whipping all around the room. He saw the Russian engulfed.

Meanwhile, the White Dragon savagely thrust and swung his sword with devastating swiftness, sending Aldric into retreat. The Knight's blade was torn from his grip; it clattered to the floor, and he fled to the other end of the Great Hall. Aldric, Simon, and Alaythia now stood in roughly the same place, cornered, in a last stand against the forces of darkness.

Aldric's sword lay under the White Dragon's clawed foot.

But Simon had his. Suddenly he threw it into his father's arms.

Now Aldric had a last chance to avenge himself, and he took it—leaping toward the White Dragon, slashing away its sword, and throwing himself at the hated beast. Aldric lunged at the dragon's chest and clutched at its heart, yelling out its deathspell. In shock, the White Dragon gaped at the Knight, trying to push him away, but the words had already been spoken, each and every one of them.

Aldric had won.

The White Dragon burst into white fire, and the white fire peeled away his leathery skin and torched his vile bones, so that Aldric's hands touched nothing but red ashes in the form of a Dragon.

At that same instant, the Venetian pounced from behind, forcing Aldric to spin and plunge his sword into the water beast. Already afire with the White Dragon's flames, the Venetian took this final blow and fell back to his death.

Aldric had destroyed two Dragons in the span of an instant.

But the fighting of the Dragonmen still surrounded them.

Alaythia closed her eyes in sheer terror.

Suddenly rubble from the quaking palace fell before them, and huge stone blocks slid over the floor to close around the St. Georges, forming a huge barrier. Alaythia was shielding them all with magic. They were protected as a tremendous blast of fire from every Pyrothrax in the world rolled around them.

The last thing Simon saw was the Black Dragon shuffling to safety.

The heroes huddled together in darkness. From inside the barrier, all Simon could see were flashes of light, as fire tried to rip through the stone cracks. The acrid stink of smoke choked him. But he had no idea what was happening outside.

The barrier rocked and nearly tore apart, but it held. Through the flashes, Simon could catch glimpses of Aldric and Alaythia's faces.

He could hear the Dragons turning on one another, hear them snarling and fighting like angry dogs, hissing like snakes. There was a tumbling of bodies, as if they were rolling against one another.

There was the chatter and crackle of fire-sprites, screeching with laughter.

And then the earthquakes really began.

The palace sounded like it was collapsing.

What Simon could not see was the frenzied retreat of the Dragonmen from each other. Their fire was uncontrollable. The firelings soared and swept over the room, attacking anything and everything, flames eating one another.

The reptilians fought, and when they could fight no more, they fled the palace. They chanted ancient magics, expanding their wings into great batlike shapes.

The palace was alive with the sound of huge wings churning the air. The force of the wingbeats was so strong it fanned the flames of the fire. Some of the creatures were wounded, some perished. Other reptilians were swooping out of the fortress, scattering to the four corners of the earth, chanting spells to speed them along faster, make them invisible, anything to get out and get away. . . . They were afire as they flew, burning, perhaps dying.

From inside his place of safety, Simon could only listen.

There was the howl of fire.

There were Serpentine screams of death, until finally the heat and the fire receded.

And the shielding barrier collapsed.

As it fell, the smoke was fanned back; the Great Hall could be seen again. The palace was in collapse. There were no living Pyrothraxes left on the premises. Several hulking lizard bodies lay inert, burning, on the torn and upturned floor. But no breathing reptilians remained. Only their fires were here, dying out in a hundred places. The firelings had burned themselves out. Fires of many colors: white, blue, black, and other hues intertwined and then faded.

It must have been a stunning battle.

"You saved us," said Aldric to Alaythia.

"No," she answered. "I couldn't have done it alone. Something was helping me."

Simon heard a violent cracking noise from a myriad of places. Looking up, he saw cracks spreading across the walls, reaching out, branching, and linking together. The entire palace was cracking into pieces, the walls crumbling in great sheets and splinters.

"We've got to get out of here," said Aldric, "or we'll be buried."

From the smashing, falling walls, a large animal pushed through, galloping into the ruins—it was Valsephany. Aldric grabbed her reins. "Stay with us," he told her. "Lead us out."

The horse trotted through the smoke.

The air was dark from the falling debris, but Alaythia managed to regain the path. She held Simon's hand and pulled him out into the light along with his father, just as her own dream had predicted.

They found themselves outside, in a London just awakening from a terrible earthquake.

Only a few people were out on the street.

The White Palace could now be seen behind them in all its glory: tall, with smooth towers tapering beside a domed center structure. It was now disintegrating. Towers fell. Huge blocks of granite tumbled from its walls. The collapsing palace hammered the streets.

Simon felt a great relief. The threat was over.

Only it wasn't.

Eeer, tik, tik, tik. Eeer, tik, tik, tik.

Out of the cloud of debris, a soaring predator tore loose. It was Tyrannique, the Paris Dragon, and though he bled fire in many places, he wanted one last victim. The boy.

Wings knifing the air in a powerful charge, the dying Dragon dove for Simon. Quick as a dream, Aldric spun with his crossbow and fired a shot into the blue-yellow flesh. The shot hit Tyrannique in the wing, but the Dragon surged forward, in a straight line toward Simon.

But before he finished his attack, the Dragon was struck by black lightning. Hiding somewhere in the rubble, the Black Dragon had put his claws together, and ebony lightning shot from his hands. It struck Tyrannique square in the face. The Parisian Dragon howled and veered away, into the clouds, exploding in blue-and-gold flame. The last blow had been struck.

The explosion spread in the sky and then burned out. Simon turned to look for the Black Dragon with gratitude, but the creature had vanished from sight in the rubble.

They searched the scene for the old Dragon. But there was no sign of him. None at all.

Wherever he was, they were safe because of him.

They stood on the torn-up street, and the horse led them away.

The land was peaceful, and they wandered on, recovering from the fury of it all.

Simon looked up tiredly, walking through the wounded city. "Cleaning up isn't part of our duties, is it?"

A rain began to fall where blue-yellow clouds marked the Parisian Dragon's death.

Now bits of black rain began to come down. The rain spattered the street, leaving huge marks of darkness. Simon watched with amazement as the black rain changed, and dark green droplets spattered the ground.

It was raining paint.

He looked ahead of him, and the city now seemed like a giant canvas, peppered with spatters of black and dark green, and now specks of red. He wanted to laugh.

The world under his feet was turning into a huge abstract painting.

Alaythia laughed in disbelief. For her, it was like landing in a childhood dream she had long forgotten. And when she smiled at him, Aldric could not help but respond.

All those painterly meals the Dragon of Paris consumed had made his death a spectacular rain of magic.

Aldric pulled a huge black umbrella from his horse's saddlebag. He raised the umbrella over them and they huddled together, protected.

"I never would've seen it," Aldric said to his son. "I never would've seen what you saw in the Black Dragon. There was a conscience there. You saw something in him."

"It was a mistake."

"It wasn't. It saved us all. I've never seen one like him," said Aldric heavily. "It will change everything. . . . "

Simon looked off thoughtfully.

"Simon," said Aldric, preparing himself. "I need to say something—"

Simon cut him off. "I know."

"I just want to tell you—"

Simon looked at him with a weary smile. "I know."

And that was that.

Aldric grinned at him. They kept walking, thankful that the world was still in one piece, impatient for rest, and wondering where they would be going next.

Together.

Epilogue

THE WORLD NEEDS ITS KNIGHTS

O N THE COAST OF New England, within sight of the Ebony Hollow lighthouse, is an old castle built by the British when they lived here. In that castle, on many days of the year, you will find the family St. George.

They are not an ordinary family.

The man of the house is a Knight of the old Order of Dragonhunters, by the name of Aldric St. George. His wife is no longer alive, but her spirit lives on in the tools of his trade. His son is a handsome and courageous young man named Simon St. George.

Their faithful friends include a beautiful woman named Alaythia who practices the art of magic. She spends her time searching for the location of a certain black Dragon from China, who, it seems from all the evidence, just might be an ally, if he still lives.

They are an odd assortment of broken, and now repairing, souls. They have each been through great and terrible trials together. They will see more.

Inside the gentle and hospitable castle is a spellbook, salvaged from a great battle. It contains the deathspells of all the Dragons left known to man. The book will be put to use in the coming days.

In the distance, the old lighthouse school warms the coast, and old man Denman and his wife still run it, sometimes welcoming Simon for an evening meal, if they can tolerate the energetic English fox that comes with him. During the day, from the high point in the lighthouse, the boys of the school can see the little fortress and can wonder what Simon is learning at home.

Beside the castle, on the green rolling hills, is a field fit to order for a great and noble horse, and not long ago, it was joined by another.

"A Knight should have a steed," said Aldric to his son.

Simon looked at him, his gratitude apparent. A horse of his own.

The white stallion, with its black mane, stood in the field and bowed to Simon, one leg thrust forward in a show of loyalty and respect.

Before the stallion, in the field, were set a great shield, a helmet, and elegant armor. Simon's sword was stabbed into the ground to greet him.

"Simon St. George," said Aldric, unsheathing his sword and laying it upon each of Simon's shoulders, "in the name of Saint Michael and Saint George, in gratitude for your loyalty and service, and in honor of your courage and fortitude, I hereby Knight thee. May the light from your sword drive darkness from this world."

Simon rose and regarded Aldric and Alaythia.

If you had seen him in that moment, you would have seen the very perfection of pride. You would have seen a boy who was now comfortable in his own skin.

He was not yet a man; but the steps he had left were short.

He was a Knight. A Dragonhunter. And with his stallion, his sword, and his shield, and with his father beside him, he would conquer evil.

He never did find out the name of the girl in the novelty shop. But life is long. There was time yet. There was hope.

His father looked at him, and if you had seen him in that moment, you would have seen the very perfection of admiration. A lone warrior no more.

You have many chances to *change* your life, but they do run out. A life is never set in stone, but grows like the roots of a tree in fertile ground. Still, over time, the strength to find new ground leaves you.

Aldric thought his chances had ended, but they had not.

He would make the most of his time now. Life is short. Time passes fast.

It was possible no adventures were left for Simon and Aldric except this one: forging a friendship between father and son.

Perhaps there were no more Dragons left.

One can hope.

Hope, after all, is the fire that burns forever.